GIMME SHEVEN

GIMME SHEVEN

Barry F. Schnell

Copyright © 2001 by Barry F. Schnell.

ISBN#   Softcover   1-4010-2426-2

All rights reserved. No part of this book may be reproduced or transmitted in any form or by any means, electronic or mechanical, including photocopying, recording, or by any information storage and retrieval system, without permission in writing from the copyright owner.

This is a work of fiction. Names, characters, places and incidents either are the product of the author's imagination or are used fictitiously, and any resemblance to any actual persons, living or dead, events, or locales is entirely coincidental.

This book was printed in the United States of America.

To order additional copies of this book, contact:
Xlibris Corporation
1-888-7-XLIBRIS
www.Xlibris.com
Orders@Xlibris.com

This was bad. This was "kissing your sister" bad. And it was their only chance to score some coin. The Chairman had made his score several months before . . . before "the Internet" became synonymous with "communist pedophile stink hole" throughout the world. He took on an Internet sales job and was bolstered with stock options up the wazoo. Then the market shot up like a pecker at the first slow dance during the junior prom. The Chairman cashed in. He went into semi-retirement working only when bored. But a new opportunity, at a brand new start-up company, dripping with STOCK OPTIONS and a Regional Buttkicker title, presented itself. So the Chairman got back in the chicanery game.

The Chairman wanted to spread the wealth and invited his long time cronies aboard what could be deemed the "USSBS.com"—a barge of bull crap that they tried to force down the unsuspecting collective buying throat of advertisers across the globe before they sniffed out the scam. It wasn't only a roller coaster ride for twelve months; it was a roller coaster ride through Satan's bowels and back again—on the company dime, of course.

Some of them got out alive. Some of them were stronger. Some of them were wiser. ALL of them were of bloated liver.

This rise-and-fall, crash-and-burn tale is no doubt one shared by thousands of STOCK OPTION salivating souls during the years 1999-2000. They took the plunge hoping for the quick score and a comfortable retirement at age 23.

A rip roaring, laugh riot, tearjerker of a company, USSBS.com, 'twas merely a reflection of the Internet industry as a whole—F'd up.

I - AMARILLO OR BUST

Jay left Los Angeles on a typical Sun Out, Breasts Everywhere, Thursday afternoon. He was still on the fence, more or less, as he moved to Los Angeles four years earlier to escape the cold, harsh, frigid weather and women of Chicago.

Life in L-A was good. Jay had friends and regular watering holes to embrace him in between soul bashings from employers and emotionally tainted gal pals. And he could sit on the beach and slurp his coffee or hooch at any time of the day or night. And he did—every day, every night.

He loved L-A and it's "whatever" attitude. It was just his style, too. The more prurient, the better. But one bad job after another made scoring some regular, serious coin somewhat of a priority. A steady diet of booze, strippers, and gourmet coffees was taking its toll. And the $1,300 monthly rent didn't help matters.

The call from the Chairman came at the right time for Jay. As much as he loved L-A, and as much as he hoped to be buried under his favorite jiggle joint in West Hollywood, he knew the Chairman's offer to leave town was one Jay couldn't refuse.

At least, he couldn't refuse it a THIRD time.

Early in November, the Chairman dangled the carrot for Jay. There was going to be a 50 percent increase in salary, a "Sales Manager Emeritus" title, and STOCK OPTIONS to be coming Jay's way. If everything broke the way it did for the Chairman and his STOCK OPTIONS only two years prior, Jay could put in his 48 months and retire a wealthy, dirty, young man!

Besides, their old cohort, Stosh, was already on board. The Chairman, Jay, and Stosh toiled away together in the print advertising industry for a few years in the late 80's and early 90's. They went their separate ways in 1992. Jay moved to Paradise and lost himself in an ocean of Heineken. Stosh bounced around fleabag companies in horsefly towns hoping interstate lottery tickets would one day lead to untold riches. And the Chairman went off and made something of himself.

Now the Chairman wanted to bring his old friends up to a more desirable tax bracket. What good is having all that money if you can't waste it on cool things with friends? But it required all to relocate to Chicago . . . in December—not exactly ideal circumstances.

When the Chairman bounced the opportunity off Jay, Jay thought about it for a few hours and then called back to accept. Then, he went out and buried his face in Trixie the Stripper's love grotto for an evening and had a change of heart. He called the Chairman the next day and withdrew his acceptance. The Chairman was not pleased, but it was certainly not a catastrophic scene that would damage his fifteen-year friendship with Jay. Jay knew what he wanted, and it was in a green bottle or hanging upside down from a brass pole near the airport. That's all he needed. That is, until his friends reminded him he needed money, too, if he wanted to keep up his preferred lifestyle.

The next morning, Jay staggered into the Sow's Hoof, reeking of Trixie and malt hops, for his standard frothy latte drink. From there he wandered out to the beach, plopped to his rump, and thought hard. He loved L.A. The sun sat on his shoulder like a warm, cozy angel reminding him of why he shouldn't go. They can't put a price on sunshine—he didn't care how many STOCK OPTIONS he was bestowed.

He sipped the latte and watched The World's Most Delectable Rump wiggle past walking a bulimic Lhasa Apso. Both were wearing tight and tiny t-shirts with "Doggie Style" emblazoned on them. Jay smiled. To hell with the sun, THAT'S why he was staying in L.A.

Jay stood erect and dialed up the Chairman on his cell phone.

"Hello?" the Chairman bellowed in his natural imposing fashion. Caller I.D. had already tipped him off as to Jay's identity.

"Hi Chairman, its Jay."

Silence followed. It was one of the Chairman's lethal tactics for putting the other party ill at ease. Three seconds seemed like three hours when the Chairman simply glared at one through the telephone.

"Chairman?" Jay quivered. "You there?"

"Yeah. What's up?" The Chairman always chose his words carefully.

"Well, I've been sitting here thinking, and I just wanted you to know I'm staying—" the signal died. "CALL LOST" blinked in the viewing window. Surely, the already unhappy Chairman was glaring even deeper into a telephone somewhere in cold, wicked Chicago.

Jay frantically dialed the Chairman's number again. No dice. As he was only a few blocks from his apartment, Jay dashed homeward to call the Chairman from the landline. Passing the Sow's Hoof, he noticed a bevy of bra-less street urchins slurping fruit smoothies on the steps of the joint.

STOCK OPTIONS can't buy a scene like that, he thought to himself. And so went Jay's line of thinking; his mind sometimes wouldn't allow him to make the connection from STOCK OPTIONS to cash to girls for hire.

Once inside the apartment, he poured himself a nice healthy glass of 10:30 AM Cabernet from the bedside Box O' Wine. Jay figured it might turn into a lengthy phone chat with the Chairman and he wanted to be relaxed. Alcohol and oral sex were the only things that could relax him these days; and the latter hadn't reared its beautiful head in over a month.

Jay sighed, took a quaff of Cabernet, and dialed.

"Yeah?" the Chairman answered.

"Sorry about that. Lost the signal," Jay said.

"I figured," said the Chairman followed by fourteen seconds of stone cold silence. "So what's up?"

Jay quaffed another gulp. "You know I've been giving this a lot of thought. It's a great offer, and with you and Stosh on board, I'm sure it'd be a great time. But I just can't—"

The phone disconnected. There was no dial tone to be heard. Jay grunted and gulped more Cabernet. He fired up the cell phone. The signal moniker with a line through it couldn't have screamed "BILL 90 DAYS OVERDUE" any louder.

Jay staggered back out of his apartment with his coffee can full of coins and set a course for the Sow's Hoof. There was a pay phone just outside the front entrance and very near the bra-less urchins!

First, Jay called the cellular phone service provider whereby they informed him that his account was, in fact, 90 days overdue. Service would not be connected until payment received. Par for the course.

Next, he dialed the local phone company which kindly requested payment on a 60-day past-due account in order to restore service.

Jay stammered and perspired. The bra-less urchins rolled their eyes and left the stoop as Jay pleaded from one creditor to the next trying to patch up the damage du jour. He rifled coin after coin into the pay phone bouncing from one department supervisor to another. They agreed to restore service if payment were made in the next 24 hours for the full overdue amount. Jay stared into the squalid copper depths of the coffee can.

"I'll have it for you tomorrow morning."

It was getting close to the 75-minute mark since the second call to the Chairman had been lost. Jay throttled his last two coins into the *L.A. TIMES* honor box on the corner. The first thing to catch his eye was the date: *DECEMBER 6, 1999*.

Goddammit, Jay thought to himself, the rent is already one day overdue. He shouldn't have tucked his last $600 into Trixie's ovaries the past few days.

Out of cash, with his next paycheck already accounted for, Jay started to listen to the STOCK OPTION devil sitting opposite the sunshine angel on his other shoulder.

"Take the Chairman's offer, Dummy. STOCK OPTIONS. S-T-O-C-K O-P-T-I-O-N-S!" the devil taunted.

Jay nodded and ran the Debtor's Dash of Shame over to his buddy Jojo's apartment. Jojo answered the door pant-less and reeking of *Milwaukee's Best*.

"Yo, Jay."

"Can I use your phone?"

"They shut off your phone again?"

Jay nodded and slipped inside. Jojo opened two beers and fell face first into the coffee table. He'd been on a seven-day binge, and it suddenly took its toll on his equilibrium.

"Could you keep it down for a second?" Jay requested with his back to the grotesque scene. He swayed nervously while the phone rang.

"Hello?" answered the Chairman.

"It's Jay. Jeez, sorry about all of the dropped calls." Jay said.

"They disconnect your service for non-payment again?"

"Er, I'm on Jojo's phone and I don't want to tie it up long distance for too long. But I wanted you to know that I was calling you earlier, because I was going to tell you for sure that I wasn't taking the job."

Seven seconds of deafening silence.

"Yeah, so," Jay continued, ". . . but then I started realizing how this was a great opportunity and the stock options and I might regret it and everything. So, I want the job."

"Oh, really?" said the Chairman, dripping with condescension.

"Well, if it's still available, that is." Jay said.

"You know, you put me in a difficult spot here. We've got one position left. Ollie is pushing for one of his friends—who he's interviewing right now, by the way—to take the last opening. I told him you were in, and then you were out. And now you want back in?"

"Uhm, yes. I'm totally positive. This is the right thing to do."

"You're SURE? And I don't ask that meaning if you say "yes" that you've got the job. I just want you to be sure you know what you're asking before I go put my testicles on the line again. So, you're SURE?" the Chairman said devoid of any jocularity.

"Absolutely?" Jay gulped and quivered.

He pried one of the beers from Jojo's cold, unconscious grip and decided to celebrate by stopping in to see Trixie. Jay owed it to himself. He made a prudent decision, and a pelvic clubbing from Trixie would be sufficient reward. Plus, if he was committed to leaving town soon, he'd best put in as many hours at "Chubbie's" strip club as possible. Turnover was high, and Lord knows if Trixie would be there were he to return in a few short years.

Jay was the only one at Chubbie's sitting rail side with a coffee can full of coins that afternoon.

About eighteen hours had passed when Jay's recently restored landline phone rang. Jay had been sloppily cramming his possessions into old, empty wine boxes and milk crates preparing for the long move to Chicago. He climbed over the boxes like a one-limbed monkey in a jungle branch-swinging contest to dive on, and answer, the call.

"This is Jay!" he said, out of breath and a tad sloshed.

Silence. It must be the Chairman.

"Hello?" Jay asked.

"Okay." The Chairman said followed by a seven-second pregnant pause. "You're in."

"I was already packing!"

"But I told you I didn't know if I could get you in."

"I was optimistic." Jay took a slug off the bedside Box O' Wine. "Besides, I'm past due on my rent, and I'd like to get out of town. That'll buy me a couple of weeks to pay them back." Jay drank again.

"Just get here. Heck wants everyone in New York by Sunday for a Sales Orientation and Christmas party," the Chairman ordered.

"Who is Heck? And what about New York?"

"Duke Heckland. He's the Big, Big Man. We report to him. And what part didn't you understand about New York? Just get here by Friday so we can all fly out together."

"But it's Tuesday already. I've still got to pack and put stuff in storage and—I've got a lot of crap to do." Jay said.

"So do it," the Chairman replied. "Just get here by Saturday."

"I'll have to drive like a bat out of hell without stopping."

Jay's complaint fell on deaf ears.

"Okay then," Jay continued. "I'll see you guys on Saturday."

The Chairman hung up the phone. Jay sucked the bedside Box O' Wine dry and continued the task at hand. He had 72 hours worth of crap to do and 24 hours to do it in. Jay put his head down for a second on a sticky stack of *Leg Stew* magazines. *Leg Stew* was the only one that specifically catered to Jay's fetish of "no feet in the photographs!" Big mistake. The clock was ticking, and Jay quickly fell asleep.

The Mother of All Intestinal episodes jolted Jay awake several hours later. He convulsed and left the business end of his angel hair garlic pasta in a pool of burgundy colored bile atop his favorite pair of Converse "gummers."

"Yo, Jay!" a voice blurted out from across the bedroom.

Jay squinted into the sunshine—the goddamn sunshine—that burst into the room through the window near where the voice came from. Jay managed to make out a muscle-bound, crew neck t-shirted silhouette sitting on a pile of dirty clothes holding a beer on each knee.

"Jojo?" Jay asked.

"You thirsty? You been asleep for almost a day-and-a-half." Jojo said.

"Goddammit!" Jay staggered to his feet. "Are you telling me it's Thursday afternoon?"

"Yeah—almost the weekend. Let's go for a ride on my boat."

"I can't! I'm moving to Chicago. I'm taking that great job. But I've got to be there by Saturday."

"That's a long haul. I don't think you can get there by Saturday. Well, wait; are you taking the northern route or the southern?"

"Southern, why? You think the northern way would be quicker?"

Jojo shrugged and drank his beer.

"I've got to make it there by Saturday. I already told the Chairman twice that I was in and then out again. If I'm not there on time, he'll write me off for good—as an employee AND as a friend." Jay paused to leaf through the November, 1997 issue of *Leg Stew*.

"Check this out. This is one of my favorite sets of legs of all time." Jay trudged through the clutter and handed the magazine to Jojo.

"How come you don't like feet again?" Jojo asked.

"I like 'em on REAL women," Jay pontificated. "But in photos, the feet become the focus. They take away from the gams. The gams are the sexy part. Way too many of these leg magazines focus on the feet. They're falsifying their genre. It pisses me off more than anything in the world."

"Yeah, those are nice legs." Jojo tossed the magazine on the floor and took another sloppy, manly sip of beer. He watched Jay stumble around the room, cram his possesses into too-small boxes, occasionally stop to smell a sock or look at an old photograph, and pack four decades of anxiety neatly away.

"You want help?" Jojo asked. "And what about your job. Don't you have to tell them you're quitting?"

"Thanks, but I'll go quicker if I do this alone. I'm going to call my boss from the road and tell her. It's all the notice she deserves."

Jay was a liberal and a pacifist and really hated no one. But he hated his boss. She was one of those over-compensatory transplanted New York Jewish broads who worked out at the gym the five hours per day she WASN'T in the office emasculating all of her male peers and subordinates. Jay could work for and get along with anyone but her. And while he showed up for work every day and met or exceeded his sales quotas quarter after quarter, Jay's boss still belittled and criticized him during the weekly sales staff meetings.

"You're only up sixty percent from last quarter?" The Witch confronted Jay a few weeks prior. "You wouldn't last six minutes in Manhattan. You'd be homeless and begging for food scraps from tourists. And I don't think you have a clue about this business! You call yourself a sales-MAN?"

An astute broad, she. Jay had only BEEN in the print advertising business for 13 years, continually getting promoted and praised in the Midwest. He took this job at an L.A. rag not because he loved the business so much. But it would afford him a regular paycheck so he could kick back and enjoy the rest of the body parts, libations, etc., California offered that he craved so much.

The boss was a part of the problem—a bigger straw on the camel's back—but she was hardly the sole reason Jay had to go after the Internet opportunity. He knew that. However, he wasn't going to give her the satisfaction of a two-week notice. Screw her.

"What about your lease?" asked Jojo.

"I'm on a month-to-month. Though I haven't paid this month yet." Jay dug his fingers into his head and looked around the room. "How am I going to get all this stuff in my car? I've already got my golf clubs and three boxes of kitchen utensils in there, and it's packed."

"Sell it."

"No time. I've got to leave town in 20 minutes or less."

"Leave me your keys. I'll round up some of the guys and we'll put it in one of those storage garages for you." Jojo said.

"How much do you think that will cost every month?" Jay asked.

"Doesn't matter. You've got to get out of here, and you'll be RICH in twelve months."

"I like your thinking. Okay, just help me take some of these clothes down to the car, and I'll take off."

Jojo nodded and plucked and armload of boxer shorts and khaki slacks off the floor. Jay took his travelling case full of techno-soul and country-rocker compact discs, and however many copies of *Leg Stew* he could clutch to his chest, and waddled out of the apartment.

A brutal arctic wind pelted the windows of the Chairman's temporary flat in Chicago that evening with lake effect snow, falling icicles, and the occasional lifeless pigeon. He relaxed with a micro brew on the sofa watching the Bulls vs. Milwaukee Bucks game. His wife was out of town for the week, so the Chairman was free to lounge about in his underpants and sustain himself on take-out Pad Thai and regional beer. Life was good.

Frost blocked out the windows and what would sometimes be a gorgeous view of downtown Chicago from the sliding balcony doors—three months out of the year, anyway. The streets were clogged with dirty snow and transients. There was little incentive to go outside until the Spring thaw, the Chairman thought. Taking the dog out downstairs thirteen flights three times per day was enough socializing within the neighborhood. In a scant 48 months, the Chairman would be able to cash in his STOCK OPTIONS, go into permanent retirement, and live in a much better climate to boot. Another four winters in Chicago would be small price to pay.

The post-Jordan Bulls were getting throttled by 27 points when the Chairman's cell phone rang. He grunted, heaved his beer-sculpted torso forward, and plucked the phone off the coffee table from underneath a bag of zesty mustard sourdough pretzel rods.

"Hello?" said the Chairman.

"Yo, Chairman. It's Jay. Listen, I've been driving for damn near seven hours now. I'm in Arizona."

"Sounds like good progress," the Chairman said while crunching a pretzel rod. "Keep it up."

"Well, that's why I'm calling. I've been doing a lot of thinking over the past 400 miles. And I hate to say this, but I think I'm going to turn around and stay here. I don't think I can absorb the risk of this Internet thing."

"Goddammit!" the Chairman screamed. "You cannot goddamn do this again! My reputation, and now YOUR ass, is on the line here. What is the problem!? You need money! This is a great opportunity. In 48 months, you cash out and do whatever the hell you want. I'm giving you a fifty-percent increase over your last salary, 25,000 stock options, and a great title. Are you goddamn nuts? Stosh had to think all of five seconds to take the offer—and he left his Old Lady and house to do it! What is the problem? What is the GODDAMN PROBLEM?" Pretzel crumbs spewed around the room as if spiraling outward from a sourdough tornado with each of the Chairman's syllables.

"I know it's a great job. And I'm thankful you went to bat for me so many times. But I don't know, you know? I've got lots of friends in California and I can walk to the bars from my apartment. And the chicks—there are no chicks like that in Chicago, that's for sure."

"Jay, this isn't Braniff in the Seventies." The Chairman's face was maroon. "There aren't strange women falling out of their stewardess uniforms and into your bed just because you're in California. After this score, I'm done. Do you get it? When you cash out here, you don't have to work for The Man ever again! THAT'S why we're doing this. Open your eyes! This is a GOOD thing."

Jay paused as his new, sleek, black Mustang convertible rumbled through the Arizona desert en route to New Mexico. He thought again about the pros and the cons. He'll miss his friends and stumbling home from the nearby watering holes at 2 A.M. without fear of getting slapped with a DUI. He'll miss the Pacific Ocean and sea of breasts that accompanied him on his morning Latte walk every day.

He WON'T miss being overdue on his rent, phone bill, electric bill, car payment, insurance payment, and miscellaneous.

And he certainly won't miss that snot rag, freaking witch of a boss.

Oh, and Carlotta... he almost forgot about Carlotta since she asked that they break up a month prior. There was a girl who wanted to have sex any time any place, could keep up with Jay drink for drink, and had a zillion dollar dowry awaiting her eventual husband. She was Jay's best friend and lay in some eight long years. All agreed that they were perfect for one another. And she broke up with Jay for the same reason why most women become hypocritical, vapid vipers of superficiality and materialism: he didn't "make enough money."

Carlotta's words ricocheted around inside Jay's skull like a .38 caliber slug from a dirty, tainted, abusive pistol. The Chairman's cursing into the telephone brought Jay back to Reality.

"Are you there, Goddammit!?"

Carlotta. Screw her.

"Don't worry, I'm in—just a temporary freak-out. I'll be in my comfort zone soon." Jay said as his foot stomped the gas pedal to the floor. "I guess I just needed another little nudge."

"Atta' boy." The Chairman said as the doorbell rang. He disconnected from Jay, wrapped a blanket around his waist, and answered the door. Stosh greeted him with a twelve-pack of OLD STYLE and a carton of egg rolls.

"Good news," the Chairman said. "Jay is definitely in. He just called from Flagstaff or somewhere."

"Cool," Stosh said. He removed his coat and plopped down on the floor in front of the TV with a beer. "Think he'll make it here by Saturday night so we can all fly to New York together?"

"I don't see why not!" The Chairman said confidently as he dropped the blanket to the floor and eased back into the sofa. "Yeah, it's all coming together."

It was 3:00 P.M. on Friday when Jay's Mustang roared over a hill on I-40 bearing down on Amarillo. He'd been driving straight since Thursday afternoon, with only three fueling and two piddle stops. Amarillo would be a good place to catch one of those "Four Hour Nap and Porn On The TV!" motels, Jay thought. The prospect of a terrific new job and STOCK OPTIONS weren't even as motivating as that.

As the Mustang purred along at 96 miles per hour, Jay noticed an odd spectacle in the distance. It looked like the Great Wall of China from ten miles away. But it couldn't be, Jay told himself, because China is south of Mexico—and the car is going east. The long drive was beginning to take its toll. Jay's eyes fluttered like bat wings. The car would erratically speed up and slow down with Jay's flirtations of unconsciousness.

He was definitely stopping in Amarillo for the nap and TV porn. And beer—he needed a few beers, for sure.

AMARILLO 40 MILES teased a sign on the right hand side of the road. The Wall of China grew closer and larger. Jay coaxed himself wide-awake by blasting the most God awful rap song he could find on the radio. Such music he did not expect to hear in the North of Texas. But it was doing the job. "Godammit!" Jay shouted, drowning out the Rap garbage. He slammed on the brakes and the Mustang skidded to a halt behind a Piggly Wiggly semi. In front of the Piggly Wiggly semi, in both lanes, were about 750 more semis, and 1,500 cars, and a few Nutjobs on motorcycles. It was a traffic jam of biblical proportions stretching Eastward for as far as Jay could see. There was no explanation in sight. The most logical conclusion Jay could draw was another conspiracy being created that would be fuel enough to have the Chairman rip Jay a new whatsis for being late.

Jay peered in the rear view mirror. Semis were grinding to a halt behind, and adjacent to him, for miles. This was getting serious. And Jay was fully awake. He kept the car on thinking that maybe it was just a spot DUI check by the Texas Highway Patrol backing things up and they'd be moving again at any minute. Or maybe a couple of bleeding heart truckers were allowing a family of geese to shuffle across the interstate up ahead. It couldn't be anything SERIOUS. In L-A, there would be 15 news choppers in the sky covering something like this from 15 different angles. And the radio stations would be chiming in with SIG Alerts every six minutes instead of letting "Ghetto Moefoes" rant on about their " . . . hoes dat blows." Jay turned off the radio.

After an hour, not one vehicle had budged—not even a foot. The prudent thing to do, of course, would be to shut the engine off and conserve fuel. Even though Amarillo was only 35 miles away, there were no signs of gas stations, stores, homes, or life—other than the stranded motorists—for miles in any direction. That being said, Jay told himself to let the engine keep running "just in case he needed to get a quick jump around the Piggly Wiggly truck when things started moving again."

One hour became three, and it was dusk in Texas. All motorists had shut off their vehicles. Truckers were strolling up and down the road swapping brown paper bags, cartons of smokes, and chaw pouches. Occasionally they'd smack one another on the rear end or try on each other's Peterbilt caps. It looked to Jay like Woodstock meets *HEE HAW*—with a sprinkling of *SPARTACUS* pinched in for flavor. There was no way he was getting out of the car, not even to drain the lizard. His sexually brutalized keester would wind up as someone's grille ornament for the next three weeks.

Every 90 minutes or so, Jay saw the passenger's side door of the semi in his rear view mirror swing open. No one would emerge from the cab. But when the fading sunlight or timely flicker of a rear truck's headlights caught it just right, Jay could detect a stream of liquid squirting outward. The chap was too lazy to hop down and relieve himself in the prairie, so he simply would kick open the door and let 'er rip.

The whiz routine left quite an imprint. Finally, six consumed diet sodas motivated Jay to emerge from the safety of his Mustang cocoon and drain the lizard outdoors somewhere. It was good to stand up and stretch out the bones again. Jay moseyed into the prairie and unzipped.

"Watch it!" a voice drawled from the darkness. It scared the hell out of Jay, and he experienced a wee bit of a premature leak.

About 18 inches in front of, and two feet below, where Jay was about to uncork crouched a denim-vested good ol' boy named Sugar. He was engaged in a bodily function of greater proportion.

"Who's there!?" Jay demanded to know.

"Just be careful where you point that thing," Sugar said. He finished his business and stood up. He left his dungarees around his ankles for an uncomfortable extra second or so.

"Sorry," Jay said with his throbbing tallywacker in his hand. "I didn't see you in the dark."

Sugar pulled up his pants.

"You gonna fire that thing or what?" Sugar asked.

Jay forgot he was just standing there clutching his joint in plain view. It was like senior prom all over again.

"Oh, yeah." Jay turned away from Sugar and unleashed himself. Not wanting to appear rude, Jay attempted conversation while Sugar spit-combed his own hair.

"Any idea what the hell the hold-up is?" Jay asked.

"Ice on the interstate. Two trucks jackknifed and blocked all lanes 12 miles outside of Amarillo. Things is backed up from here to Tucumcari!"

"Shouldn't somebody radio the police or something?"

"Hell. This is Texas, boy. Police can't do nothing about an ice patch. They don't have no equipment to deal with it."

Jay dribbled, shook, and packed himself back up.

"Isn't there *ANYTHING* they can do?" Jay asked.

"God put it there, and God is gonna have to take it up."

Marvelous, Jay thought and fumed.

For the next twelve hours, Jay was one of the umpteen hundred prisoners of cellblock Interstate 40. His gas tank was at one-quarter full after allowing the engine to run for ten minutes every half-hour to pump some heat and friendly radio voices into the car. He could've turned the key to the accessory position and kept the radio running non-stop for company, but he didn't want to take the chance. He'd occupy himself the remainder of the time leafing through the May, 1996 edition of *Leg Stew*—a classic—and thinking about what kind of killer 2 bedroom apartment he'll be able to rent in Santa Monica after he cashes in the STOCK OPTIONS in, gulp, 2003.

Though the primordial survival instinct kept Jay wide-awake during the traffic jam crisis, he'd occasionally suffer a slumbering lapse. But the lapses never lasted more than a few seconds. After the most recent one, his eyes were drawn to a light in the rear-view mirror. He tilted the mirror upward for a better look-see.

It seems as though in the cab of the semi right behind him, there was a little "party" going on. Two truckers sat facing one another. All Jay could make out for certain is that they had their respective shirts off. They drew closer to one another and the chap in the driver seat reached up and turned off the cab lights.

Shivers ran down Jay's spine. He double-checked to make certain his door was locked and slunk deeper in his seat. Yes, the road to STOCK OPTIONS-ville was a surly one, indeed.

II – NEW YORK BASH

"So where's this new guy?" Ollie asked the Chairman en route to the airport.

The next person to ask the Chairman that would be eating knuckle hair for lunch with his coach class peanuts.

"Don't know," grumbled the Chairman.

"We haven't heard from him since, what, Thursday night?" Stosh asked.

"Yep," grumbled the Chairman. The Chairman was not pleased. Jay's disappearance was making him look very bad. The last thing he wanted was a flake under his wing. He knew Jay wasn't the most responsible of sorts, but he always answered the bell for work. He was of upstanding character—despite the fact that inebriation often left him short of standing up. Even for all Jay's follies, this was unusual.

"Listen," the Chairman barked. "Let's just get to New York, make a strong showing for Chicago, and have a good time. If Heck asks me about Jay, I'll just tell him his old job wouldn't let him go early or something. I'll deal with it, and it's the last I want to hear about it."

When the Chairman said he didn't want to hear about it anymore, he wasn't kidding. There was no gray area. Everyone sat silently while the airport mini-van taxi sputtered and skidded its way to O'Hare.

The whole Chicago office of USSBS.com, save for Jay, was wedged into the taxi. In addition to Ollie, the Chairman, and Stosh, were Rennie, Jeeves, Hot Pot, and the Regional Big Cheese—Swifty. When, and if, Jay got to Chicago, that would make a staff of eight—a lethal and lean sales killing machine.

Each character had a story, of course. They were assembled a little bit because of *WHAT* they knew and a lot because of *WHO* they knew. Heck, the National Sales Overlord, hired Jeeves to open and run the Chicago office. Jeeves had a career in advertising that some thought even pre-dated the Golden Age of Radio. But he was sharp, articulate, and took good care of himself the past seven decades. Others often described Jeeves as " . . . a cross between Moses and Charlie Sheen," thanks to his full lustrous crop of silver hair and never-resting libido.

Jeeves was very popular with the ladies. But he also knew his stuff; he could talk the talk with the best scheisters in the game. Sure, this Internet grifting would have a bunch of new terms to learn and throw around. That's small potatoes for a man who could sell meatballs at a Vegetarian rally.

So Heck put Jeeves in charge of getting the Chicago office up and running in May of 1999. And from May to September, Jeeves collected bi-weekly increments of his whopping six-figure paycheck but did little else. Oh, he did manage to set up some office space in an executive suite type building on North Michigan Avenue—the priciest rent district in town. It was also a convenient walk to Jeeves' $3.7 million townhouse a few blocks away.

Jeeves made it already. He didn't need the work, but he needed the job. One can only travel to Aruba and taste wine and cheese with Kennedy and/or Roosevelt stepchildren so many times per week. A regular job would break up the monotony quite nicely. Besides, there's a lot of new, young tail out in the world. The tail craves Jeeves, and he craves the tail.

Heck was a fierce competitor, former high school and collegiate gymnast, had 20 years in sales under his belt with some of the most powerful corporate monikers in the business, and lived to fight the fight. He was given a tremendous salary, hundreds of thousands of STOCK OPTIONS, and a carte blanche to kick tailbone throughout the sales ranks. So the fact that Jeeves hadn't actually DONE anything in four months was a tad irksome to Heck.

Heck heard ramblings in the industry about Swifty. He, too, was already "made" financially. He came from a lineage of wealth and also scored big in the STOCK OPTIONS game with his previous two Internet sales job. He was a tireless worker, with a touch of Attention Deficit Disorder, which made it sometimes entertaining or frustrating for everyone else. Swifty knew the value of hard work and loved the thrill of the hunt. Heck approached Swifty secretly about taking the reigns from Jeeves in Chicago. Jeeves would still stay on in some bogus capacity, but it would be Swifty's show to run. Heck made Swifty one of those hard-to-refuse offers that kept trickling down—an outrageous salary, a lofty Regional Guru title, and gobs upon gobs of STOCK OPTIONS.

Of course, there were no STOCK OPTIONS—yet. But that was merely a formality. Like the Chairman said numerous times over the next year, " . . . Venture Capitalists are the drunken sailors of the world right now; they want us to make a million, so they can make a BILLION." USSBS.com was initially funded with about $4 million. That was enough to get a bare boned operation up and running for a few months while awaiting a hefty infusion from the Drunken Sailors.

The whole stock market was going nuts for these Internet start-ups. An IPO would launch at $3 in the morning and skyrocket to $81 by noon. There was so much money to be made during this gold rush of bull crap, and the higher-ups at USSBS.com wanted theirs. They would go IPO in February of 2000 while the market was still red hot. And wham-bang, everyone from the four company founders on down to Jay and Stosh would be pig stinking rich. It was the perfect plan, and too easy.

So the STOCK OPTIONS were the big lure to get everyone on board. Many of them left stable, decent paying positions at credible businesses to take the plunge on this young, unproven, mysterious Internet company. But every OTHER young, unproven, mysterious Internet company was going IPO and making an entire generation of slackers and ne'er-do-wells millionaires. It was a legitimate pattern developing in the eyes of the business savvy and ignorant alike: open Internet company with any kind of lame idea, sucker some Drunken Sailors into funding it, go IPO in 90 days, cash out six months later, and retire.

In its defense, USSBS.com didn't have a completely lame idea. It was actually better than a lot of the schemes cooked up at the time. In essence, they would compensate "members" for sitting at their computers while being bombarded with advertising messages via a bouncing "Ad-Ball." Every 30 seconds, a computer generated pixel "Ad-Ball" would come bouncing, hopping, or zooming in from a different part of the computer screen. The Ad-Ball displayed the message from a different advertiser each time. When the member clicked on the Ad-Ball at the completion of the message, it would disappear—and the member would get a dime credited to his USSBS.com bank account. If the member corralled friends into joining up, the original member would be awarded and extra three cents per Ad-Ball click per recruit. It was a new twist on the old multi-level marketing schemes. Members movements on the Internet were also being tracked and recorded so that more relevant based messages would appear on the Ad-Ball depending on where they surfed. If they went to a website about food, messages from a competing food website would appear on the Ad-Ball.

The pitch to advertisers would be along the lines of, " . . . imagine Kentucky Fried Chicken putting their signs in the window of the Burger King down the street! We will put YOU right on your competitor's cyber front door!" Advertisers get to put their message anywhere that they want on the Internet; members get paid just to sit around and surf the net while clicking on the Ad-Ball; and USSBS.com gets to go laughing all the way to the bank. Everybody wins.

Swifty happily agreed to Heck's terms, and he took charge of the Chicago office in September, 1999. He needed a couple of floor generals to assemble a sales staff for him and quickly brought on the Chairman and Ollie. They were both bestowed with the big salary, STOCK OPTIONS, etc. Things were now at "Internet

Speed." They couldn't take weeks looking for a sales staff. Swifty's orders were to get people NOW.

"Offer them the top salary, but first sell it with the STOCK OPTIONS." Swifty instructed Ollie and the Chairman in mid-October. "Everybody knows this is about the STOCK OPTIONS, but a good salary should motivate people to make the jump over to us." Right Swifty was. Rennie left his job at a 75-year-old storied and stable ad agency the next day to work under Ollie. The Chairman got a verbal commitment from Stosh who said he would leave the West Coast and be in Chicago within a week. Ollie also knew of a girl, though currently working as a waitress at a pancake house in a west suburban truck stop, who had a previous sales background. She often pined on about getting ". . . out of the friggin' wiggling-for-tips business, and back into some kind of lucrative sales thing." Hot Pot was her name—well, it wasn't her name, but that's what everyone called her. And Ollie had her on board within eight hours.

So three-fourths of the sales staff was in place, and things were totally happening at Internet speed—until the Chairman made an offer to Jay. That derailed the recruitment locomotive for a several weeks. But for all intents and purposes, the Chicago office had its core in place. And now it was time to show Heck in New York how smoothly everything was coming together.

Swifty was oblivious to the conversations going on in the taxi as to Jay's whereabouts and everything else being discussed, for that matter. Being saddled with A.D.D. had Swifty looking for stimulation anywhere he could get it. He barked on his cell phone, fiddled with the taxi radio, read the newspaper, and sought out naughty vanity plates on passing vehicles all while balancing his portable D-V-D player on his knee to enjoy *Ishtar* for the umpteen hundredth time. He had every line of dialogue and camera angle committed to memory and often performed both for whoever was within view or earshot.

Despite the distractions, Swifty was still one of the sharper knives in the drawer. He could jump into any conversation at any point and run with it until he got bored. It was certainly a talent that fueled his success as a salesman over the years. How it would work to his credit as the Midwest Regional Guru was yet to be seen.

Swifty, Ollie, and the Chairman were all knowledgeable, competent, confident beings. It helped them transform from successful salesmen into sales managers. They were the big cocks of the hen house. Conversely, Hot Pot, Stosh, and Rennie were a little tentative, clumsy, and still overly polite. None had sold the dark, nefarious Internet demon to anyone before. Big things were expected from them, and while each had a game face on, their stomachs churned with all the fury of mating cats in a pillowcase. Around Swifty, the Chairman, and Ollie, every word had to be perfect, all body posture had to exude confidence, and any question had better not be a "dumb one."

Jeeves was kind of just along for the ride. He didn't have to worry about impressing anyone, and the Chairman and Ollie made it clear to the subordinates that they didn't have to worry about impressing Jeeves. He had a gig and was basically just waiting for the vesting date to kick in on the STOCK OPTIONS. Jeeves was well liked by all, but the managers wanted him to understand in no uncertain terms that he was more of a figurehead on the payroll. And his storied background at major networks and publications around the globe were only serving as credibility markers to be dangled before advertisers in order to give this start-up racket some legitimacy. It worked well, many times over.

The flight out to New York was uneventful. Everyone flew coach and got saddled with a middle seat. But they had to give the company props for picking up the tab on a major carrier and getting each a private room in an Upper East Side, four-star hotel. Yes, this Internet baby was certainly spending! Money schmoney, was the prevailing ideology; the VC's would be rounding the sweet money mountain at any moment.

Given that the Chicago staff was spread all over the plane, there was no quality time to be shared. They'd be arriving in New

York having worked together as a complete unit for only a few days. They hadn't yet been given the proper amount of time to pigeonhole the other coworkers into convenient little stereotypes: Who was the pervert? Who was the bigot? Who was the nymph? Who was the snitch? Who was the drunk?

As it turns out, each would be the drunk. But the other labels would have to sort themselves out in New York.

Stosh entered his 17th floor room with a bursting bladder and a little tickle in his throat. The Chicago folks agreed to meet in the hotel bar in 90 minutes, so that afforded Stosh ample opportunity to drain the lizard and catch a quick nap. The room was typical by New York standards: small, sparsely furnished, and smelled pre-Truman. The room would certainly suffice for two nights of acid reflux and gaseousness.

After tending to the lizard, Stosh plopped down onto the saggy queen bed and lost himself in his delusions of Internet grandeur. Oh, the stories he'll tell one day about that saggy old queen bed in the cramped New York hotel room—before he became a rich and powerful Internet STOCK OPTION stepchild. How difficult it was to get along back then when the company was still just a suckling sapling struggling its way through the abyss of the anomaly that was the "World Wide Web." One day, Stosh will tell his grandchildren of hardships overcome much the way his grand-pappy did with talk of the depression long ago and the way his pappy did of the advent of T-V dinners years before.

Or maybe Stosh was overestimating his importance in the Big Picture. Maybe this was going to crash and burn like everything else he tried. From selling petunia seeds door to door at age 15 to selling embellished death notices in the local Chicago rags at age 28, nothing ever put him over the hump. Hell, sales sucked! What the hell was he doing in another sales job? He told himself that his next career move was going to be something that didn't drip with rejection every goddamn second of every goddamn day. It was going to be something where the ever-declining masses didn't get to give him their sixth-grade education level opinions about heaven and earth and what kind of soil was best for transplanting—the petunia seeds—OR the corpses. Goddammit! Stosh left his wife back in California to give this Internet House of Cards a whirl and for what!?

STOCK OPTIONS that's what.

When Stosh fully vests in what was now 3 years, 11 months, 3 weeks, and 2 days, then he'll have the last laugh. Then he could kiss the pathetic sales life good-bye once and for all. He could pay off the house, get a second suit, groom the cat, cover the wife in birthstones, and bowl until his plant leg snapped like a chopstick on an awkward blind date maneuver.

Stosh was right-handed, so his plant leg was the left one. And the more he went bowling, the more his plant leg throbbed and hurt. It was a good kind of hurt. And it was all for the sake of bowling—one of the few pure sports left where pathetic, cowardly men and women, and their ever-declining morals couldn't cheat during the heat of competition.

Stosh quit playing basketball because everyone began suffering from a disease he coined "Jordangotti-ism." Every schmuck who stepped on the basketball court since 1982 fancied himself as a "whiter, slower" or "stockier, more feminine," version of Michael Jordan. When combined with the fact they were raised by MTV instead of parents, it eroded their overall judgement and sense of decency and fair play as well. The misguided, dorky, criminally insane fools transformed into Michael Jordan Wannabes with John Gotti's character traits on the basketball court. Whoever cheated quicker and better was the victor, and if you could get both feet off the ground at the same time, hey—that was sugar on top. And should one of these precious darlings be taken to task for their alleged hooliganism on the basketball court, the accuser would buy a knife to the eye in the street after the game.

Stosh couldn't stomach the declining caliber of competition by 1997 any longer. He had played organized or pick-up ball for going on 20 years and it just got worse every year. So Stosh gravitated back towards his first love, bowling. It was just Stosh, his plant leg, a 15-pound emerald Ebonite, and ten honest victims—perfect competitive harmony. And with the advent of automatic score keeping, the up and coming generation wouldn't be able to impart its MTV ethics on the game. It was as pure a competition as could be had in this day and age.

An excruciatingly loud telephone ring brought Stosh back into the here and now. He was a little groggy, but it could be the Chairman or Swifty calling with some last minute tips on how not to embarrass the Chicago office in Heck's presence the next 48 hours. It was a must-answer call.

"Hello?" Stosh said.

"Yeah, Stoshy!" said an exuberant Swifty. "So, did you get a suite, too?" *Ishtar* was blaring away in the background.

"A suite? It's kinda small, but I guess by New York standards it could be—"

"Heck's downstairs. He wants us all to hit the bar so he can get to know you guys before we officially go out for drinks. Put on your sport coat and remember to zip up from the Spank-O-Vision. We'll see you downstairs in five." Swifty hung up.

Stosh looked at the phone and shook his head.

"Okay, five minutes." He hung up the phone and finished his thought aloud looking at his pillow-creased face in the mirror. "I knew this Internet Speed stuff was gonna drive me to drink . . . more."

The tickle in Stosh's throat was burning a tad bolder now. He groped for his tonsils on the way out of the room.

"So this is the Chicago crew, eh?" Heck's voice boomed above everything else in the already raucous ambience of the hotel bar. He looked them over in a poorly lit, back booth. "There's somebody missing, right?"

Nothing gets past Heck. The Chairman rolled his eyes.

"Yeah, where's Jay?" Swifty chimed in.

"He had trouble wriggling out of his gig in L-A. So he couldn't make it here this weekend. But he'll be in Chicago when we get back," the Chairman said. He could tell Heck was making a mental checkmark; whenever Heck squinted real hard with no focal point, he was making a note to himself. "So, what's going to happen tonight?" The Chairman attempted to change the subject.

"Are you sure you can count on this—this—what's his name?" Heck asked in his cynical best.

"Jay," the Chairman blurted. "No worries, he's the real deal. We're lucky he's on board."

"Alright. You guys know that I'm empowering you to call all the shots in Chicago."

"Hey, let's drink already!" Swifty's tone was akin to a kid in a candy store. But nobody dared speak out in favor of partaking of the demon rum—at least, not until Heck said so.

"Good suggestion, Swifty." Heck said.

Swifty stood half-way up, cocked his head towards a waitress, made a walloping circle in the air over his head with his index finger and gave the order: "DRINKS!" Hindsight being 20-20, if USSBS.com ever invested in a corporate logo, Swifty ordering drinks for the group would have been perfect.

Heck, the Chairman, Swifty, and Ollie all ordered the hard stuff. Still wanting to project a professional image, the others opted for light beer. And Jeeves never drank ANYTHING BUT, " . . . Chivas and Maalox, with a twist." The Big Honchos finished their first round in about six minutes with Heck serving as the Pace Liver. The others tried to stay a round or two behind, but Heck would have none of it.

"What's with you Chicago guys and girl!? You sure as hell don't drink like your from Shee-cago!!" Heck said, slightly slurring for the first time. But that would change over the course of the evening as he made the same comments every 21 minutes until 3:00 AM.

Heck pontificated the whole evening about the great state of the Internet, and advertising as a bona fide life form, and how

Mary Lou Retton would still be racking up gold medals today if she were under Heck's tutelage. Heck also asked everyone to stand up and say a little bit about him or her self. But since he waited until the eighth round of drinks, nobody could actually stand up. Plus, Heck would rather he told them what he thought their past and future lives were all about instead of having to listen to them mutter and stutter their way through sugar-coated bull crap.

"Rennie! I can tell you're a fighter. You're a killer. You want ish!" Heck wiped his mouth on an empty water glass. "I'm not shaying that's good or I'm not shaying we can't stop you. But we're family now? Does everyone underschtand that?!"

Nobody could understand a goddamn word, but Heck continued. He stared at Hot Pot for several uncomfortable seconds, blinked really hard, then began again.

"And how come they call you 'Hot Pot?' Wait, I'll bet ish because you're going to go out there and do what's besht for the family so Shy-ca-gooo has a great year, right? Right!?"

Hot Pot, sloshed to the gills and barely awake, somehow managed to pick her slant-eyed skull up from the table and nod on cue.

Swifty had been playing games on his Palm Pilot for damn near two hours while Heck ranted on. He had more to drink than everyone at the table combined, but still appeared quite lucid. Swifty looked at his watch.

"We want to be fresh for the meetings tomorrow, Heck. What do you say we call it a night? We can pick things up right here after business tomorrow, huh?" Swifty said.

Heck had a glassy gaze like a mounted blue catfish at the end of the table. He buried his chin into his throat, smiled without showing any teeth, stood up, and bulldozed his way through the bar and on up to his room.

"I guess that's it everyone," Swifty said. "Get a few hours of shut-eye, and let's look good and sharp tomorrow. Heck doesn't forget anything, not even after eleven Rob Roy's. He'll have plenty of questions for us tomorrow. And the founders will be here, too.

Somebody carry Hot Pot up to her room. And Jeeves—no ascot tomorrow. Just a sport coat!"

It was a miserable morning. Everyone was legally drunk, comatose, or contagious when he wandered into the eighth floor meeting room. About 80 chairs were crammed around a horseshoe table set-up that would've comfortably seated about 35. At the front of the room was an ancient, dusty overhead projector and projection screen. Pitchers of water were available every 14 feet or so on the table. The lucky or semi-coherent souls gravitated towards seats within reach of the 64-ounce oases. Inside temperature hovered near 85 degrees.

Like hapless veal entering the slaughterhouse, each new face was a little nervous, unfamiliar, and barely 22 years removed from the womb. They clustered in packs. The New York and California folks sat mostly upright near the front as they would be doing most of the talking. The adolescent looking reps from Atlanta and Dallas sat in semi-attentive fashion along the flanks of the horseshoe formation. The more "mature" Chicago people slouched in the back of the room. Sure, they looked presentable enough like Swifty wanted. But collectively, they possessed the blood alcohol level of Ireland after dark. Oh, and the stench!

Thanks to the drinking and sleep deprivation, Stosh was now in full-blown Strep Throat mode. He carried a fever of 104, his skin was a pasty purple, and his throat burned and scratched like a raccoon on fire. He was a zombie for the duration of the day.

One by one, the Top Tunas stood, introduced themselves with a mini-job description, and threw terms around the room that were unusual to industry newcomers like Rennie, Hot Pot, and Stosh.

"CPA, CPC, are okay, but we're a CPM shop," said some arrogant New York nobody. "And if you can't sell that on the street in this market, you shouldn't be here. We only want the best of the best. You can walk out of here right now if you're not fully confident of bringing in $1 million each in the next six months!"

One million DOLLARS? Stosh and Hot Pot exchanged looks never having heard such a figure bantered about in any previous sales life. It's a world gone mad, they thought.

A steady stream of condescending, arrogant, suddenly empowered bastards took turns "motivating" the room through threats and intimidation. But none of them, no matter how vile or angry, could hold a candle to Heck. He stood in the very back of the room, with Wayfarers on to deaden the light seeping into his alcohol saturated optic nerves, quietly making his mental notes. When finally introduced in hour number four, he tucked the sunglasses away and stomped to the front of the room. He yanked the overhead project cord out of the electrical socket and angrily pushed the machine against the wall where it made the first of many violent thuds that were to be heard during his 120-minute diatribe.

"I've been standing here all morning, dammit, and I don't like what I see!" Heck pounded his fist into the projector screen jolting even the comatose upright in their chairs. "There's a lot of goddamn money to be made out there, and there's a price tag on each and every one of you. I'm listening, and I'm watching. I don't want to see any more slouching, blurry eyes, tears, confused looks, or smiles until we are a company with a one billion-dollar market cap. I've done it before, and I can do it again. And I say we can be there in twelve—" Heck stopped himself. He looked up at the ceiling and counted to himself while his lips moved for all to enjoy. "—no, make that eight months."

He paused for effect ala the Chairman and looked over the troops. Even when Heck wasn't making direct eye contact, each felt the hellish embers of Heck's fiery glare smoldering on the bridge of his nose.

"A billion dollar market cap company in eight months. We WILL do it. You have the tools, you have the product, and you have the support. And supposedly, you have the know-how, because I told all of the hiring managers to only bring in the best of the best of the best of the goddamn BEST. I don't want any excuses. People are spending money, and I want a commitment from you that you will find out who they are and take the money from them. Do I have your commitment?"

A smattering of unsure nods and low audible "yes's" slapped Heck in the face like an Ike Turner tribute. Heck punched the projector screen to the floor.

"Do I HAVE YOUR COMMITMENT!?" he shouted.

"Yes!" resonated the room.

"Good. Remember, I'll be watching. I'll be watching." Heck thumped himself on the chest, adjusted his crotch, and returned to the back of the room. The good chewing out obviously stimulated him, Stosh thought.

After a 45-minute lunch break, where most, save for Stosh, mingled by playing the Name Game and comparing his grasp of this whole Internet thing versus everyone else's, the barrage of babble from the Mucky-mucks continued.

Each of the four founders took an hour telling the same story of how the company was conceived at Denny's restaurant in Silicon Valley while they brainstormed for a way to strike while the Internet irons were hot. Eventually, one of them pantomimed a routine with a pancake and two pork sausages that served as the syrupy prototype for the "Ad-Ball." And each grabbed his share of the credit for the whole concept. But it was the financial backing and God-given pitchman talent of the CEO, Jimmy Jim Johnstone, which eventually brought the half-baked idea to fruition.

Jimmy Jim was a very well to do, slick speaking, aging Hippie with powerful friends, a colorful track record, and about three-quarters of a billion dollars in the bank. He figured his take after bringing this baby to market and going IPO would comfortably tuck at least another half-billion away in his personal offshore accounts. Besides, it was another lark to add on the resume, so why not?

Jimmy Jim Johnstone had a history of being on the ground floor of initially captivating businesses that eventually went belly up long after he had pulled his own money out and cashed in. That chain of drive-through vaccination centers in Florida and

Texas? Those were Jimmy Jim's at one time. He sold the chain to some Cuban businessmen, and the Kennedy administration eventually shut them down. Then there were the Pet Rock Babysitter Labs in the late Seventies'. Parents dropped off their children in trailers all over America where face-painted boulders "babysat" the kids while Mom & Dad went about their daily business. The kids were enraptured with the boulders and behaved like angels in their presence—until the whole pet rock fad ended and the kids chose to smash or urinate on the boulders and then trash the trailers. But by that time, Jimmy Jim was cashed out and gone again.

There were about 30 such businesses he was a party to over the years. Rarely did he lose money on any of them. Though he did take quite a hit on the clothing-optional auto repair centers that folded up before he could get his investment back.

Stosh was on the verge of passing out. Nine hours of rhetoric and poppycock, and all he had in his stomach was churning phlegm. He still didn't understand a damn thing about the Internet, the company, or how he was supposed to convince people to give him a million dollars when he couldn't even convince himself this was any more legitimate than a hack P.T. Barnum tent show knockoff. But that skill would separate the men from the criminals, he gathered.

All were fidgeting in their chairs. The water pitchers had been bone dry for hours. Sweat stains were the only common trait this "well-oiled sales team" shared. Everybody wanted to know what happened to things going at "Internet speed" when the day was just dragging on.

By 8:00 P.M., even the Top Tunas had enough. Tessie, the gangly Australian woman with the "Vice President of Indeterminate Essentials" title, took nearly two-and-a-half hours to try and convince the rank and file that she was something legit. No one cared, and no one bought it. The dissention was apparent on the collective furrowed brow of the room with each of Tessie's cursedly accented utterances. Heck had seen and heard enough. He had no stomach for Tessie. She didn't know what the hell she was talking about—and she had the chest of an eleven-year-old boy, to boot. But she was hand selected by Jimmy Jim for her position, so she was there to stay.

"Alright!" Heck interrupted her. "I think we've sponged up all we can for today. Why don't we all take 30 minutes or so to freshen up and return messages, and we'll convene across the street at Club Le Poof for drinks, dinner, and what not."

If they didn't think there'd be hell to pay for it, a "Hallelujah!" would've erupted across the room. Instead, all stretched and exited quietly. Yes, the life had been sucked from this bunch. And it was only the first of two days of "meetings."

"Pssst!" Swifty whispered to the Chairman. "I got through *Mystic Pizza* three times today!" The Chairman noticed a tiny wireless earplug in Swifty's head after Swifty proudly displayed his DVD player tucked inside the depths of his briefcase. But the only part that surprised the Chairman was that Swifty actually took *Ishtar* out of the DVD player after 18 months.

"What happened to *Ishtar*?" the Chairman asked.

"Eh." Swifty shrugged. "It was never one of my favorites. I'm more of a Traci Lords guy."

"I don't think she's in *Mystic Pizza*."

"I know. Good tunes though."

Why Swifty called for a limo instead of a hearse for the Monday morning ride back to the airport for his Chicago troops will be debated about in war crimes tribunals for centuries. The crew was a total mess—alcohol ravaged, sleepless, germ laden, and trembling from the effects of Heck's psychological sodomy. There was barely a pulse among them. Even Jeeves looked like a dapper cadaver in a $1,500 jogging suit.

How each made it to the car by departure time was nothing short of Divine Intervention. Reports were sketchy as to what, exactly, transpired between Saturday night cocktails and the here-and-now. Suffice to say, the Chicago Seven took out their feelings of metropolis-envy rage on the poor, unsuspecting Big Apple. Sidewalks were regurgitated upon; mailboxes were urinated upon; passers-by were spat upon; and that was all just from Hot Pot strolling on the boulevard.

As his head throbbed and tonsils sizzled like generic brand, thick cut bacon, Stosh asked probing questions during the limo ride to try and piece together everyone's respective antics from the past 36 hours. They had split up into smaller drunken mobs at some point. Stosh was able to rage for a few hours each night, but spent the majority of the time sweating through his underpants under the blankets in bed. Something had invaded his body on a serious and microscopic level. And it just wouldn't go away. Stosh had become the poster boy for pathology.

His personal recollections were few, but Stosh did remember a few things: Heck holding a horse in a "Full Nelson" headlock on Lexington Avenue; Swifty and the Chairman playing "keep away" with Jeeves' Bruno Magli money belt; Rennie giving a homeless woman a hickey; and all of the aforementioned Hot Pot ditties as the group galloped en masse back to the hotel from SCORES—the grand mammy of all jiggle joints.

"So, what'd everybody do last night?" Stosh asked hoping to elicit an answer from any life form.

Silence. And it was more than just one of the Chairman's communication tactics at work.

It was a compartment full of stone-faced corpses staring blankly out of the windows. Perhaps in their minds they were replying with all sorts of witty banter. But not a single mouth had motor skills, nor a brain to chauffeur.

It was the end of round one, and Life at Internet Speed had the Chicago office on the ropes already—with its teeth bleeding, ankles wobbling, and corner man out for a smoke. The first week together being the barometer, this was not shaping up as a pretty fight.

Even Been-Everywhere-Done-Everything road warriors like the Chairman and Ollie were reduced to quivering epidermal rubble.

Was this the end of USSBS.com already, Stosh asked himself. How could he hitch his wagon to this train wreck? What will his wife say when he tells her this new once-in-a-lifetime opportunity lasted eight days? And what became of Heck and the horse? Too much information to process now.

The limo slithered out of Manhattan towards LaGuardia. Stosh closed his eyes and tilted his head up against the window. The others followed suit, except for Swifty.

This would be a good time for Swifty to get some work done. He took a sloppy hit of Triple Sec off his trusty flask, "Stanley," fired up an Internet connection on his Palm VII and *Mystic Pizza* on the DVD player. He inserted the wireless earplug and surveyed the limp bodies around him.

"Good team!" he thought.

III - DIGGING IN:
8 BECOME 24

Even though the Chairman didn't expect anyone to show up for work before 9:00 AM, Stosh made sure he was there by 7:00 AM every morning. He sure wasn't going to have any job security based on his ABILITIES, but maybe he'd have a little by being a punctual and immovable cancer in the workplace.

The Tuesday morning after the New York weekend was no different. Clutching his high-octane brew from the Granny Bean's franchise down the street, Stosh moved quickly into the seven by seven-foot office on the fifth floor overlooking a building under construction 36 inches from the soot streaked window. Oh, and the sweet part of this whole "executive office" set-up was that he'd be SHARING the office with Jay—eventually. There was barely enough room for ONE person to lean back in his seat with his feet up, let alone two. Also in the nicotine scented paradise were two pressboard desks, a jalopy bookcase, and the official, impenetrable "office supply cabinet" all circa 1971.

This was the space Jeeves envisioned as the nerve center to a young, hot, upstart Internet company. Never send an Octogenarian to do a live person's job. Nobody could figure out WHY he committed to this suite of eight offices for two years. He was an immaculate man with high brow tastes who had nary a soiled fingernail in the several preceding decades. But there they were—LOCKED IN to a long-term lease. They had to make the best of it—at least until the IPO money afforded them the opportunity to build something swank.

And USSBS.com wasn't the only operation using the "executive" offices. There were about 25 offices in all on the floor. And the occupants ran the gamut from a fussing and feuding, newly married insurance schleping couple—to another insurance dealing gay fellow who made sure all of his intimate phone conversations were heard at a higher decibel level than Henry Rollins taking a dump. And Brick, the chain smoking freelance writer who looked like the lovechild of the Marlboro Man and wife mummy to King Tut, and whose office was right next to Stosh's lungs, was just the icing on top.

While his HP craptop computer booted up, Stosh reflected over the weekend that was. Though the symptoms of his illness left him barely able to speak until returning to Chicago, Stosh held on as long as possible each night trying to display the "Chicago Office Solidarity" like Swifty, Ollie, and the Chairman demanded. And against his better judgement, he did slurp a few cocktails. He knew it was the worst thing for his immune system at the time. But dammit, if Stosh was going to have to stand around all night covered in his own mucous listening to Heck rip everybody a new corn shoot, he may as well have a buzz going. He couldn't get over the fact that this was supposed to be a big team-building, cuddly-wuddly; get-to-know-you schmoozfest weekend. But in retrospect, it turned out to be more like a virtual reality, 3D version of *Shindler's List*.

And Heck was watching, and Heck was listening. So results had better be forthcoming. Stosh didn't dare take a sick day. His symptoms had cleared up somewhat, but the lingering sore throat and listless blahs would hold on the entire winter. Heck would get his results. Right after Stosh finished reading the morning *Sun Times*, though. He'll sacrifice only so much for STOCK OPTIONS.

True, there were only seven employees in Chicago . . . TODAY. But if/when Jay arrived, that would be eight. And the Campaign Coddling Department was supposed to have somebody report in and hire a separate staff to support the sales team. Plus, a

Bogus—ahem—BUSINESS Development wing was pegged to launch soon with several representatives in Chicago.

So with only eight offices, that meant pairing-up. Ollie and the Chairman took one office. Swifty and Jeeves, much to each other's chagrin, shared a window office with an exquisite view above Michigan Avenue. Hot Pot and Rennie were paired-up as they were "Ollie's Team." And Stosh and Jay were to co-exist as "Chairman's Team." That left four offices to split amongst newcomers in the next few weeks and months. USSBS.com was poised for growth; only the companies which grow the biggest and do it the fastest go IPO!

Stosh finished reading his newspaper and slurping his steamy liquid bean in about 20 minutes. One could get away with reading the newspaper on company time because it was "prospecting," allegedly. Stosh preferred to get it out of the way before the office filled up with judgmental eyes, just the same. It was a lot easier to convince onlookers that one was ostensibly "working" by gazing at a computer screen and dancing one's fingers on a keyboard than it was leafing through the NBA box scores just above the massage parlor ads on page 77.

By 8:00 AM, the early birds in the other offices on the floor began showing up for work. Brick, the perennially smoking man on the other side of the wafer-thin walls from Stosh's lungs, was typically one of the first in. He entered the building smoking a cigarette, sat at his desk all day smoking a cigarette, and probably drilled his Old Lady at night with a cigarette dangling from his mouth. The four offices adjacent to Brick's reeked of his no-filter, double tar goodness. And the odor quickly seeped into clothing, hair, papers, food, coffee—anything within a three-cough radius of Brick's esophagus.

Long about 8:55, the Chairman kicked in Stosh's door left ajar clutching a donut and a 64 ounce bottle of tap water.

"Where's Jay, dammit?" This would simply become the Chairman's stock way of saying, "good morning."

The Chairman was angry, disappointed, confused, and hungry. Such a combination does not make for cheery morning conversation. He took a seat behind Jay's future desk.

"I wish I knew," Stosh replied. "I hope nothing bad happened to him."

"Please," the Chairman said taking a vicious bite off of his jelly filled victim.

Almost as if on cue, Jay flung open the office door and spread his arms wide.

"So this is the Internet speed I've been hearing so much about!" Jay said looking at the Chairman and Stosh slouched in their respective chairs. Jay appeared no worse for wear from the long trip, though his clothes were severely wrinkled and he sported a 4-5 day growth of whiskers, tomato sauce, and sesame seed bun crumbs.

Stosh shook Jay's hand and hugged him.

"You made it!"

"Yeah," Jay said offering his hand to the Chairman. "Sorry I didn't get here for the New York thing. The trip was a nightmare."

Silence.

More silence.

Then the Chairman shook Jay's hand.

"Your cell phone not working or something?" the Chairman asked.

"Not actually. I had no signal for most of the trip, and a dead battery for the rest of the trip. My charger is still in L-A and—"

"What about a pay phone!?" the Chairman interrupted.

"By the time I got to one, you guys were already in New York. So then I figured I'd just take it slow the rest of the weekend and stop in at a few strip joints along the way and stuff."

"Goddammit, Jay! You're off to a bad goddamn start. Heck was asking all sorts of questions. Even Swifty started to wonder, and he doesn't focus on ANYTHING! And what do you mean 'take it slow?' You were three days late getting here. Well?" Chairman then punctuated the tension by rapidly squeezing and flexing the plastic water bottle in his left hand, followed by more silence.

"Well," Jay said taking off his jacket. "Here's what happened." He told the tale of his journey to an enraptured Stosh and skeptical Chairman. He included every detail about packing up, or the lack of it, and the inner turmoil he was experiencing about the life change. Rennie and Hot Pot had arrived right when this "stranger" was telling the tale of being stranded outside Amarillo, Texas, for fifteen hours without a phone, food, or toilet, and all of the homo-eroticism that went with it. The Amarillo incident ended when Jay barreled into town and right inside the first liquor store he could find, checked in to the cheapest motel on the highway, shot-gunned six Heinekens in 35 minutes, and passed-out on the crusty, pastel bedspread for the next 18 hours.

The tale of the journey continued with lengthy anecdotes about stops in Oklahoma City, Tulsa, Joplin, Springfield, MO, St. Louis, East St. Louis, Springfield, IL, and Peoria for "gas or SNATCH." Jay was oblivious to Hot Pot standing in the door with Rennie listening on and really belted out the word "SNATCH" every time. Having grown up with two older brothers, Hot Pot was pretty much desensitized to the use of the word "SNATCH," so no harm done. The most telling phrase of Jay's pre-occupation during the drive?

" . . . you wouldn't think the quality of SNATCH would go down so far from St. Louis to East St. Louis. But let me tell you, if you're driving west, hang on to your money until you get to the premium SNATCH in St. Louis. The East St. Louis SNATCH is a total rip-off. I've seen better SNATCH on *Animal Planet*!"

This was a man who knew what he wanted out of life, and it took singles from off his nose every time the deejay changed the song. That's what Stosh liked about Jay; he was what he was. And that's what the Chairman didn't stomach so well sometimes.

While there was a speeding ticket issued from a wisecracking Missouri State Trooper, Jay suffered no real serious setbacks since pulling out of Amarillo.

"So why is it you didn't call again?" the Chairman asked.

"Well, like I said. By the time I got to a phone at the SNATCH patch in Oklahoma City, you guys were already taking off. And I knew you wouldn't be coming back until Monday afternoon. So I'm sorry I didn't make it for New York, but that was totally out of my control. And I'm here now. So let's get started. Where's my office? And where do I sign for those STOCK OPTIONS?"

"You're standing in your office," the Chairman said rising to his feet. "But first I want you to meet Rennie and Hot Pot who have been standing in the doorway for most of your story. Come up for air next time."

Jay, always the gregarious one, offered up a big smile and handshakes for Rennie and Hot Pot.

"Hot Pot? I had one of those in college—I used it to sanitize and deodorize my stinkables and what-not." Jay said, attempting to break the ice/get some new tail.

"I know you're thinking crazy hippie parents, but it's just a nickname. However, it's what everyone calls me."

"Even clients?" Stosh asked.

"I try and avoid the issue with clients," Hot Pot said smiling. "To them, I'm just 'Honey,' 'Darling,' 'Sweetie,' or 'Toots'."

"Damn," Jay said. "I was going to use those."

"Rennie and Hot Pot are on Ollie's team. We'll all catch up later with a mini-meeting when Swifty gets here. Stosh, help Jay settle in," the Chairman said marching off in the direction of the men's room.

"We'll talk to you then." Rennie said nodding to Hot Pot to follow him back to their office. Rennie was the quintessential one-syllable word communicator. One always knew where he stood with Rennie.

Jay eased in behind his desk and queasily eyeballed Stosh.

"Why does it smell like a French whore's ashtray in here?"

"Shhh!" Stosh said whispering. "It's the guy next door. He smokes all damn day. But the walls are real thin. You can hear everything everybody says. I'm sure he heard your story!"

"Whatever. So, is the Chairman really mad?"

"Hard to say. I've seen him worse. And remind me to tell you about New York later."

"Yeah, I want to hear about that."

A few moments passed without anyone speaking while Jay rummaged through his rickety old, corkboard desk pulling strange, abandoned things from every drawer.

"Who do you think this electric nostril trimmer belonged to?" Jay asked while tossing the thing in the trash basket.

"We'd better get you a craptop and get you going. Heck wants results and fast!" Stosh said.

"Craptop?"

"Oh, you'll see after a few days. Obviously Internet speed must mean crashing six times in an afternoon with the closest technical support person 2,000 miles away."

"Great. Well, maybe we'll be able to do this Internet stuff without computers?" Jay said.

Maybe he was kidding, maybe he wasn't, Stosh wondered. Neither of them knew enough about the Internet to really know for sure.

That first week together, the Chicago office hummed along like a blender full of broken glass and ball bearings. Along with the office space came the complimentary "administrative personnel." There were three bodies, and each was named "Nicole!" (Though one of them acquiesced to being called "Nikki" to make things less confusing.) Together, they were the three-headed, bleach blonde, GED deficient, foul-mouthed, daydreaming monster in charge running the switchboard, processing mail, and basically making sure the office operated in perfect harmony for every company within renting space.

The reception desk and mailroom were conveniently located one floor below all of the offices which they served. And there were no stairs between the floors—only elevators. That meant every time someone had to run to the copy machine, get a stamp, or SEND A

FAX, he had to call for the elevator each way. This did not make the one-floor jumpers very popular with the folks who had to go a much further vertical distance in the 23-story building. A stop for every elevator at the fifth floor was almost assured at every time of day because so many people were sending so many faxes, etc. One cannot possibly elicit a more hateful look of contempt and disgust from others than by taking only a one-floor elevator ride. It just can't be done. It's far more piercing and lethal than the look given from holding up the grocery checkout line for any reason. Anyone can live through the Grocery-line Glare and live to tell about it; but the repeated Elevator Glare will pummel one into therapy after a scant four incidents.

The office of the building flat out REFUSED to supply a copier or fax machine dedicated to the fifth floor. It was 1999 going on 1954. And there were no "fat pipes" (high-speed access) to the computers in the building. Everyone had to limp along at 56K—it didn't matter what company he worked for on the fifth floor.

It was certainly not a boon for the USSBS.com employees who represented the Midwest headquarters for the new, young, hot, upstart Internet company on the scene. As far as connectivity went, it didn't get much more embarrassing than 56K in the workplace. To the outside cyberspace world looking in, they were Pong!

One Monday at 4:45 PM, the Chairman asked Jay to take a FedEx envelope, containing some very important mortgage papers, down to the Three-Headed Nicole monster for delivery. Upon Jay's arrival, the central administrative office was empty, put he left the FedEx on the desk. At least TWO out of six eyes would see it for sure, Jay figured.

Long story short: the envelope didn't go OUT until the following Friday for one reason or another. Monday night, the Three-Headed Nicole monster decided it was a slow day and thought it would be a good idea to knock off a little early, so the envelope sat where Jay left it overnight. On Tuesday AND Wednesday, they allegedly "just forgot" about it. On Thursday, one of the heads called in sick leaving only two skulls to sort through the daily workload—this caused the Chairman's envelope to be "misplaced."

Finally, on Friday, the FedEx successfully left the building. Yes, the Chairman knew he could have taken the FedEx parcel for processing himself since the contents were so valuable. The first couple of days, blind faith allowed the Chairman to send the parcel through "normal office channels." The next couple of days it became a matter of goddamn principle to see if the Vapid Rag Squad could execute the task. If they ultimately didn't, the Chairman was going to use that as leverage to somehow break the lease so USSBS.com could get the hell out of there.

Breaking the lease had fast become a priority after the first of the New Year. The mandate came down from Heck that he wanted more feet on the street. He told Swifty to get four more warm bodies out there selling. The Business Development charlatans were up and running with a couple of new reps. And the Campaign Coddling department appeared out of nowhere with ten new employees.

There was literally not enough room for all of the Campaign Coddlers to sit. Some days, they were told to work from home. Other days, when attendance was mandatory, they were told to just pace up and down the hallway until a chair became available.

Elfie, tagged the Supervisor-by-Default since she was the first to interview and accept one of the Campaign Coddling jobs with USSBS.com, ran the department with an iron fist, forked tongue, and heavy eyes. It wouldn't become known for months, until well after this 24-year-old going on 68-year-old's $110,000 annual salary kicked in, that Elfie was a raging Narcoleptic! Elfie had the mouth of a disgruntled lumberjack and the stamina of a bludgeoned tortoise. She was IN CHARGE of the Coddling wing for Chicago, which on paper, gave her as much "virtual power" as the Chairman or Ollie! She reported ONLY to Tessie, the gangly Australian woman in New York, and only had to cooperate with Swifty when she deemed necessary.

This, of course, did not sit well with Swifty. And Elfie was immediately slapped back into place over the first internal power struggle over who had the right to command the Campaign Coddlers: Elfie, or the sales reps? Since Elfie made herself scarce two days per week by allegedly working from home, combined with her habit of snoring and drooling in the workplace with her head wedged between her thighs, Heck told Tessie that Chicago was Swifty's show to run—period. Embarrassed by the rumors of Elfie's abusive language towards subordinates and slumbering ways, Tessie didn't put up much of a fight since she handpicked Elfie for the job. She didn't dare draw attention to herself on a higher corporate level for fear of anyone on the board finding out what a $200,000 per year fraud she was.

So Elfie was slapped on the knuckles early on, and they thought it might induce her to stay awake for eight straight hours. But reports of Elfie dozing off during conference calls, brainstorming sessions, riding the elevator, or on the toilet kept rolling in.

Because of the "go, go, go, hire, hire, hire" Internet climate at the time, even Elfie had a little job security for the time being. In any other industry, she would've been out on her saggy rump after the first nap. But like every other Internet company at the time, USSBS.com needed to keep and retain as many bodies as possible during the push to go IPO.

Elfie hired her subordinates in the most effective means possible given her maladies: over the phone. Though none was outwardly grotesque, Elfie did seem to coincidentally assemble as many battle axe neurotics on her staff as possible. She likely didn't know she was doing it at the time. But something innate obviously "clicked" each time she hand-selected another disembodied, muffled voice to be on the Campaign Coddling team at a very nice salary.

One of the first aboard was Gabby. She was a typical Midwestern girl: brown hair, brown eyes, no accent, and could stand to lose 15 pounds. She was joined by Sharon, Sherrie, Cherie, Kathy, Cathy, Juleen, J'Ndana (pronounced who the hell knows), Knockers, and Big G (the only male on staff). They invaded the floor each within 72 hours of one another. It took the sales people weeks to learn their names. Swifty never quite did.

The Business Development, or "Biz Dev Grifting Machine" as it would come to be known, department was made up of two eclectic, hungry, young, fast talking lads by the names of Josh and Brad. They were the best boldface liars the Business Development head based out in California could find during his four-hour layover at O'Hare one day. Each was bestowed with a six-figure salary, six weeks vacation, and license to fleece any entity that had a checkbook. The bigger the fish, the more they'd be rewarded in heaven or via STOCK OPTIONS. They were accountable only to Kweeg, the Biz Dev Overlord in the Bay area. That was another thing that irked Swifty, but he didn't contest it—yet.

The new crop of sales people the Chairman and Ollie brought on board at Swifty's request was pretty much all the market would bear at the time. There was Babs, the 20-year-old daughter of a friend of Swifty's mother at the country club. Along with Babs came Kippy, a 21-year-old, Cocky-As-All-Hell punk of a bastard whom DEFINITELY was raised in a four MTV household. A few days later they tapped Noah, a smarmy perfectionist with successful track records in sales and making enemies. Finally, during Happy Hour at the Billy Goat Tavern, they found Gerard-Generation X's six-foot tall, hairy-knuckled answer to scratching one's bum. Time constraints and all things being considered (ex. blood-alcohol level), the management team felt pretty well about all of the pawns they had in place by the end of January.

As Swifty put it, "I wouldn't want to wake up in bed next to any of these people, but maybe they can sell. That's all that counts. Let's go drink."

IV - THE BOOM

"Alright, here's the drill one more time." The Chairman's voice was raspy from drinking for half a day and the smoked-filled atmosphere of Café D.O.A., one of the Lincoln Park neighborhood's favorite after hours hangouts for Goth and genetically awkward types. The Chairman liked "the fringe" late at night, and he wanted to turn Jay and Stosh onto the scene to let them know there were more than just " . . . trendy sports joints and old-man bars out there." The Chairman took a healthy gargle off his sixteenth OLD STYLE and continued.

"We're dinosaurs, boys. You, me, Ollie, Swifty—and definitely Jeeves—are all dinosaurs in the Internet business. The industry is young—young and computer savvy. The median age at the companies and interactive agencies you'll be calling on is about 22. You won't be dealing with traditional media buyers or clients. At the agencies, the girls will be named Lisa, Amy, or some version of "Jennifer;" the guys will all be Dave, Jeff, or something Indian. They're going to talk in a lot of terms you guys don't understand yet. But Ollie and me will try to help you. And read the trades, goddammit. Read the trades!"

Jay's eyes were welded shut from inebriation by the 2:00 AM hour, but he was still listening and ordering drinks with a limp fist. Stosh was groggy but didn't dare let out a yawn in the Chairman's presence opting instead to oddly pucker his cheeks and flutter his eyelids when the urge to yawn arose.

"That's why we brought on Babs and Kippy. Hell, they're each making sixty-grand right out of college, and they don't know a damn thing about selling. But they do know the Internet. I'm counting on you guys to help them out in the ways of the world, and for them to help you guys out on this whole Internet scene thing."

Jay let out an effeminate belch.

"Where wish you Chairman," Jay slurred while slapping the Chairman on the back.

Stosh politely nodded.

"Look, we know they weren't the most qualified. But to be honest, neither were you guys!"

One could always count on the Chairman to shoot straight from the hip.

"There is, or has been, nepotism in every industry. Right now, the Internet is hot. This is the Gold Rush. This is where the fortunes are to be made. And this is where we needed to recruit bodies, but at the same time, maybe throw our friends a bone while we had some kind of power to do so!" The Chairman was short on breath. He paused to gulp some beer.

"So, how do those STOCK OPTIONS work?" Stosh asked.

"Yes, that's the sweetest part of it all. Okay, you guys are making a damn good salary, but that will never make you rich," the Chairman said.

Two portly Goth girls perked up at the end of the bar as this was the most articulate conversation ever overheard inside the establishment.

"When I started at Poopydoopy.com, they gave me a mess of STOCK OPTIONS. But I didn't really realize the value of them. You're getting a strike price of, like, a nickel. Then after the IPO, the stock shoots up to fifty bucks. You do the math!"

"If I could do math," Jay stammered, "I would've been an accountant."

"Just trust me," the Chairman said firmly. "There are no guarantees, but we're in the right place at the right time. These venture capitalists are the drunken sailors of the world right now. They want us to become millionaires so they can become billionaires. It's too easy! It's all tied to the STOCK OPTIONS."

Stosh was buzzed. STOCK OPTIONS . . . STOCK OPTIONS . . . STOCK OPTIONS resonated in his head with each thump of the ear splitting beat emanating from the deejay booth. Stosh would normally never be caught dead in a place like this. It was dark, cold, laden with mildew and demonic drumbeats—uncomfortable to registered voter sorts. The two portly Goth girls disappeared behind the deejay. And Stosh was certain he saw a guillotine back there so the parent-hating masses could off themselves in a trendy way.

"Let's get out of here," the Chairman said after shot-gunning his seventeenth.

Stosh sighed with relief and picked Jay off the barstool by his armpits. He could drag him out to a cab, go home himself, and sleep off the alcohol.

Alas, the Chairman wasn't finished thinking out loud. "There's another joint I want to check out in Wicker Park with a 6 A.M. license. It's got a biker/parolee motif."

On the rare occasions Rennie spoke out loud, his words were carefully chosen bearing three constants: one-syllable when possible, no smokescreens, never say more than he would want to have to listen to.

"What do you think is up in there?" Rennie asked Hot Pot.

"Dunno," Hot Pot smiled. She knew the correct answers to very few questions in life, opting instead to skate by on her striking face, platinum locks, and firm caboose. A quick smile from a cosmetically appealing face often softened the blow of such a noncommittal response. Maybe she knew, maybe she didn't; it was for the one doing the querying to lose sleep over.

"Well, the door has been closed all day. Most of the time, the door is open." Rennie replied.

Rennie turned back to his computer and resumed prospecting after being unable to entice Hot Pot into some kind of conspiracy theory discussion. Truth be known, the closed-door meeting was scaring the hell out of Hot Pot.

No good comes from closed-door meetings of the higher-ups. They were all in there on a conference call with Heck: Swifty, Ollie, Jeeves, and the Chairman. Since nobody had sold anything in three weeks, save for Rennie's $500,000 deal with a major insurance company, Heck must have been chewing everybody out but good.

Stosh, having been dubbed the "temporary office manager" by the Chairman and Swifty, came down the hall to see if Rennie or Hot Pot needed any office supplies. Stosh poked his head in their office. Hot Pot was nervously twirling her hair with her index finger, and Rennie was rocking back and forth mumbling ever so softly to himself.

"Anybody need anything from Officecrap.com?" Stosh asked.

Rennie's phone rang.

"This is Ren," he answered.

Stosh whispered the question again to Hot Pot.

"Just get me what everybody else is getting. What do you think I'll need? Just whatever I'll use is fine."

"Everybody needs something different," Stosh said glancing down the list. "I need pens and tape. Jay wants some of those ink stamp inkpad things and manila envelopes. Babs wants a paper shredder, thumbtacks, and kite string—"

Being unfamiliar with office supply vernacular and becoming more insecure with each new word, Hot Pot flashed Stosh a smile and a zippy " . . . yes, that stuff. Me, too."

"Oki dokes," Stosh said.

Rennie hung up the phone, stood up, and rubbed his bowed forehead slowly with his palm. To the casual observer, it looked like the pose of a boy looking at his dog who just got pasted by the ice cream truck.

"We don't have to do the office supply stuff now if it's a bad time." Stosh said in his empathetic best.

"Huh? Oh, yeah. Just get me all of the same stuff as her." Rennie nodded towards Hot Pot.

"Is everything okay?" Hot Pot asked Rennie.

"That was Schmutz.com. They want to test out the Ad-Ball for $100,000."

"That's awesome!" Hot Pot said feigning glee though green with envy. "Why do you look upset?"

"Oh, I think I said the guy's name wrong. I hate when I do that. It sounds bad. I like to sound good."

That being said, Rennie sauntered over to Swifty's office. He could hear Heck shouting via the speakerphone through the closed door. He knocked anyway.

"We're in a meeting!" the Chairman shouted.

"Who is it?" Ollie barked.

"It's Ren. I just got a deal—ten weeks, ten grand per week."

The door quickly opened and Rennie was welcomed inside. All Hot Pot and Stosh could hear were a couple "Atta boy's!" and "You da man's!" before the door slammed shut behind him.

Stosh returned to his office where Jay had been tutoring Babs on Sales 101 just minutes before like the Chairman requested at Café D.O.A.

"How'd the tutoring go?"

"If she's supposed to tutor us on the Internet like the Chairman said, we're in deep hog piss. She knows less about the Internet than you and I did in 1974. And we'll have a major struggle teaching her about sales, too. She asked me why we're going to all this trouble to ask people to put their 'message thingies' on the computer when they can just put them in the Sunday paper or, and I quote, whatever day that real fat paper comes out."

"Well, we'll have to make the best of it. Swifty juiced her into the job," Stosh said.

"I have no problem with that. But they'd better not expect us to wipe her nose for her when we're trying to sell. We've got quotas!"

"Rennie just signed another deal with Schmutz.com—one hundred K!"

"Alright!" Jay responded.

"I don't know. Don't you think it's going to turn up the heat on the rest of us to start selling something fast? They're still in that meeting, you know. And Rennie's in there getting his back slapped like he just sold a lifetime supply of aluminum siding to the Egyptians to put on the pyramids."

"Chill out. Didn't you read the Cyberskuttlebutt today? The VC players are throwing tons of money around in all of these start-ups. The money is out there, and we'll get it. We've only been at this six weeks or whatever. Just focus on sending out twice as many e-mails today," Jay encouraged.

"I can't. My computer is still locked up from trying to send that two-page PowerPoint file to Korndog King."

"He has a website?"

"A damn good one!"

"I don't know. How many people do you think want to order corn dogs over the Internet?"

"Ours is not to question why. He's got $4.5 million in VC money under his belt dedicated just to the website, 30 percent of which is earmarked for interactive marketing. They're the best damn corn dogs in Chicago. And he's the only one to return my call in weeks!"

Jay picked up his phone handset for a quick listen. A dial tone confirmed they were allegedly working properly.

"You know what," Jay hung the phone back up. "I don't think I've gotten one incoming call since I've been here."

"Not possible," Stosh countered. "We're the fastest growing Internet company on the scene. The Chairman said only yesterday we signed our six millionth member!"

"Have YOU gotten any incoming calls?"

Stosh thought for a moment, then checked his own phone for a dial tone. "Now that you mention it, Korndog King did call me on the cell."

"Quick, call the general number and ask for my extension." Jay said.

Stosh followed through. After an unnerving eight rings, a Newport 100 tainted orifice of the Three Headed Nicole Monster answered the phone. Stosh asked to be connected to Jay's extension at USSBS.com. While the phone rang in Stosh's ear, Jay's phone did not ring at all. Stosh gestured for Jay to answer his phone anyway suspecting a bad ringer-doohickey. Nobody there—just a dial tone. Both hung up.

"This is nuts," Stosh said. "You call me now!"

Jay placed a call to Stosh via the switchboard the same way. This time Jay heard the ringing in his earpiece, but Stosh's phone didn't ring. They attempted the process again using their respective cell phones. The result was the same—no normal connection.

"We'd better look into this!" Jay said. "I've been sending out a ton of e-mails, too, asking people to call me back!"

Upon further investigation, it was determined that while half of the USSBS.com offices were hooked up with live phone connections, the other half were logged into some kind of phantom switchboard abyss. Any calls transferred to eight of the phone extensions given to USSBS.com by the executive suite office support personnel weren't really hooked up to anywhere. And since nobody complained early on, Listeria, the office manager for the executive suites, did nothing about it.

Jay and Stosh decided to surprise the Chairman and Swifty with this little tidbit knowing full well that they'd been looking for even more excuses to break the lease with this current outfit. It would also take some of the heat off of them not being able to close a deal yet. "God only KNOWS how much business we lost because people couldn't call us on the phone or e-mail us because our computers crashed . . . " is how they'd position it.

At 4:45 PM, while they lay in wait outside Swifty's door for the all-day conference call to end, Kippy strode past with his chin up, chest out, and par-for-the-course slacker backpack slung over his shoulder.

"Later, losers!" Kippy chuckled.

Quite the cajones that Kippy had insulting two people he barely knew, who were both older than he, and who could've beat him to slacker dust with his own pulmonary system if they'd had a tough-guy molecule between them. Furthermore, this was a START-UP company. Everyone was to put in a minimum of ten to nineteen hours every day—no exceptions. Combined sacrifice is what was needed to take USSBS.com over the hump to be the leader in its field, and consequently, deliver the employees into STOCK OPTION nirvana.

"I'm taking my bitch to the Phatty Phat-Phat concert." Kippy said while exiting the premises. "Then we're gonna screw."

Jay and Stosh were aghast. That punk hadn't shown an ounce of respect to anyone since joining the company. He wasn't being a team player. And to top it off, he had comely lass at the ready to give him sex that night after the show.

"It's been so long since I've been with a woman, I think I've forgotten where all of the biological ports o' call are." Jay said a little louder than he should have. Swifty's door swung open. The Chairman stood there with his arms folded across his chest.

"Heck's not happy," the Chairman said.

"Well, it's really Jay's problem to deal with," Stosh offered.

"Heck will be here next Tuesday. He wants to know why Rennie is the only one selling anything. Every other company is signing multi-million dollar deals every week except us, and Heck wants to know why!" The Chairman paused and gestured for Jay and Stosh to follow him over to his office.

The Chairman proceeded to give the duo a tongue lashing for several minutes. They didn't want to snitch on Kippy, but did drop the bomb about the phones not working to take a little of the heat off of themselves. As expected, the Chairman flew into a rage and marched back over to Swifty's office to form a plan of attack against Listeria.

It was 5:30 PM by now. Any attempt to reach Listeria would be futile, as she was already safely tucked away inside her dilapidated bungalow on Crack Alley making love to one cancer stick after another with her throat until the sun came up. They'd have to confront her when her yellow-toothed, stained finger, tar-hacking skeleton showed up for work in the morning. No wonder she never came down on Brick for smoking in his office despite how many city ordinances and Ms. Manners etiquette rules he was breaking. Brick's penchant for smoking in the workplace cast any suspicion away from Listeria herself. Except for the fact that she worked one floor below him and was often out of the office for days at a time, it was the perfect cover in Listeria's mind.

"Well, nothing more we can do around here if the phones are down," Swifty chirped to most of the staff assembled in the hallway. "Let's go get some vodka gimlets! Somebody tell Babs and Kippy to meet us down there—we've got to build some team unity. Heck's coming to town next Tuesday. He just wants to say hello."

That was a tad different than how the Chairman put it. And over time, everyone would learn that was one of the greatest traits about Swifty. No matter how hot the fire got from Heck, or anyone, Swifty took all the heat to protect his people. Nothing was ever as bad as it seemed after Swifty put his spin on it.

Hot Pot looked like she had been hit by a beer truck, then crawled around lapping up all of the spilt beer all damn night, when she burst into Stosh and Jay's office a couple of days later.

"Rumor! Rumor! Rumor!" she teased.

"What? What is it?" Jay and Stosh asked in unison.

"Okay, first, headquarters told Swifty to go ahead and move to a bigger office because this place is a nightmare and we need room to hire fifteen more people. Second, we're getting $150 million infusion from some big Japanese Internet investment company. And last, Rennie just inked another insertion order with Fizzyburst Cola for three hundred thousand cracks!" Hot Pot hopped up on Stosh's desk and did a dance that was part Ickey Woods touchdown celebration, part stripper being eaten by school of Piranhas.

"Whoa! Take it easy!" Jay was so excited seeing a live woman writhe so close in front of him he didn't care what was happening the rest of the year.

"That's big news," Stosh said. "What's a crack, anyway?"

Hot Pot hopped off the desk. "Just dig it. We're on our way to the big time. I heard from reliable sources is all you need to know. Hippy! Happy! Hoppity! Humdinger!"

"Not to change the subject, but have you sold anything yet?" Stosh asked.

Not one for entertaining such straight-laced conversations about business or the lack thereof, Hot Pot became flush and dashed out of the room.

"What was that all about?" Stosh asked Jay.

"Hell, if I did a dance like that, I'd have to race out and have a cigarette, too."

"Have you even SEEN a woman in your building yet?"

"Doesn't matter. I'm moving into One Bodacious Place—it's a vanity address. You know, the new hi-rise over on Superior? That place will be crawling with trim!"

"No kidding? That's an awesome building. I thought you were subletting for six months at the joint on Dearborn."

"It was month-to-month, except they just decided to go condo. So I'm getting kicked out in ten days."

"Ten days? Is that enough time to move?"

"No sweat. I'm fully up to Internet speed. And I'd suggest you learn to adapt by the time Heck shows up." It didn't make any sense, but Stosh heeded it as good advice. They plugged away on the phone and e-mail for many hours without a break hoping to snare a "live one" to impress the Chairman. Concentration was at an all time high. The craptops hadn't locked up more than twice between them, so the boys were making major headway, technologically speaking.

Although initially unconfirmed, Hot Pot's tasty rumor report about the big Japanese company investing in this little USSBS.com operation was a major boost to their confidence for the longevity of the company. Later on in the afternoon, the rumor was confirmed on the Cyberskuttlebutt report, which everybody in the office received via e-mail daily.

Swifty looked upon the issuing of the news as a reason to celebrate, yet again, after work with a few rounds of margaritas. Attendance was mandatory. Even the Campaign Coddlers were invited. The USSBS.comer's were experiencing their proudest day as a dotcom play; they had been legitimized to the tune of 150 million cracks!

Rennie was the last to join the crowd at El Chorizo es Diablo later on. They were all half in the bag when he entered. It was a familiar scene by now.

"What took so long?" Ollie asked him. "You're already three frozen mangoes behind!"

"Oh, I had to talk to this guy. He read the news about us. He wants to spend twelve thou' a week with us for the next three years. I said yes, he could."

The place went up for grabs. This was too much good news too soon. Nobody even remembered Heck was showing up the next morning for a cattle prod session. The television was on behind the bar. And although they couldn't hear the newscaster's voice, the graphics verified what the industry buzz had been saying for many weeks. The NASDAQ was going through the roof. Twenty new Internet companies went IPO just that day. And the weakest of them opened at 6 cracks and increased 250% by the close of the market.

The Chairman pointed at the television and shot an "I Told You So" look over to Jay and Stosh. Swifty was holding court with a margarita in each hand boasting about prosperity for all and having fun and drinking faster and drinking longer. He looked more like Jackie Gleason in his prime than Jackie Gleason ever did. Fully anticipating the sales goons would pick up the tab, the Campaign Coddlers were having a ball inhaling as many mini-burritos and drinks at Internet speed as their bodies could digest. Hot Pot had a gut-full of tequila shots commensurate with the volume of a

Wrigley Field, six-man urinal trough. Elfie dozed with her head between her knees on a barstool, but she appeared to be having more fun than usual. And Babs nursed a beer while watching Kippy feel up his bitch under the coat rack.

Somewhere in Silicon Valley, Heck was boarding a plane with human gray matter from the West Coast sales office stuck to his penny loafer.

The Gods must've been smiling upon Stosh the next morning. An unknown number was ringing his cell phone. The caller was a man from downstate Illinois with a rural drawl by the name of Tom Jango. He had been hearing quite a bit about this " . . . dadgum Ad-ball," and wanted to advertise. Stosh didn't ask how Jango came about getting his cell number, and he didn't care. Stosh had his first sale!

Jango wanted a small test of $3,000 to begin with. It was a far cry from the umpteen hundred thousand dollar deals Rennie was landing every other day. But it was SOMETHING. And anything that was something in this world of selling intangible NOTHING'S was a big deal indeed.

Jay congratulated Stosh, and Stosh broke the good news to the Chairman. The Chairman was pleased, naturally, because SOMETHING was better than nothing was. But in the Chairman's mind, the SOMETHING's had better start coming in with more tonnage and of greater frequency. And a $3,000 deal was NOT going to ease any of Heck's wrath; hell, his tie tack cost more than that.

Stosh started to become a believer. If one guy can call him out of the blue all psyched about the Ad-ball, there must be a thousand more guys like that. Stosh filled out all of the time consuming, nuisance paperwork so the Campaign Coddlers could get to work on Jango's campaign. And then he sought out more marks, er . . . clients, with renewed vigor.

This made an impression on Jay, who then started calling a few more agencies. By mid-day, the fever pitch had spread around the office with the consensus school of thought being " . . . if

STOSH can get a sale, ANYBODY can!" Babs, Kippy, and Hot Pot were dialing for dollars with reckless abandon. Even Josh and Brad came sniffing around once the scent of blood was in the air. As Biz Dev Vultures, their second duty, when unable to con a client on their own, was to find out which clients were spending money with USSBS.com already and then steal away the account citing some foreign or biblical precedent.

Subconsciously, maybe Heck's impending arrival was finally motivating everyone to push a little bit harder . . . to stick their cyberfoot in the virtual door before it could be closed. The intense focus on siphoning fresh blood also made everyone oblivious to the devastating winter blizzard crippling the city.

Only Swifty and Jeeves had a window to look outside at the sub-arctic chaos. Jeeves was on a last-minute holiday as of midnight the night before. He didn't want to be around for Heck's blitzkrieg and told Swifty about a " . . . one day lift ticket in Lake Geneva he had to use before it expired . . . " at the end of the raucous margarita party. Swifty approved it, but knew it was a load of butt grease. Jeeves had only been in the same room as Heck once in the past eight months, and that was in New York in December. Jeeves was never happy about the fact Heck took his power away and gave it to Swifty. And he made it a point to become scarce whenever Heck was scheduled to appear.

And Swifty was too engrossed in a director's cut of *Porky's Revenge* on his DVD player to notice the howling wind and slush tidal wave activity in his peripheral view on the other side of the window.

Most traditional companies or brick n' mortar operations already sent their employees home by 2:00 P.M. The dotcom peasants in wacky lofts and moldy basements around the city continued to forge ahead with martyr-like zealousness figuring they had STOCK OPTIONS at stake and had to rise above it all. Blizzard schmizzard. However, specifically to sales types—advertising sales types—this all but shut them down for the day. If 9 out of 10 offices were closed, who would be left to contact? Nobody important, with a fat marketing budget, that's for certain.

The Chairman began making the rounds up and down the hallway telling everyone the GOOD news: Heck's plane had been diverted to Kansas City. And he wouldn't be coming to Chicago that week, because he had to be back in New York for meetings. A reprieve!

All of the sales reps had gathered in Swifty's office soon after to exchange sighs of relief and talk about Stosh's grand day!

"Well, it's just a $3,000 test." Stosh said.

"By the time Heck hears about it," Swifty commanded, "it will be a $60,000 test! In fact, that's how I want you to fill it in on your weekly report. We'll worry about the specifics later."

"But—" Stosh said confounded.

"You heard Swifty!" The Chairman interrupted. "Don't worry, we know how to position these things for the bean counters."

Stosh nodded and cast his worried gaze out the window. Through the flying snow and pounding sleet, he thought he saw the fuzzy image of a large octopus sitting on the street curb repeatedly poking itself in the head with a different tentacle. Leaning forward and staring more intently, it was something far more gloomy: the Three Headed Nicole monster, Listeria, and Brick were huddled together at the bus stop for warmth passing around their last collective cigarette.

"Hey, while you guys are here now, I guess I can share some good news. But keep it under your hat until after it becomes official." Swifty said, motioning for Kippy to close the door. "We're out of here effective April 1. We're breaking the lease because we need to add some more people. And hell, getting some T1 access might be good for business, too. Anyway, the board OK'd it. Ollie, me, and the Chairman are going to start looking at places next week."

"Alright!" Jay shouted.

"Hip, hip, hooJay!" Hot Pot deadpanned.

"Bitchin'." Kippy said.

With Heck out of the picture for a many business days, Stosh and Jay decided to kick up their heels and blow off some steam—nine consecutive nights in a row. Each time, the tab was no less than $185. That's a lot of money when it's sometimes just two guys drinking $1.25 draft beers, but they didn't see it that way at the time. Each was making the best salary he'd ever been paid, so who cared what the pithy bar tab was? If the Venture Capitalists were the drunken sailors of the world right now, they'd be the naval reserve.

Every night was the same. Jay would buy the first two rounds, then Stosh would buy one or two. By that time, they were too blitzed to remember the system. And one would think whoever possessed the motor skills to retrieve cash or credit card from his pocket typically paid the rest of the night. But contrary to physics, it was usually Jay who spent an eternity fumbling for his American Express card night after night and ended up paying for the bulk of the hooch. And if there was even a slightly attractive female form in the bar, her drinks were on Jay. And if the slightly attractive female form was with two or three friends, their drinks were on Jay, too. They never said squat to him, but they always took his drinks.

"Ish okay, I'm an Internet executiff!" he would blurt out at different unrelated points in the evening. In a perfect world, such a pronouncement at that point in time would have trim raining from the sky down onto one's face. But this was Jay's world, and the casual sex clouds never yielded a drop of anything.

Many nights, even Jay's pulmonary system couldn't absorb any more and his survival instinct kicked in. His brain instructed his legs to become rigid enough to carry him home, and he would just wander off into the night. Sometimes Stosh would find him in the street just outside the bar, sometimes Jay would make it all the way home to his comfy, cozy, twin inflatable air mattress.

Jay and Stosh each had an inflatable air mattress as the cornerstone of their furnishings. Stosh bought the deluxe brand with the built-in air compressor attached to the mattress. Jay purchased the outdoorsy, Blow-It-Up-With-Your-Mouth-Till-You-Have-An-Aneurysm kind. Why an air mattress? They were practical in that neither wanted to waste money on furniture or had women to bed. Stosh's wife was 2,000 miles away, and any potential strange Jay might score had to be much further than that. This was just a temporary venture, after all. In 46 months, one week, and some change, they'd be back out West sleeping on whatever overpriced conversation piece they picked up at the Puff Daddy bankruptcy auction, thanks to the STOCK OPTIONS. Four years on a more-comfortable-than-one-would-think inflatable air mattress was nothing!

The bottom line was that they were under heavy stress and drinking to excess to cope with it. It was the same workout regimen adhered to by their fathers before them, and their fathers before them, and so on. The system must breed success, they gathered, because look at them now: two highly paid Internet executives hammered to the hilt in a corporate world that previously used them as whipping boys for half the money. They would have the last laugh for sure.

The remainder of Q1, the term corporate pigeonhole thinkers give to the months January through March, absolutely rocked for USSBS.com and most other dotcoms. The NASDAQ recorded record highs day after day. More and more Internet IPO's were executed. Companies that had no right to exist outside of someone's perverted imagination like Roadkillclothes.com were replacing grand old retailers and oil companies on the S&P 500 Index.

Every night on the evening news, the lead story/ journalistic gang bang revolved around some wacky dotcom rags-to-riches corporation. It was accompanied by related stories about how the company's two 13-year-old founders had become billionaires on paper just by developing a way for people to order designer toilet plungers from behind the Iron Curtain. Also, insulting "Internet for Idiots" pieces filled with factoids, lame puns, and pictures of Bill Gates were thrown in to make it all palatable to the typical TV watching mind.

"Membership," an official sounding but laughably impossible to verify measurement in Internet terms, was multiplying at USSBS.com to the tune of 40,000 new "members" per DAY. Members translated into eyeballs that became dollar signs to Internet advertising players. The more eyeballs, the more potential coin to be swindled; TV perfected the scheme, and the Internet was just taking it to a new level.

Everyone at USSBS.com was taking advantage of the Boom. Rennie had booked $900,000 worth of business for Q1. Hot Pot and Jay broke their cherries, and then joined Stosh to build a list of no less than a dozen paying clients each. Stosh even landed Korndog King to a $5,000 per month campaign after overcoming every client objective in the Sales 101 manual. Despite his gutter mouth and condescending nature, even Kippy scored a few clients. The Biz Dev Grifting Machine was in full force talking with several major airlines about decade long commitments to the Ad-Ball; there were even whispers about a $100 million deal with General Motors in the works!

Babs, however, struggled with it all.

"Why do people say they'll call me back, and then they never do?" She asked dejectedly once during a team meeting.

In everyone's eyes, she was heavy, rotting dead wood. But so far, the rest of the team was bringing in enough money to carry her. If she didn't turn things around in Q2, which was a definite long shot, Swifty would have to make a tough decision. He'd have to keep her on board as a liability and get an earful of venom from Heck or drop her in the summer and soil his mother's good name at the country club for a good six generations.

Trade magazines and papers picked up on the buzz USSBS.com was creating and ran multi-page articles about the phenomenon. Jimmy Jim was being elevated to Mother Teresa-like proportions while captions such as "This Man Is Paying You To Look At His Ball!" and "Quit Your Day Job and Just Surf, Baby, Surf!" ran atop his smiling photo. The "members," all 11,000,000 at last count, were making money because they were letting the Ad-Ball violate the computer screen while they meandered around the web. The more the Ad-Ball appeared, the more each member got paid. The more friends and acquaintances each member coaxed into joining the Ad-Ball universe, the more money for EVERYONE. Some chap down in New Mexico received checks to the tune of $8,500 every month from USSBS.com because he had aligned so many warm bodies "under" him.

"Don't fret," everyone at USSBS.com was used to saying by now to advertisers, potential members, and media vultures, " . . . it's *NOT* a multi-level-marketing scheme. It's INTERNET marketing."

"Ohhhhhhh," they would usually respond, totally placated. Like the man said many years before: "You don't sell the STEAK, you sell the SIZZLE." And human beings transformed into lemming-brained zombies when somebody before them gave good sizzle.

USSBS.com was on the upsurge. Sales offices were popping up all over the globe in every U.S. city that had a population greater than 500,000 and every European or Asian city that maintained a population of at least 750,000. Crates of marketing tools, toys, and collateral material arrived weekly. In Chicago, they wouldn't have any place to put the stuff until relocating to a bigger office. So every Chicago employee had to haul at least three boxes of pamphlets, pens, rate cards, or edible jock straps—all bearing the USSBS.com logo—home with them per week. (Kippy took nothing but the jock straps).

Stosh and Jay were on the top of the world. They had never known the good life as sales people. One-hour lunches were scoffed at; usually they went for two-and-a-half hours at a minimum. They dropped $20 to $40 each on Oriental buffets, imported catfish sandwiches, expensive wine, and the most succulent Hot-Fudge-

Sundaes-On-A-Stick the local eateries had to offer every afternoon without guilt. With notions of STOCK OPTIONS dancing in their head, they racked everything up on credit cards that would easily be paid off when the IPO hit.

The good vibe of the Bull market was effecting everyone in the office. Swifty bought new condos in Aspen, Colorado, and Wisconsin Dells. The Chairman moved into a 1920's mansion on the Northwest side of town and completely gutted the place for renovation. Hot Pot was purchasing three pairs of new shoes every evening after work and dropping the bulk of them off at warming shelters after one wearing. Even Rennie splurged and increased his crew cut visits to the barbershop from twice per month to every 10 days.

Jay was in his new apartment at One Bodacious Place and decided to fill it with the most expensive wicker or wax furniture that money could buy. He bought two bamboo folding chairs at $195 each, a coffee table sculpted from the world's biggest block of petrified head cheese, a sterling silver shoe horn for each foot, and a computer desk with a built-in bidet. He was on the top floor, unit 5525, and had a better view of the Loop than St. Peter. If an Internet Executive title and the most overpriced apartment in the city (425 square feet at $2,800/month) didn't help him score some fresh tail, then nothing in this dimension would!

The burgeoning sales reports coming out of Chicago convinced Heck to postpone his motivational speech tour indefinitely. Chicago was doing something right. Out of the 250 or so USSBS.com worldwide sales offices, Chicago was bringing in the most revenue per salesperson head. Swifty, the Chairman, and Ollie were looking good for the personnel choices they made. This made them happier. And while they were never micro-managers, they felt the reps would be best left to their own devices. Nothing was broke, so nothing needed fixing—if they ignored the whole Babs portion of the equation.

Jeeves was opening up to everyone a little bit more now, too. He was conversational, witty, naughty, accommodating—a real pal to everyone. Though one dark day, he tried to be more of a pal than necessary to Hot Pot when he rammed his tongue in her mouth on a quickie elevator ride down to the copy machine.

It didn't bother Hot Pot as much as it did the other four people riding the elevator. But it did confuse her as Jeeves said little more to her previously than idle workplace chit chat drivel—the non-touchy/feelie-kind of talk mandated in the workplace now by the federal government everywhere outside of the Oval Office or Congress. Gosh, Jeeves was old enough to be her Sugar Daddy three times over.

The office romance never really blossomed beyond the elevator peck. Jeeves was heavily into dating services and seeing many different girls a week. And Hot Pot's life was filled with perpetual spastic episodes of one kind or another; she was being pulled in too many different directions, professionally and by women's footwear retailers, to devote concentration to a relationship. Still, she'd be moving up the social ranks by dangling from the diddler of a rich, sophisticated, Boul Mich gentleman.

After toying with the notion in her head a few days, Hot Pot was convinced a May-December romance would never last between unstable lives at Internet speed, especially between raging alcoholics. At best there would be shared remorse and biological carnage. At worst she'd end up humiliated, solitary, and abandon with a strain of herpes from the 1930's raging through her bloomers.

V – ALL HAIL THE "AD-BALL"

"Goddamn, no-talent, vapid piece of neurotic waste!" Jay screamed at the television while hosting a small Grammy Award watching party at his place—really small, as a matter of fact. He was alone until Stosh showed up just after his outburst.

"Who are you calling a neurotic waste?" Stosh asked upon entering.

"Pick one," Jay said pointing to the television.

"Oh, I thought maybe you were talking to your reflection in the wine glass again."

"Talent isn't based on skill, creativity, or ability anymore—just MARKET-ability!" Jay fumed.

"Sounds kind of like the Internet," Stosh said.

Jay nodded, and they slouched in the expensive bamboo folding chairs sipping a fine 1997 California Cabernet—the best year for Cabernet in the last 25, according to Jay. After twelve minutes, they could take no more of the self-congratulatory, oratory masturbation, 35-second sound bytes thanking Jesus, and feeble attempts to communicate in English.

Jay turned off the tube and put an "Outfellers" CD on. The Outfellers were a local Chicago band that had experienced some notoriety in the early 1980's with a couple of songs that received national radio airplay. Jay became enraptured with their sound and stalked them at every live show between 1986-1996 before moving out to California. He also turned many friends, including Stosh, on to the band though none pursued them to the extremes Jay did. Jay liked the Outfellers because they did have true talent and a conscience and bled if pricked. They weren't a contrived, talent-less pretty boy quintet preening to the unsophisticated masses. The Outfellers put their souls on the line with every composition. That was to be respected. And stalked.

Jay and Stosh retired to the outdoor balcony with their wine to enjoy the crisp winter evening. Precipitation loomed. Stosh looked down at the pool 55 stories below.

"Man, in the summer, that thing will be filled with bouncing breasts!"

"I hope so. I plan to fall off of here after drinking too much on the 4th of July."

But it wasn't even Spring, and they were in Chicago. Bouncing breasts were a long time away. Not wanting to depress the other, each avoided pointing out that obvious fact. They sat silently sipping their Cabernet looking at the twinkling magnificence of the Chicago skyline for a few minutes. Jay's stomach gurgled.

"Hungry? Want to get a bite?" Stosh asked.

"Nah. I'm kind of broke until next payday. I just had to pay rent. And I bought three bottles of this wine at $125 a pop. It's a 1997 Cab—that was the best year, you know. Plus I had to send the bulk of my check to American Express to cover bar expenses for last month." Jay emptied his glass and went inside for a refill.

Stosh sighed and took a mental panoramic note of the glorious view that he could replay in his mind's eye when looking up into the water damage stained ceiling at his apartment later on—his reality. To the East was the cool darkness of Lake Michigan serving as backdrop to the architectural charmers known as Tribune Tower, Amoco Building, and Navy Pier. To the Southeast, the wicked hellhole of Gary, Indiana looked almost tranquil with its dozen or so working streetlights twinkling against the shoreline in the distance. Directly South stood the grandeur of all that was "downtown"—the Chicago Theater, the Merchandise Mart, the Sears Tower, and forty other skyscrapers that changed names from one Japanese word to another every couple of years. To the West, there was Midway Airport, the United Center, and an unnamed nearby building that was good for peering into with binoculars. All in all, it was the breathtaking scenery deserving of an Internet Executive. And the Outfellers were laying down a perfect soundtrack for it.

"Hey, I can make some onion dip if you're hungry." Jay said.

"Nah. I'll have some cheese popcorn when I get home. I'm good."

Jay sat.

"Nice view, huh?"

"I can't believe you don't sleep out here. I can't get enough of this."

"Maybe I will when the temperature gets above 35."

"Yeah, that will be sweet. A summertime slumber party on the balcony should soothe your savage beast."

They dinged wineglasses in celebratory fashion.

"So, not to bring up work, but what are your clients saying about their results with the Ad-Ball?" Jay asked.

"I guess everybody's happy. Nobody has said they weren't. And you only really hear when they're not happy, you know?"

"Got'cha." Jay said knowingly. "I hope Elfie gets canned soon. I cannot believe she's still on board. Do you know everyone in Campaign Coddling doesn't even loop her in on campaigns or anything any more?"

"I believe that. She does more damage when she is looped in. She used the back of one of my insertion orders this week to sketch little Satanic triangles and things, and the folks at headquarters needed the I-O to start the campaign. She folded it up, put it in her backpack, and alleged she never saw it. It only turned up because she lost her smelling salts and tore the backpack inside out looking for them."

"Nice. Did I tell you she tried to target one of my campaigns just to our members in SPAIN? It was for Flufferflixxx.com, that adult video store in Wicker Park. They want to only target Ad-Ball users in five neighboring zip codes, naturally, and she calls me up and tells me she's got the campaign all ready to start on Monday just in SPAIN! I went flying down the hall screaming. I would've slapped her into a coma if I didn't think she'd enjoy it so much." Jay emptied his wineglass again. "You ready yet?"

Stosh shook his head. Jay was on a breakneck pace tonight, even for Jay.

"Better catch up. This good stuff goes quick! Hey, you want to get a pizza?"

"I thought you didn't have any money."

"I'll just put it on American Express. My commission check should make up for it—and then some, I hope."

"It's time to give a little something back," the Chairman opened the weekly staff meeting. "We're going to throw a party, invite all of our current and potential clients, and generate some new business out of it."

"If I could interrupt," Swifty was accustomed to saying, "we want this to be a huge blow-out. Go down your entire client lists. I don't care if you've never talked to these people live before, get them an invitation. Now we need a theme, any ideas?"

"Wine and cheese?" Jeeves said. Nobody dignified his suggestion with a reply.

"Any ideas, any ideas at all," Swifty repeated.

"Too cold out for a boat ride. How 'bout if we do it in and not out?" Rennie contributed.

"Good, Rennie, good." Ollie encouraged. "Now if we can just expand on that. Any other ideas?"

"Super Bowl!" Hot Pot barked.

"That's over," the Chairman scowled. "Goddammit, this shouldn't be so hard!"

"Could we maybe rent out a bar and just have sort of a mixer with wine and snacks and everything?" Jay said.

"Yeah, that is like what I said." Rennie followed.

"Good, Rennie, good!" said Ollie.

"Stosh! What do you think? And no stupid answers!" the Chairman commanded. Nothing like a little extra pressure in a public forum.

"Well," Stosh stalled. "I like to bowl."

"That's IT!" Swifty shouted. "A bowling party! I love it! We can get those little shirts made up and give prizes."

"And it will be in, not out, like I said." Rennie boasted.

"Yeah, remember Rennie said something in instead of out. I think bowling is the perfect combination of ideas!" Ollie concluded.

"Think you can organize this for us Stosh? We want to do it in about three weeks so we'll have a big push on for Q2. People open their checkbooks when you oil them up real nice with open bar and 'comp' hot wings! Get in touch with somebody at headquarters to iron out the budget. I've got to go fly out to Titmouse, Colorado, and hire a new rep. Thanks, everybody!" Swifty was almost out of the room when he let the good news slip out. "By the way, I'm not supposed to say anything. But that's crap. We're moving April 6. We found some tasty digs on Wacker. And the IPO should be happening in six weeks. All of the papers are filed. Don't count your chickens, but don't start fretting you'll have to retire on that 401-K garbage, either! Later!"

All were elated down deep but hesitated from any outpouring of emotion in front of the managers. They could almost taste those STOCK OPTIONS now.

"You heard Swifty," the Chairman said. "Stosh, get this party together. Everybody else get your client lists to Stosh to compile. He'll send them to Ollie and me for final approval. We want this to be big . . . huge! Heck is going to be invited, and so are the founders. Don't let us down. The big day is right around the corner. The wheels are in motion. All of the pieces are in place. It's going to happen, and it's going to happen because of YOU!"

The Chairman should be in politics, everyone thought. Either that or the special teams coach for the Green Bay Packers. His rhetoric was sufficiently multi-faceted.

Among the perks/fleecing tools utilized at USSBS.com were season tickets for Chicago White Sox and Cubs games. A free ticket to a sporting event was a common, lowly sales carrot dangled before customers in all industries over the years to further the shameful, insincere ploy regarded as "client bonding."

A sign-up list in the Chicago office at USSBS.com was posted so the sales reps could reserve tickets for specific clients. The rule imposed by Swifty was that if a rep requested the tickets, he had to accompany the client to the game and foot the bill for everything, no exceptions. Though the expenses would eventually be reimbursed, it was typically a $300 outlay for each game. There were five seats in all, and the rep was responsible for wining and dining the client before, during, and after the game. What was supposed to be a cool perk turned into nothing more than a weekly financial liability for all.

And if the Chicago crew didn't have enough excuses to go out and get crocked, the baseball games provided 5-7 more opportunities every week. Rennie reserved most of the dates, as he had the most clients that needed to be stroked. Jay spent more money than anyone did at each outing. Stosh consumed more sausage-based products than all other reps and clients combined. Hot Pot filtered the most beer through her bladder during the season, easily outpacing Jay's standard of "One Beer per Every Half Inning."

Some days a client just couldn't be tapped for a day out at the old ballpark. And in such cases, Swifty OK'd the use of the tickets in-house for whatever sales rep wanted them plus four friends or co-workers of his choosing. This was always a last minute decision, though, 20 minutes before game time. Up to that point, the Chairman and Ollie cracked the whip to get their respective team members cranking on the phones with a "terrific last minute opportunity that has opened up" for a ticket to that day's ball game. A more desperate spectacle the sales world cannot recall.

Some weeks, 2-4 days worth of drumming up business were lost because the majority of the Chicago sales team was bending Budweisers at Wrigley Field and Comiskey Park. Budweiser would never have been the first choice it being the bland-headed stepchild of beers and all. But Budweiser is what the vendors peddled in greatest quantity, and quantity far superceded quality when in an Internet frame of mind.

A client or guest never attended half of the game dates. Far too much of the time, Kippy absconded with the tickets to enjoy beer bongs at the game with his old, delinquent frat rats.

"I'll take those, Jackass!" Kippy would usually say when ripping the tickets out of one of the manager's hands.

The novelty of the whole baseball scene had worn off for Stosh after seven games. Baseball was palatable to him when dramatized on film or viewed in a historic black-and-white newsreel—when players at least had the façade of being decent human beings. This modern day joke of the sport dominated by pampered Panamanians marketed to the American buying public was less appealing every day. And the uncultured thugs that filled the stands seemed to morally erode before Stosh's very eyes with each foul ball that sprayed off into the crowd. People were actually choking and thrashing one another for the rights to a $4.99 piece of sewn up cowhide inadvertently dropped at their feet by non-English speaking, convicted spousal abusers who would be unemployed and more marijuana than men within three years. The stands were filled with rowdy, cursing, selfish, gluttons poised to do battle for something as inconsequential as pinching a mustard packet the wrong way over a hot dog.

Ultimately, the fans and players deserved each other, Stosh figured. But he had to go the games to demonstrate to Swifty that he was working just as hard at bending over for the clients as anyone. Stosh certainly developed his Cheddarwurst eating disorder as a direct result of stress brought about by having to be put in such an undesirable environment on a regular basis. Often he'd sit with a juicy, steaming Cheddarwurst in each hand, regularly having reinforcements delivered five to seven times per game.

But at least Stosh was being reimbursed when he dropped a few hundred dollars each game day on the Korndog King and his guests or whoever. Jay wasn't too keen on completing excessively anal tasks like expense reports. Despite the Chairman's pleas and directives for Jay to do so, he just couldn't bring himself to sit down and do a bi-weekly expense report. Jay had weeks upon weeks of cab and restaurant receipts, not to mention baseball game charges, stacked up in a holding pattern on his American Express card. He'd always pay the charges, but hadn't yet gotten reimbursed for any of it. The prospect of losing so much money forced Jay to drink more on game days, and alas, his personal Cycle of Despair and Fiduciary Downward Spiral was steadfastly in place.

More praise was being heaped upon Jimmy Jim and the Ad-Ball founders in ink and on television. The company didn't dare spend a dime on traditional advertising. USSBS.com was still just a "start-up," and all funds had to go towards more necessary things like product development, employee salaries, and the edible jockstraps with the emblazoned USSBS.com logo.

And true to Swifty's word, the banker dudes had all the ducks in a row ready to take the company public in early April of 2000. Employees were each issued the double-secret stock related papers to be filled out and returned for SEC compliance. About 5,000,000 stock options were bestowed to paying clients, friends, and family. Their strike price, or "nut" as the Chairman commonly called it, would be $1.25 per share. Since all expected the stock to rise to $45-$75 in the first few days, that wasn't a bad deal.

Everybody was getting his. The big group of Japanese drunken sailors that infused USSBS.com with the huge chunk of funding took 40 percent of the available options. At USSBS.com, everyone at the management level was bestowed with 50,000 to 100,000 options; and every other employee across the board at USSBS.com was bestowed with 25,000 options.

The traditional marketing players, at both companies and agencies, were including the USSBS.com Ad-Ball on all future campaign buys. After listening to the USSBS.com pitchmen, the buyers were convinced that there wasn't anything the Ad-Ball couldn't do. When Jimmy Jim spoke publicly about the product, he often alluded to the notion of the Ad-Ball replacing television, billboards, blimps, and penicillin within 36 months as it became more fully developed. Businessmen and women alike swooned at Jimmy Jim's feet as if awestruck groupies at a Tom Jones concert when he pitched the company at trade shows.

The Ad-Ball was going through some improvement, to boot. The upgraded version of the Ad-Ball had a built-in search engine, horoscopes, compass, and "skin." The idea behind adding the search engine, horoscopes, and compass was to indirectly force the members to keep the Ad-Ball on their screen longer so more advertisers could be presented. The "skin" was the look of the Ad-Ball. Members could personalize it to initially look like a bouncing ball of bricks, a bowling ball, the sun, or one of sixteen deceased ex-presidents. The Ad-Ball's "skin" would dissolve soon after appearing so advertisements could appear. One hasn't lived until he's seen the computer-generated face of JFK dissolve into a static pixel advertisement for cat litter.

With demand from advertisers to have greater presence on the Ad-Ball came higher rates they were forced to pay. They did so without question. Every advertiser had the satisfaction of knowing that they were a part of the process way back in the day before the USSBS.com company bought out Microsoft, Cisco, Wells-Fargo, McDonalds, and two-thirds of the Western Hemisphere. There was prestige now tied in to being an Ad-Ball advertiser.

The demand also created the necessity for additional USSBS.com products to be developed so the potential advertisers could be gouged in a more timely and greater manner. Heck put some slick, arrogant alcoholic named "Bungleman" in charge of coming up with new ways of siphoning funds into the USSBS.com coffers. And these funds would only be credited to Heck and the sales team; the Biz Dev Grifting Machine had it's own bottom line to pay attention to. For the pre-IPO surge, Heck told Bungleman to come up with something within one week's time.

Bungleman locked himself inside a grotesque Queens motel room with a bottle of Everclear in Mid-March. He'd been on the payroll in a quasi-sales capacity for seven months but never actually had to sell anything or do anything. He was an old friend of Heck's, and Heck mostly kept Bungleman around so he could pick his brain. Fueled by the super proof alcohol and 21 hours per day of pay per view porn, Bungleman soon emerged with USSBS.com's Cadillac of Scams: Premium Tentacles.

The Premium Tentacles would be pitched to, and initially reserved for, the big spenders. When the Ad-Ball zoomed or dribbled onto the user's screen, small green circles—twelve in all—would appear on the outer edge of the Ad-Ball so as not to get in the way of whatever advertiser message was appearing in the center of the Ad-ball. When a surfer clicked on an outer green circle, .20 cents would be credited to his USSBS.com bank account, and a long, green, slithering octopus-like tentacle would shoot out from the Ad-Ball and present the "premium" advertiser's message. So as not to go broke, USSBS.com limited Premium Tentacle clicks to five per surfer per day.

For the privilege of being on one of the tentacles, three options were given to the advertiser. A commitment of $1,000,000 would secure the advertiser its tentacle of choice (ex. Noon position, three o'clock position, etc.) for one year. For $500,000, an advertiser would be guaranteed 100,000 tentacle "clicks" in six months. And for $375,000, an advertiser's message would appear on any given tentacle for no less than 250,000 impressions. Heck was satisfied. Bungleman had done well. Now all Heck had to find out was if the software boys could actually ADD tentacles to a bandwidth-eating beast that was already triple its original content size.

For his efforts, Bungleman was given a new title, National Intermediary of Sales, along with a $15,000 salary bump, and an additional 15,000 stock options. Swifty never liked Bungleman and cursed his name every time Bungleman was coming to Chicago to "check things out." A one time Chicagoan, all Bungleman was really checking out were his old Rush Street haunts from his grammar school drinking days and using the company expense account to pick up the airfare under the guise of a sales meeting in Chicago. He also had family still in the area; that was convenient so someone could drive Bungleman home from the Area One Police Headquarters drunk tank. Swifty knew the lethal drinking and a concurrent erection fueled Bungleman's whole "tentacle" idea. Furthermore, he had a disdain of Bungleman's obvious abuse of the expense account system. But Bungleman was Heck's boy. It was another thorn the regional VP's had to deal with.

April had arrived. It was to be a big month indeed. In the first week, the Chicago office finally got to say good-bye to Listeria, the Three-Headed Nicole monster, Brick, and the whole Dumpster full of human misery that made up the executive suites on Michigan Ave. Plus, there was the client schmoozing Bowl-o-Rama party. And certainly most importantly, the IPO was imminent—STOCK OPTIONS!

The moving of the office couldn't have come at a better time for Kippy and the Campaign Coddlers. They occupied offices on each side of the Gay Insurance Man. In those final couple of weeks, he was fighting with his current lover while trying to seduce a new lover at 120 decibels over the speakerphone with his door wide open. The man pulled no punches on either extreme cursing as loudly to one as he would playfully moan to the other. This had nothing to do with homophobia, as these younger kids were all raised as accepting Homosexuality as a second language by MTV. It was just that it was difficult, and occasionally embarrassing, to have a lispy, baritone voice shouting, " . . . go to hell, and cram it with walnuts in your happy hole!" or "Yes! Yes! Oh God, Yes!" in the background while on a conference call or telephone sales pitch.

Everyone else was relieved to be packing up, too, of course. They had had enough of the characters and the elevator death-stares and stale nicotine atmosphere for a lifetime. It was time to get this red-hot Internet start-up into a trendier, user-friendly set-up.

Swifty, the Chairman, and Ollie dedicated many hours into finding just the right space. They shied away from a loft-type deal, because every unimaginative, trust-fund baby stockpiled start-up was doing the "loft thing." Lofts were also too hot in the summer, too cold in the winter, and even the slightest flatulent noise would echo around in the place for days. They found a place about a mile south from the current digs, so it was still centrally located and convenient to all transportation. The building was an early 1980's black and silver glass monstrosity designed by a famous German architect who went blind soon after; many speculated he didn't want to look at his final project any more and took an ice pick to his corneas. The space, all 6,500 SQUARE FEET of it, was on the 35th floor, providing an excellent view—for the time being. A fifty-story office building was slated to go up right next door forever obstructing the view. But since they had barely broken ground there, the management team figured the view could still be enjoyed for a couple of years.

By comparison to the old place, this new office was cavernous! And there was very little build-out to be done. The space was complete with offices for the executive boys on the outer perimeter (window views for all) and cubicles already built in the center of the room for the sales reps and Campaign Coddlers. The current staff would only occupy half of the available space, but they had to be poised for growth.

One thing that was lacking now, with the separation from the Three Headed Nicole monster, was an official Office Manager. Stosh had that designation for a while at the old place so Swifty, the Chairman, and Ollie could ask him to take care of things they didn't trust the Three Headed Nicole monster to take care of. But Stosh was on board to be an Account Executive. He couldn't be bothered with that kind of nonsense now. Certainly there was someone out there more qualified to book Swifty's airline tickets and stock fresh feminine products in the ladies can. The budget was there and headquarters approved it, so as the last act of business before moving into the new office, the management team hired, gulp, an Office Manager.

The wording of the classified ad for the Office Manager, initially scribbled out on the belly of a Penthouse centerfold by Swifty, was very straightforward:

"Person wanted to manage affairs, and engage in occasional grunt work, in sales office of Internet start-up company. Salary, STOCK OPTIONS, benefits, STOCK OPTIONS, flexible hours, casual environment. Did we mention the STOCK OPTIONS?"

The recruiting climate for workers at Internet companies was still amazingly aggressive. It was definitely a candidate's market. USSBS.com wasn't exactly getting the picks of the available litter. Yes, they were a wacky, Good Time Charlie, Internet start-up company with a few eccentric characters. But they needed a body with its feet on the ground and head in a perpetually nodding motion now. And it HAD to be a woman so the male sales staffers—and maybe even Hot Pot in an experimental phase—could continually say boorish things and use the office manager as a barometer of virility.

The classified ad was pulling the absolute dregs of entry-level office work society. Luckily, no men applied for the position. But Swifty, Ollie, and the Chairman had their fill of eye-patch wearing, twitching, casual expletive using, Feminist bent, whack jobs in the first 15 interviews. They needed somebody yesterday, but somebody who they could trust clutching a letter opener while standing behind them.

Finally, Swifty threw down the gauntlet: the first person in the office to successfully recruit a competent Office Manager would receive a $5,000 bonus and 5,000 STOCK OPTIONS. It didn't matter if the person was a friend, relative, or stranger; they just had to be in position within five business days. Oh, and if this candidate were on the attractive side of the bell curve for Comeliness, the recruiter would get an ADDITIONAL $1,500 bonus.

This launched Stosh and Jay into the streets with the speed of stock male foreplay. Kippy would use the offer as a ploy to try and " . . . do his bitch at work, you know, like it was an interview." Hot Pot would try and be more "in your face" in the women's locker room at the health club. Rennie agreed to keep his eyes and ears open, but he wasn't comfortable talking to women that weren't two-dimensional and on a 19" television screen. Jeeves might broach the subject on his weekly blind dates, but was typically matched with women who were above working for a living. Noah felt such a challenge was too pedestrian for the cut of his jib. Gerard was indifferent to the whole concept. And Babs repeatedly asked out loud, "How about my brother who's coming home from college for the summer?" which only aggravated everyone.

But for all of their collective efforts, they could entice nary a person to come for an interview. Stosh and Jay approached strange women in strange bars in their strange patented way. But each time, the only thing accomplished was paying for the strange women's drinks on Jay's American Express card. He tallied up about $700 worth of bourbon, vodka, and Amstel "Chick Beer" Lites in four nights of gonzo-interviewing. Luckily, Swifty let him submit the tab as a business expense. Nine out of ten times, if a meeting involved alcohol and the words "Internet" or "penis" were used, Swifty would sign off on it on an expense report.

Finally, on the official office moving day, a demure, slim lass who had responded to the original classified ad wandered into the office as the last scheduled interviewee. If she didn't work out, Swifty was going to either call a temp agency or mail order bride service in Laos to fill the role.

She was polite and proper clad in a conservative gray business suit wearing her hair up in a bun. On the surface, she was the Office Manager dream candidate. Her name was Zela. The men who saw her seated in the waiting area agreed she was attractive in that Small-TV-Market-Midday-Newscaster kind of way. She was certainly DO-able, er, if the opportunity ever presented itself. As the Chairman often advised: " . . . be in position to be in position!"

And maybe it was the frenzied timing of things around the office with boxes being packed, people shouting, the Gay Insurance Man crooning a speakerphone duet of Sheena Easton's "Sugar Walls" with someone, etc., but Swifty offered Zela the job on the spot. And although Zela said she was looking for a salary in the mid-$20's, Swifty offered her $39,000 and 25,000 stock options. She had until the end of the day to decide. Zela went home, and after discussing the matter with her trusted confidant, Maw, she called back in 40 seconds and accepted the job.

"Has anybody seen the goddamn bowling party prizes?" Stosh shouted on the verge of tears. It was the last thing anyone from USSBS.com uttered in those groty, hallowed halls of Startupville. A caravan of taxis whisked the staff en masse up the road of respectability to the new USSBS.com digs 35 stories closer to God.

VI – YUMMY!

A far cry from the sport of choice for the cultured elite, bowling was still an honorable way of life in Chicago. Whether one worked at a bowling alley or just spent the entire day hanging out in the neighborhood lanes, provincially it was an accepted way of passing the time during the bitterly cold and inclement months of September through June. If someone in Chicago made it to his thirteenth birthday without ever having stepped inside a bowling alley, it was considered a peculiar upbringing. Not everyone was expected to bleed bowling pin white, but they'd better damn sure know the difference between a "turkey" and a "Brooklyn" if they want to eat Polish sah-sage in that town again!

Serious bowlers all had a noticeable, wobbly gait in their step from years of stress on the plant leg. Every one of the USSBS.com Chicago folks had one, except Elfie. Like she needed another strike against her with the others.

The big USSBS.com Bowl-o-Rama and Client Schmooze took place in one of the smaller, older bowling alleys on the north side called "Bowl Here;" the name was short on creativity but long on conveying an effective message. There were eight lanes in all. The joint was very quaint and full of character. Legend had it that Bowl Here was the FIRST building erected after the Great Chicago Fire had leveled the town back in the late 1800's. Even then, the locals had their priorities straight. There were absolutely no computer-like mechanisms within the four walls of Bowl Here. Everything was mechanical or run by coal. Scoring was kept on each set of two lanes at a small wooden pedestal no wider than four ashtrays laid end-to-end. The bartender sold *OLD STYLE* by the bottle or *HAMM'S* on tap. Anyone caught drinking something non-alcoholic or smuggled in would be politely asked to leave by having a 16-pound Black Beauty whacked between his shoulder blades. It wasn't the Ritz Carlton to the outside world, but it was to bowlers. This is where the party HAD to take place if USSBS.com was going to score some points with the local clients.

Stosh worked overtime coordinating the party with a woman named Burmese from the Promotions Department in the USSBS.com California headquarters. She approved the budget, reserved the bowling alley, processed the invitations, ordered the prizes, and arranged for catering. Stosh certainly couldn't have done it all without her help.

Out of over 250 issued invites, 16 advertisers agreed to attend the party. It was fortunate the projected turnout was going to be lower than anticipated, because nobody actually paused to consider how 300-plus attendees, when including the USSBS.com people, would successfully navigate an eight-lane bowling alley and ten foot long buffet table. Party planning at Internet speed means never having to care too much about the details.

Swifty and the others lauded Stosh for organizing such an impressive event in so short a time. Stosh accepted the praise though inside felt a tad guilty as all he really did to pull the whole thing off was say "yeah, uh-huh" to Burmese a few hundred times over the phone while she put all the pieces in place from 2,000 miles away. Stosh ultimately figured what the hell; that's what she's getting paid for.

The place looked, well, as good as a 130 year-old wood frame structure in need of a delousing could look all dolled up in USSBS.com sticky note pages, blue balloons, and dangling, shredded paper remnants (mostly from PowerPoint presentations Babs had misspelled company or contact names on). Babs volunteered to head up the decorating committee for Stosh. Swifty thought it would be a good idea, as it would keep Babs off of the phones and shield innocent clients from her for a couple weeks.

The kickoff time for the party was 8:00 PM, at least, that's when the open bar officially began. By 8:45 PM, the "client schmoozefest" amounted to little more than the buzzed USSBS.com staffers shuffling around looking at one another and rehashing the same old anecdotes they'd already discussed the full week preceding. Topics of discussion included, and were definitely limited, to: new office better than old office; Elfie's new favorite napping position; and the bad taste Listeria left in everyone's mouth.

Swifty, the Chairman, and Ollie, were eyeballing Stosh in that "If You F'd This Up We'll Fingertip Roll You Into Next Christmas" look one sometimes sees around a bowling alley.

"You're sure the right date was on the invitations!?" the Chairman cornered Stosh.

"Definitely! I don't know what's up. We went over everything a bunch of times."

"How do you explain nobody showing up then?"

Even Heck, Bungleman, Jimmy Jim, and many other USSBS.com notables were no-shows. All claimed "prior commitments," so their attendance wasn't *REALLY* anticipated. But in the back of everyone's mind, a quiet little fantasy of Jimmy Jim crashing through the back of the bowling alley toting bags of bonus money was being harbored.

Stosh's face was saturated in flop sweat. He shrugged and turned to nibble on an eight-ounce hunk of fried Limburger cheese. It was all he could do from letting the Chairman see the tears well up in his eyes. They're going to take away his STOCK OPTIONS because of this, Stosh convinced himself. The first thing they always go after are the precious STOCK OPTIONS!

Enter Korndog King. Stosh wiped his tears away with his bowling towel and greeted Korndog King with a snappy welcome and a big, fat, firm handshake. "Korndog King" wasn't actually a birth name; in real life, he was Herschel Skoalburg.

"Herschel! You made it!"

"Yeah," Herschel sighed. "I figure it should kill a few hours before I have to go home to the wife."

Before Stosh could work in a reply, Swifty and the Chairman pounced on Herschel.

"Hi, I'm Swifty." The boss introduced himself. And for the next minute, his tongue prattled off at warp seven. "I kind of run things here in Chicago for USSBS.com. We're so damn glad you got on board with us a few weeks ago. How is the campaign working out for you? Listen, let's renew you for a full year, and I'll cut the rate in half for you. Ever been here before? It's pretty cool, from what all the hardcore bowlers tell me. Stosh is a stand up guy; he'll do you right! Want a beer? Stosh, get him a *Hamm's*. This Internet stuff is pretty wild, huh? Have you noticed a significant upturn in business since getting on the Ad-Ball? We're making some unbelievable upgrades to the software in a few weeks. The new product will knock you on your hairy Jew ass!"

Herschel tried to sponge it all up, but Swifty dashed off to greet a second arriving guest before Herschel could get a retort off.

"Sorry," the Chairman said to him. "Swifty is just a go-go-go type guy. He'll come back for a chat a little later. How is the campaign working for you though, seriously?"

Stosh returned and handed Herschel a frosty 32-ounce mug full of *Hamm's*. Herschel nodded thanks while addressing the Chairman. In the back of his mind he was still trying to determine if Swifty said something about his "hairy Jew ass," or if he misheard him due to all of the ambient bowling noises.

"So far, so good. We seem to be sending more dogs and baked bean party packages out of town—into the sticks and overseas. I'd say I'm content with things to this point."

Herschel could overhear Swifty giving the new arriving guest the same exact schpiel he just delivered to him moments before. Herschel would pass it off as insincere sales leech pabulum—*IF* Swifty didn't do such a damn good job of delivering it. Instead, Herschel gave him props for being more of Sir Alec Guiness on speed.

"Hungry? Let's get a nibble," the Chairman said consciously leading Herschel out of earshot of Swifty.

A few more clients trickled in by 9:30 P.M. The full sixteen that RSVP'd for the event didn't show. But enough clients did follow through to distract Swifty and the Chairman and got them off of Stosh's back. Most of the USSBS.com hosts were a little too sloshed to hold a healthy sales dialogue. Besides, this was a catered social affair, not an all out offensive on the respective company marketing budgets. It was time to put the hard sell peckers back in their pants and engage in a pleasant, non-threatening game of Business Footsie. It was exactly the type of behavior that made Stosh wretch. But, for the good of the party, Stosh pretended he was excited to be there exchanging "Hollywood Hello's" and pretentious Internet jargon with a toothy smile like everyone else. If not for the whole bowling tie-in, he may have phoned in sick to the event.

In no time at all, the nine clients who did feel comfortable enough being seen in smelly rental shoes were as blitzed as the USSBS.com folks. Serious bowling was not to be had now. This, of course, is the norm any time a butt kissing business connotation or six kegs of beer is at the root of a function. Everyone was at least having a good time. Jay was making the most of the open bar, yet still somehow wound up with $242.60 being charged to his American Express card that evening.

When the smoke finally cleared at 2:15 AM, the clients were happier about the Internet, Internet people, the future of the Internet, and the Ad-Ball. And all vowed to increase their spending with USSBS.com in the next coming months, which was the point of the whole party, really. Sure, USSBS.com wanted to thank them for being Ad-Ball test subjects initially. But now that they were ostensibly Ad-Ball junkies, it was time to turn the screws and get a firm commitment to the Ad-Ball for all eternity! Heck wouldn't only expect it, he would demand that $9,000,000 in business be realized from this $9,000 outlay from the marketing budget.

In itemized fashion, the $9,000 marketing budget mirrored the list of Secret Santa gifts exchanged at an insane asylum Christmas party. The guests all received free bowling (though only a few actually attempted to do so), free beer, free fried cheese and blanched chicken thighs, numerous other unidentifiable fried munchies, a commemorative sky blue polyester bowling shirt, an USSBS.com pair of trap-door jammies (with a strategically placed, silk screened picture of the Ad-Ball on the keester), and a titanium back-scratcher where only the middle-finger was extended to do the scratching (Swifty's idea). For this bundle of wampum, Heck expected big commitments in return from the guests with future marketing dollars.

All of the USSBS.com troops that were able helped Stosh break down the decorations and clean up. The best thing about that for Stosh was that he might be able to persuade someone into helping him carry Jay home instead of dragging him by the armpits four miles by himself like he'd done so many hundred times before. Jay was propped up in a corner by six pool cues while awaiting later transport.

Swifty, the Chairman, and Ollie had made quick exits once the last sentient client, Herschel, tripped off into the night with Crazy Sadie. Crazy Sadie was a local Chicago homeless legend famous for exposing her breasts and private parts up against windows of reputable business establishments all over town. Sometimes the "audience" would reward her with two bits or half of a smoked cigar. In her prime, Crazy Sadie's routine was kind of cool to tourists and locals alike. But now, at age 61, she seemed, well, desperate.

But she was still shapely enough to catch Herschel's half-open peepers at closing time. Hopefully hindsight wouldn't allow him to hold Stosh, USSBS.com, or the Ad-Ball accountable in the morning when he woke up covered in tainted bodily fluids on a bed made from hamburger wrappers and pigeon beaks.

Swifty did express his genuine thanks to Stosh on the way out for throwing together such a raging, rock rolling soiree, once again. The Chairman offered up a token, " . . . you did what you were supposed to do. Nice job." And Ollie simply parted with a " . . . this 'in instead of out' was a good idea. Nice job, Rennie! You too, Stosh."

Nobody wanted to wake Elfie, who was sleeping "spread-eagle" face down on lane number six. But management refused to let them leave her there. With the aid of some vile drunken peer pressure, the rest of the group coaxed Babs into hoisting Elfie over her shoulder and carting her to the nearest bus stop or warming shelter.

Hot Pot expressed aloud more than once how "horny as a prisoner in CellBlock 69" she was. However, thinking the ride on the Hot Pot Grinding Train would definitely end up with her head in a bucket thanks to the half-keg of suds coursing through her veins, no man took advantage of her beguiling bent. She's the one that should've bellied up to Crazy Sadie at the end of the night.

Stosh was satisfied. He did his part and scored a few points with Swifty and the Chairman in the process. Though he didn't get any serious bowling in, the lanes were too dry just the same. His patented mini-hook was all over the place and uncontrollable. He later found out from the proprietor that the lanes hadn't been oiled since the Arab oil boycott of 1974 just out of spite.

"Hey, Rennie!" Stosh shouted to Rennie who was staring down a dartboard an inch from his nose wedged between autographed pictures of bowling great Earl Anthony and crooner Iggy Pop. "Can you help me carry Jay back to his apartment?"

"Yes. I want to see his place." Rennie said breaking his bullseye trance. "I had a good time here. We should do this at least twice per month."

One good thing about having a buttload of semi-attractive, or downright homely, women in the workplace is that their VERY attractive friends will often come around to visit. And since the very attractive friends aren't company employees, they are "fair game" in the paws of any man in the office; at least that's how Swifty's lawyer has been instructed to argue on more than one occasion.

There's something about Asian women, the boys in the office all agreed, that was so desirable. They couldn't put their finger on it, exactly, but spending the night with a demure female who is subservient and aims to please was a tad more palatable than a night of getting lectured, criticized, and ridiculed by a typical American broad. Maybe they had all seen one too many James Bond films over the years. But stereotypes exist for a reason!

Such an Asian woman did materialize in the USSBS.com offices in early spring. She was a friend of Juleen's, one of the more competent workers in Campaign Coddling. Her name was Yummy—supposedly a derivation of a Japanese word for "edible flower." She worked nearby, and her visits to Juleen at the end of the workday became quite regular.

Yummy knew about 165 words in English though she had been in the country for eight years. Still, she knew several multi-syllable words, which put her one up on Rennie. At 21-years-old, word rapidly spread around the office that she was old enough to " . . . get drunk AND give consent." She worked as a Japanese-English translator for a 70-year-old Japanese businessman/pervert named Yoshi Noshagumi at a brokerage firm. Given her limited vocabulary on the English side, the Chairman was quick to surmise that the man likely kept Yummy around for her ample bosom—a trait uncommon to most Asian women. Yummy was also a 'size 2;' that meant nothing in male lingo, but it made the women in the office fume. So it had to be something GOOD. Yummy's face was also not to be sneezed at; she was cute and in a dangerous-sexy way that was good for carnal daydreams.

Low and behold, Noshagumi began to pressure Yummy to "soothe him long time." Many nights he called her at home in the evening and insist she meet him for drinks after 10 P.M. to "bone up for tomorrow's plan of attack, etc." Not one to be rude, Yummy did partake of the overtures on a couple of occasions. But things never got physical beyond the Peck-on-the-Cheek Goodnight level, much to Noshagumi's chagrin. The pressure for a nooner started to intensify, and Noshagumi all but said Yummy had better " . . . put out, or get out."

She loathed the man and wasn't that hot for the job, so Yummy did get out. Yummy wasn't the combative type and didn't even consider a sexual harassment suit. Without a job to distract her, Yummy turned to the bottle. A worldly aunt back in the old country taught Yummy to drink when she was only twelve. Her reasoning?

"Learn to control your alcohol intake," the aunt said, "because boys want to get you drunk and take advantage of you. If you can out-drink them, you will be in control."

Damn, meddling aunt!

Out of work and stone drunk most of the day, Yummy wasn't meeting her fiduciary obligations. She was six weeks overdue paying on the six-by-nine foot room she was renting from an old-as-dirt Vietnamese woman in Wicker Park. The woman kicked Yummy out on her perfect little tush. Juleen came to the rescue and took Yummy in until she got back on her feet.

"Who IS that!?" Swifty said to the Chairman while peering through the blinds of his office.

"I think she's a friend of Juleen's."

Yummy wisely made herself up like a Catholic schoolgirl on this day, right down to the plaid skirt and sans panties, while bending ever so slightly on Juleen's desk outside of Swifty's office.

"We've GOT to give her a job!"

"As what? We already hired the office manager."

"I don't know, but we need to keep her around. Tell Juleen I want to talk to her."

After a brief seven-minute audience with Swifty, Yummy's assets were hired. She was going to be a "Sales Assistant," which put her in a netherworld between the sales staff and the Campaign Coddlers. She was given a salary of $35,000 and 5,000 STOCK OPTIONS. That was about double the salary she was receiving from Noshagumi. Swifty beamed as he professed to the Chairman that the negotiation was "his finest hour."

Under the guise of an "emergency sales meeting," the men, minus Hot Pot and Babs, assembled in the conference room to exchange high-fives and Cro-Magnon pelvic gyrations while Swifty broke the good news.

"Who will she report to?" asked Jeeves.

"Whoever needs her!"

"Did Heck approve this?" Jeeves countered.

"He will when he sees her next month!"

"Er, is Heck coming to Chicago?" Stosh asked.

"Oh, yeah. Didn't I tell you guys? He'll be here for a week. He wants to go on some calls with us, so everybody had better line up their biggest fish for that week. He was bummed about missing out on the bowling party, and he wants to see the new office. Don't worry, we're kicking tail, and Heck knows it. Since they're rolling out the new Ad-Ball with those tentacle things, Heck just wants to make sure we're selling it the way Bungleman designed."

A frantic, heavy knock on the conference room door interrupted Swifty. Ollie opened the door to see Zela taking full liberty of the "casual Friday" wardrobe guidelines: she stood there with legs spread apart, hands on hips, wearing tighter-than-skin blue jeans and an optic orange tube top. From the middle of her sternum, a nine-inch tattoo of a wandering sea urchin wiggling up, around, and fully covering the top half of her right breast commanded the attention of every eyeball in the room. Her long brown hair cascaded down to rest atop her bare shoulders. This was certainly not the same Zela with the military background who wore nothing but conservative business suits her first several days of full employment. This was a probe from the planet Sluttron taking on a human form.

"Sorry I'm late," Zela said. "I had to take my Mom to get her new dentures."

"Dentures? I thought she was only in her mid-40's?" Swifty asked.

"Thirty-six, actually. But her teeth got knocked out at the 38 Special concert after a monster truck rally in Shreveport about 15 years ago when I was only nine. Anyway, Juleen just told me the good news about her girlfriend coming to work here. I'll get started on the paper work!"

"Yeah, great. Thanks."

Ollie closed the door, and with a puzzled look, faced the gang.

"Can anybody do the math on that one for me?"

"Her mom is young," Rennie said.

Swifty snickered. "Hey, nice recruiting there, boys. What's wrong, wasn't Lizzy Borden available?"

"She sure seemed okay when we interviewed her," said the Chairman.

"Yeah. She was in the Army for two years, and she seemed real quiet. But bar none, she was the best candidate we interviewed!" Ollie said.

"Well, I probably shouldn't have been so generous with the salary and stock options. We could've given that much more to Yummy!" Swifty said. His cell phone rang and he left the room cackling some memorized dialogue from *Ishtar* to whoever was on the other end. Meeting adjourned.

The following Monday, the Chairman arrived at the opening of Stosh's cubicle with a present: Yummy.

"Train her on PowerPoint and the Ad-Ball," the Chairman said.

"No problem!" Stosh said on the verge of orgasm.

Yummy was just as the boys had imagined underneath the big rack and tight caboose: demure, submissive, eager to please, etc. At least that was Stosh's initial reading. He remembered how Zela had tricked more worldly men than himself into thinking she was real Office Manager material. Women are born to deceive, he cautioned himself. So Stosh wouldn't lose himself in Yummy's blouse just yet.

"Do you know PowerPoint?" Stosh asked.

Yummy tilted her head slightly and nodded with all the uncertainty of an inbred Dalmatian at obedience school.

"How about the Ad-Ball or what we do here?"

Yummy shook her head.

Oh boy.

Stosh had a price tag on his head. And as much as he enjoyed this business sanctioned flirting, he still had to produce. Trying to teach Yummy about English, let alone the Internet, could prove to be a daunting and time consuming task. Heck, Swifty, and the Chairman still expected Stosh to bring in the cash while taking on whatever tasks they deemed.

"I know to drink, Mr. Stosh!" Yummy blurted.

"Huh?"

"Men like to see the naked woman. My aunt teach me to drink when I twelve so the boys can no take advantage." Yummy smiled and forcefully nodded once with supreme confidence.

"Well, maybe that's true in Japan," Stosh kidded her. "But here in America, we don't allow women to drink for that very reason!"

Yummy was confused.

"But I drink much in America. All the time I drink. I like the vodka lemonades."

Stosh smiled. "You'll go far here."

For the next three quarters of an hour, Stosh described for Yummy, in his best layman's baby talk, his version of what exactly was going on in the world, what the Internet was, and skimmed over different kinds of PowerPoint trickery. Yummy caught Stosh's eyes wandering down to her bountiful bosom each time it happened, too, dammit. She didn't outright condone it, but she didn't fold her arms across her chest either.

"Hey, hey!" Jay burst into Stosh's cubicle. "What's going on in here?"

"Oh, we're learning PowerPoint and the capabilities of the Ad-Ball."

"Is that what the kids are calling it nowadays!?"

Stosh stood up and stretched.

"Yummy, I have to take a break and then go talk to the Chairman. Would you like Mr. Jay to teach you for a little bit?" Stosh asked her.

"Okay, Mr. Stosh. I go with Mr. Jay for now, and then I come back to you."

"MISTER Stosh?" Jay asked.

"Get used to it, Mr. Jay."

"Follow me!" Jay said to Yummy leading her to the office he shared with Rennie on the other side of the room.

Yummy bowed and swayed like the Universal Sex Kitten prototype behind Jay. It was just her natural, God-given walk. And the walk alone confirmed that yes, there IS a God.

Upon moving to the new office, Jay and Stosh no longer had to fall on top of one another, but still served as part of the Chairman's cohesive sales team. Jay and Rennie were granted a shared window office while Stosh sat adjacent to Hot Pot, Kippy, and Babs in center cubicles. The rest of the reps were spread around the room in different shared offices or isolated cubicles. Stosh also sat next to Zela's cube, which put him within listening range of everything going down in her world. As he would later find out with one of Zela's friendly exchanges with the building maintenance thug, Kenny, it was usually Zela that did most of the going down.

Stosh was in the midst of draining the lizard and reflecting about his training session with Yummy when the Chairman hitched his pony to the adjacent urinal.

"So, how did the training go?"

"I let Jay take her for a little while."

"What did she learn so far?"

"Mostly that I have trouble looking above her neck."

"Seriously. Is she going to work out for us?" the Chairman said, unzipping with authority.

"She's perfect for the Internet, I'll put it that way."

Yummy's assets aside, big things were happening around USSBS.com on the business front. At the home office headquarters, Jimmy Jim was able to convince the PRESIDENT OF THE

UNITED STATES to come to his house for dinner in a media orgy blitz benefiting both parties.

Each had something to gain, but of course. A visit from the PRESIDENT OF THE UNITED STATES would give Jimmy Jim's humble little Internet start-up company a bold dose of government sanctioned commerce credibility. In theory, the government would finally be printing Jimmy Jim a license to steal! He will have one-upped the competition once again causing brokerage houses all over Wall Street to drop to their knees. This presidential endorsement stuff was a greater semi-legitimate reason to get into bed with USSBS.com.

The Japanese drunken sailors were always looking for more inroads to the White House by hook or by crook; and those were the only two ways of doing business the current White House occupants understood. The USSBS.com financiers fully appreciated the gravity of the world's most powerful, and arguably shifty, man giving a thumb's up to this Ad-Ball company. With such a man behind the concept, the Japanese drunken sailors would eventually have more yen to burn than they even anticipated on the initial funding of USSBS.com!

The president, by accepting Jimmy Jim's dinner invite, was demonstrating to the American people that, yes, he GOT it. He understood how big this Internet dominance stuff was getting, and the PRESIDENT OF THE UNITED STATES was down with it. The president would surf. The president would approve. The president would assimilate or perish in approval ratings. Furthermore, being a lame duck leader meant the world's most powerful flim flam man would be looking for work in a few months. Connections to the powerbrokers in an industry like the Internet were a must. What a logical, natural progression it would be for one to go from populist president to "Internet Consultant." Lying, slithering from coast to coast, and sleeping around for two terms was like Internet Consultant Training Camp for crissakes!

Jimmy Jim issued a directive to sales people across the board to invite their clients to his house to meet the president as well.

What a shot in the arm it would be for the coffers if the gullible buying masses were to dine with Internet royalty and the PRESIDENT OF THE UNITED STATES. The Fleeced would assume they were invited as insiders to become part of the Fleecer's Universe that would no doubt become America's most powerful corporation by year's end through mergers, acquisitions, high tech piracy, and a slap on the back from the executive branch of government.

The caveats to the invitation were few. The marks had to pay their own way to Jimmy Jim's 44-room Silicon Valley mansion. The marks had to pay $15,000 to reserve a seat, maximum of two. The marks had to commit to $100,000 worth of business on the Ad-Ball in the next six months. No marks came.

Still, the party was successful in achieving its core goal of stroking the President and vise versa. About 200 non-client people partied the night away at Jimmy Jim's house in hippie chic style while the surviving members of the Grateful Dead, Iron Butterfly, and Deep Purple performed or served appetizers. The story made a grand tie-dyed splash in the papers and on Internet content sites. Jimmy Jim stood photographed arm-in-arm with the PRESIDENT OF THE UNITED STATES. The following day, every employee at USSBS.com sat around waiting for the phone to ring. Surely clients, family, friends, long lost lovers, and the like would be calling to talk about the wingding at Jimmy Jim's and the photographs with the president. USSBS.com was positioned to be the envy of the Internet, and a heartbeat away from validity.

Rennie, Stosh, Jay, Hot Pot, and all of the USSBS.com sales staffers had their own style when it came to selling, pitching, and fleecing. The key was to be comfortable with one's style. It wasn't going to work on every potential mark, but a least the salesperson would look more confident and credible if not fumbling through homogenized, rehearsed dialogue and perspiring like a convulsing mosh pit groupie.

Stosh sweat through his clothes either way. He was uncomfortable trying to talk people into buying goods or services that he himself would never buy. Jay shared that moral dilemma, but didn't end up moist and trembling like Stosh on sales calls. Stosh definitely liked to do his pitching, closing, and schmoozing over the phone. He could hold his own when hiding behind a telephone. Plus, it saved a ton on dry cleaning costs.

Early on in the game, Stosh rode along with Rennie on a call at Ollie's urging to pick up Rennie's pitching style, etc. They went to one of those cookie cutter Amy-Lisa-Any Variation of Jennifer agencies just west of the city where the median employee age was 22 and everyone looked like Tori Spelling and spoke with a white suburbia forced gangsta rap accent. What outsider wouldn't be embarrassed for them?

Sure enough, Rennie and Stosh sat across from two comely bottled bleach blondes named "Jenniy" and "Leesuh." Rennie had worked with the agency numerous times on different accounts in previous sales incarnations, so the lame get-to-know-you formalities were blown off.

"What have you got for us Rennie?" said the assertive Jenniy, overcompensating for any number of psychological shortcomings.

"Here," Rennie said, as he handed them both some glossy printed collateral bull crap sheet about USSBS.com.

They took a few minutes to read through it. Both moved their lips as they read silently to themselves.

"Interesting," Leesuh said to Jenniy, kind of unsure. "Right?"

"Very interesting!" Jenniy said.

"I knew it."

"Who's your friend there. He hasn't said anything."

Stosh, calm and dry as he was unnoticed up till then, began to perspire from the brow, waist, and teeth. He stood and shook their hands.

"I'm Stosh. I'm kind of new with the company. I'm mostly here to observe. Rennie is the man. He'll handle any questions."

Put off by the unsightly droplets oozing from Stosh's pores, both girls were sure to focus on Rennie from that point on. Rennie's pitch was no different than his regular means of communication. He said as little as possible in the most compact way imaginable. Stosh would never be able adapt Rennie's style into his own; he used more syllables stuttering on the word "cyberspace" than Rennie did on an entire face-to-face sales call.

"Well, that is what we got. If you want to do a deal, call me." Rennie stood up and put on his coat.

That's IT, Stosh thought?

"Always good to see you Rennie. Like I said, this looks very, very interesting. We'll definitely talk it up to our clients." Jenniy stood and shook Rennie's hand.

"As usual, you really left us spellbound." Leesuh said without an ounce of facetiousness in her voice.

Stosh stewed in his own juices and soaked it all up while his mind pointed out a few facts. Are they kidding? All he did was hand them a slick brochure! And that chick only used the word 'spellbound' because it's in the title in every new piece of crap hour-long weekly occult serial featured on network television. If that's all there was to going on Internet sales calls, Stosh was sure he'd be able to keep the sweating at bay while the potential mark read through the glossy propaganda.

But Stosh would learn that there was certainly more to sales calls than that. Rennie simply had a client base of people who knew his style and dealt with him on his terms, not theirs. They were comfortable with his near silent, almost telepathic, approach to selling. Because the clients were comfortable, Rennie was comfortable. He kept selling, and the clients kept buying. Rennie allegedly worked years on perfecting his style, boasted Ollie, and it showed through in the results.

The absolute masters of the art of pitching were Swifty and the Chairman, hands down. Their styles differed, too. But Stosh was in awe each and every time he watched them in action. As managers, it wasn't their job to sell. But they would go along and aide whichever rep requested their presence on a call if the potential mark merited the heavy artillery.

By nature, neither Swifty nor the Chairman could sit in an on-deck role on a call and watch somebody like Stosh sweat and stutter his way out of a deal. Everyone soon learned that if Swifty or the Chairman were going on a call, HE would be the one driving the bus.

The Chairman would just ask the sales rep for a few specifics about the company on the way to the call. He wasn't looking for anything too detailed—maybe just the company name, their business model, and how much they want to spend. From the moment they entered the mark's office, the Chairman took control and had everyone eating out his palm. He would spout facts and figures about the mark's company off the top of his head that only an insider would seemingly know. He touted the Ad-Ball as an all-knowing, all-seeing, Internet elixir only the grandest of fools would not at least test out on a trial basis. There was no question he couldn't answer. If he didn't know the answer, the answer he fabricated would sound better than the correct answer being anticipated. The Chairman would leave a roomful of skeptical marks sometimes questioning their own understanding of the universe, and most times clamoring for an Ad-Ball contract on the spot.

Swifty took more of the "Life's Too Short, So Shuddup And Listen" approach. He, too, could deflect any damaging question or comment away with ease. In pitch mode, Swifty crammed as many words between breaths as he could as fast as his tongue could flap them out. He'd go off on tangents about the Holy Ghost, Big Macs, *Ishtar*, tight underwear, etc. And no matter which direction he went off in, he was exuberant in getting there. Sales 101 manuals since the beginning of the marketable corruption of man have stated that transference of energy is what gets most deals done. Swifty incorporated the tactic better than anyone did.

But Swifty and the Chairman were managers in the company, not salesmen. They were supposed to guide and nurture the flock.

Their presence on calls was ordered diminished over time. Heck had spoken.

Why be so foolish as to let the BEST sales people the company has actually appear in public and talk up the product? It was a point Jay questioned to Stosh six beers into the night, seven nights per week. Stosh never had an answer. He was just mad he'd have to make most of his future face-to-face appearances solo. His glands would never make it another 43 months, 1 hour, 58 minutes.

VII – HERE COMES THE FUNK

It was late April. Something funny happened on the way to the IPO. The technology driven Internet market, which had been riding a 36-month high day-after-day, decided it was time to cool down. The cow was still kicking, but not as feisty as it had been. Sure, the Internet is the future, most drunken sailors agreed. But should they be putting all of their barnacles on the same boat? The investment bankers and brokerage houses began thinking the same thing—maybe they should go back to a more conservative approach in taking these Internet start-up companies public after only three weeks in existence.

Based on Wall Street projections, only one in every 400 Internet companies would be profitable by year 2065. And only one in every 1,600 Internet companies would be in business after 72 hours. And the average life span for Internet employees, both male and female, would be 33 years.

These numbers sure were contrary to the figures Wall Street had been prognosticating about only a month earlier. In March, if you weren't investing in, or working for, an Internet start-up, you may as well start living in Hobotown and learning to eat from city sewer pipes. Because that is where the shortsighted, cynical, investment ignorant blokes will DESERVE to be for not sinking every available nickel into the Internet IPO market! Only the damnedest of fools wouldn't hop aboard the Cyber Gold Rush Express.

This, of course, didn't bode well for the USSBS.com IPO. The bankers were nervous. They didn't want to have the company go public on a Tuesday and declare a liquidation sale the following

Monday like several other Internet companies had done in the final days of April, 2000.

All 35 USSBS.com Chicago employees were assembled in the conference room when Jimmy Jim broke the news to the 750 USSBS.com employees worldwide via conference call.

"First thing y'all need to know," Jimmy Jim began, "is that the company is doing great, and we're all very happy at headquarters. During the road show for the IPO, we were getting standing ovations from stuffy investment people who normally wouldn't show any emotion under any circumstances at all. The new Premium Tentacle version of the Ad-Ball is going to be released this week, and everyone is gaga about it. The software development people really did a great job in getting that together in a short period of time. You won't believe the capabilities of this thing when you see it; I think it can even reach out and scratch where you've got an itch."

All emit a token laugh.

"But I wanted you to hear this from me, first. The bankers have advised, and we all agree, that we postpone the IPO for a few weeks while the market is being a little skittish."

The utterance sent hearts sinking into guts around the world. Everyone had been busting butt to this point, save for Elfie maybe, and a postponing of the IPO was a definite setback. It would totally derail everyone's "retire in 48 months" plans for at LEAST another 30-60 days. So many companies had gone public with far inferior business models. It didn't make sense to the average working stiff brain.

"Again, like I said, there is nothing to worry about. We've got a great product, a great team in place, and the investors aren't losing faith. But why risk issuing the IPO and ending up with a $15 stock price when we can wait a couple of weeks and be at $30 or $40? The world is not ending, and no one is going to lose his job over this. We're going to tell the SEC our plans today. And I'll be updating you all weekly either on a conference call or via mass e-mail. Until then," Jimmy Jim slipped into a hokey DJ voice, "keep on rockin'!"

"The man makes sense!" the Chairman bellowed while disconnecting the speakerphone. "Listen, it's simple: we're playing it safe. This can't even be considered a minor setback. If it's worth doing, it's worth doing right. And we're going to do it right. Any questions?"

Big G raised his hand then spoke publicly for the first time since being hired. "Yeah. Do this mean we not be going public and sheet?"

"Good question, Big G," Ollie patronized. "We do still plan to go public, just not as soon as we anticipated. Everything is still all-that."

"A'ight." Big G said before scarfing up a Ding-Dong.

Swifty had been enjoying MYSTIC PIZZA the entire time but still absorbed the gist of Jimmy Jim's message. He reassured everyone without looking up from this DVD player. "You guys, it's nothing. The Chairman and me have been through this a number of times before. They just want to—" Swifty interrupted himself by howling and pointing at the screen resting on his lap. "Oh, that's rich!"

"Now, if anyone needs to talk more about this, come and see the Chairman, Swifty, or myself and we'll discuss it one on one. While we're all here, Kippy has something to say, so I'll surrender the floor to him."

"Thanks, Jag!" Kippy's attempt at addressing his immediate superior with a colloquialism over-saturated in his usual peer circles didn't elicit the big laugh he was hoping for. But not knowing the meaning of the words "humbled" or "humility," Kippy pressed on. "Yeah, so, we're going to be doing this softball team. It's an Internet league, so we'll make some good contacts. The season starts tomorrow. And we need half of the team to be bitches, so make plans."

"Tomorrow!?" Hot Pot exclaimed. "How about a little advance notice? Some of us have plans tomorrow."

Hot Pot's furor started murmurs amongst the staff. The Chairman and Ollie liked to maintain control, especially in Swifty's presence, and quickly quieted the crowd.

"People! People!" Ollie pleaded. "Let's not freak out here. This is another GOOD thing. We'll make contacts and get our name out there. Besides, it's 16-inch. It's fun. Don't bust Kippy's cookies. It was big of him to organize the whole thing for us."

"Listen, this isn't a lifetime commitment. It's what six, seven—" the Chairman looked to Kippy.

"Twelve weeks, dude."

"—okay, twelve weeks. And everybody doesn't have to play every week. We've got 35 people here, so we should be able to field at least ten people, half of them ladies, once a week." The Chairman folded his arms and leaned back on his black leather swivel throne.

"Uh-uh. No way you're getting me to play no punk ass softball." Zela's words sizzled out like fingernails dragging across hot coals.

Swifty closed the lid on his DVD player and looked up. "Cool it, people. Whoever wants to play can play. Whoever doesn't, can come and watch and drink while the others play. I'll provide or pay for the booze every week, no problem."

A collective cheer and they were a tenacious team once again. Swifty looked at his watch.

"Christ! I've got to get to O'Hare in 20 minutes. I've got a Regional VP meeting in San Francisco the rest of the week."

Swifty jumped to his feet and grabbed his sport coat off the back of the chair.

"Good luck at softball tomorrow, you guys. See you next week." He stopped himself in the doorway and spun around.

"Does anybody know if that place in the lobby sells beers to go? It's about a three-beer ride out to the airport."

In the grand scheme of things, the Chairman had an answer for everything. And if he didn't, he could at least concoct a conceivable one in a split second based upon his amassed knowledge of the contemporary world. He was also able to soak up knowledge like nobody's business. The Chairman knew a little bit about everything, and a great deal about most things in particular. This wealth of stored facts, formulas, human behaviors and the like were articulated as necessary to whomever the Chairman was addressing at the time. If he needed to dumb something down for the likes of Jay and Stosh while in the same breath speak on a more educated plane worthy of Jeeves' attention, the Chairman had an uncanny ability to do so. No question about it, he was born to lead.

In a previous sales life, Stosh spent a little time as a pitchman for a manufacturer of high end cooking appliances. This is the sole area where he maybe knew a little bit more about this particular topic than the Chairman.

The Chairman was still refurbishing his 1920's mansion, and it was time to do the kitchen. So he came to Stosh for his take on things. What differentiates a good cook top from an inferior one? What kind of ventilation is needed over a professional type range? Where does fire come from? Unlike questions about the Ad-Ball from clients, these were all questions Stosh felt confident in answering.

Annually, the Super Big Cooking Show committee selects a different city to hold the event. For whatever misguided reason, in 2000 they decided a springtime show in Chicago would be the cat's meow. Obviously none on the committee had ever spent springtime in Chicago. It was no different than spending a week at Ice Station Zebra. But like most that pass through Chicago, they came for the city's most redeeming quality: food!

The show was held at the grand McCormick Place convention center, which accommodated about 2,500,000 people at any given time. Conveniently, parking accommodated 1,200 cars. Every convention or show ends up as mass chaos with claustrophobia, baby stroller head-on collisions, and cock fights reigning the day. The anticipation, as usual, is greater than the event itself.

Through connections, Stosh had two free admission badges into the Super Big Cooking Show. He knew the Chairman was looking for kitchen ideas for the rehab project and offered the badges to the Chairman so he and the wife could go. The wife was out of town on business. But the Chairman insisted Stosh use one of the badges, as he could offer some insight on different cooking appliances and manufacturers.

Snow was still piled high along the curb. Stosh stood knee deep in a dirty drift on Madison St. when the Chairman picked him up in his new BMW 980—which just arrived days before from Germany. The sky was typically dull and overcast, but the silver metallic paint job still brightly glistened somehow.

"I can't believe you're taking this out on the dirty streets," Stosh said. "Why don't you wait until everything dries up?"

"I can't wait until June. I need to get around."

Stosh looked and sniffed in awe at the computerized gadgetry and leather entombing the interior. This was what it was like to drive rich. Who woulda thunk a vehicle could be so opulent? Stosh thought to himself. There was even a rotisserie in the glove box for small fowl or swine to be prepared.

"I didn't know BMW even MADE a 980 series."

"It's a prototype, actually. Swifty got me a deal through an expatriated uncle in Affenbutter—that was a town on the East Side before the wall came down."

The Chairman's reply was passionless and quick. Stosh was afraid to soil anything for fear of scolding and remained motionless on the ten-minute ride to McCormick Place. They motored along in complete silence—even more than when the Chairman is using it as a communication tactic. This silence was heavier and more resonating. Something wasn't right. This caused Stosh's stomach to churn like Splash Mountain on Kiddie Weight Watcher Day; he waited for the other shoe to drop. And naturally, Stosh figured, it would be something that affected his STOCK OPTIONS.

"Alright, keep your eyes open for a spot."

That was all the Chairman said until they were once inside the building and swept up by the cooking hoopla.

"Let's go look at those jet-fueled ovens you were telling me about," said the Chairman.

"Okay." Stosh's knees were knocking.

They waded through the muck that was the overfed general public from one exhibit to the next without the Chairman saying a word. He would only nod or cringe as Stosh talked about the features of various brands and cooking appliances. After a few hours, neither could take being throttled in the ankles by baby buggies or watching Joe and Betty Sixpack devour free pork samples any longer.

"Let's go have a beer," the Chairman demanded.

About four seconds later, the Chairman's $110,000, hand crafted, German rocket chariot was tearing up Lake Shore Drive. The ride to a delightful "old man's bar" on the northwest edge of the city limits would've taken about 25 minutes in the common man's automobile. The Chairmanmobile burned up the asphalt in a third of the time. But again, it was a ride of complete silence. The coins in the ashtJay were even afraid to jiggle as they peered upwards at the Chairman's steely glare.

The old man bar was called Reinhard's. True to form, it was filled with old men passing away a Saturday afternoon hiding from their wives and talking to the proprietor in voices thick with German accents. Surely somebody would be asking about the Chairman's new car parked out in front of the joint at some point.

The Chairman and Stosh each quaffed two draft *DABS*, the working man's beer of Deutschland, while taking in the other conversations and some Tiger Woods slaughterfest on the circa 1969 television behind the bar. A couple of slovenly youths from the neighborhood, clearly fourth or fifth generation American pigs, wandered in and commenced shooting pool in the back of the bar.

An hour had passed. Still not one patron had made a comment about the Chairman's super snazzy vehicle parked in clear view of the barstools right out the immense street side glass window. Stosh was certain it was irksome to the Chairman, and it even started to peeve Stosh a little bit as well. Two more *Dabs* were downed. Finally, the Chairman parted his lips in a conversational manner.

"There's been something heavy on my mind the past couple of days," he lamented.

OH NO, THE STOCK OPTIONS! OH NO, THE STOCK OPTIONS.

The Chairman continued, breaking Stosh's internal paranoia train of thought. "I've got to have a talk with Jay. Somebody has lodged a complaint against him."

"Who, a client? What kind of complaint was lodged? Is somebody unhappy about their Ad-Ball campaign?"

"No, it's internal. And I'm not going to get into naming names or too many details, but I trust you to keep this to yourself. Swifty and I have to make a call here. We've got to quash this thing before it gets any bigger or out of hand. Heck wouldn't be pleased with any type of litigation levied against the company."

"Jesus. What happened?"

"Let's just say Jay made some inappropriate comments to one of the Campaign Coddlers."

"That's nuts!" Stosh belched. "Jay makes inappropriate comments to everyone! That's Jay! That's me. And that's even you, when you're feeling buzzed or naughty!"

"I know. And you and I know Jay and how he operates. But we sometimes forget that he's a forty-something-year-old man. And off color quips or jokes of a sexual nature can have a different effect on a 22-year-old girl who barely knows Jay, than they do on me or you, you know?"

"Goddammit!" Stosh wanted to finish the sentence with " . . . who is it, I'll slap her into the Deserving Wench Wing of Cook County Hospital . . . " but thought better against it in a public setting.

"Keep it quiet and to yourself. I'm just going to have to sit down and talk this out with Jay. We're not sure what might happen next, if anything. But we were advised to handle it internally, and make the accuser happy."

"This is total garbage. Jay makes jokes, but that's all they are. He would never say anything wrong to anyone or do anything to embarrass you or the company."

"I know, I know." The Chairman glanced over Stosh's shoulder out at his car. "It's the goddamn, psycho-reactive times we live in. If Jay is 20 years younger, ten pounds lighter, and remembers to zip up his pants more regularly after draining the lizard, I doubt we'd even be having this conversation. But this chick is one of those deranged sexual militant empowerment bastards who want rules to apply only when they're to her convenience. This isn't the first time she's complained to us about SOMETHING. She usually has one a week. But this one I have to take seriously, because it can go higher than Swifty and me. That's what sucks."

"What did Jay say, and who was it, goddammit!?"

"It was totally stupid. He overheard—okay, it was Gabby— and he overheard her say to someone, ' . . . hold on, I'm coming.' And Jay stuck his head out of his office and said, ' . . . gee, I didn't know I was THAT good.' It was totally stupid, totally freaking stupid."

"What a psycho. I knew something was off about her. She always walks around with headphones on, never smiles or anything. She's no charmer that's for sure. Nice rack, though. Ever notice her nipples are, like, always outward?"

"No duh! Swifty and Ollie call her 'Highbeams'."

While spit cleaning the downwind end of the bar, Reinhard noticed the Chairman's sled parked out front. He said something in German to Fritz, an old man making love to a tumbler of Jaegermeister, and they went outside for a closer look-see. This pleased the Chairman; Stosh could tell because he finally unclenched the fist of his non-drinking hand for the first time all day.

"But you're right," the Chairman said. "She is a whack-job. And I'll tell you something else for free: she's about as popular as

Elfie is in that department. Nobody really likes her. She moans if she doesn't get to work on big accounts. And when we do give her big accounts, she screws them up, louses up the reporting and flat-out refuses to work any overtime. Overtime '... conflicts with her bongo lessons and continuing education...' or so she says."

"Continuing education in what?"

"Twenty-first Century Dementia would be my guess."

With that, the Chairman hopped off his barstool and went outside to showcase his ride to Reinhard and Fritz.

Stosh remained inside and held a mock three-beer wake for Jay.

"Listen up, Ass-wipes!" Kippy said on a frigid evening in the middle of Grant Park. "I am the manager of the team, and I am calling the shots. You go in when I say you go in, you go out when I say you go out. And you old guys, try and keep up, okay?" Kippy then inhaled a light beer, smashed the aluminum can on his groin, belched, and dashed out to left field.

Not exactly inspired by his pep talk, the rest of the team slowly trickled out to their positions on the diamond. Thirteen USSBS.com people in all turned out for the inaugural game. Luckily, five of them were women so the game wasn't automatically forfeited. Noticeably absent from participating were Swifty, the Chairman, Hot Pot, Zela, and Yummy. Swifty was out of town. Both the Chairman and Hot Pot had their prior engagements. Yummy wasn't exactly the athletic type, but the men all wanted her there for obvious reasons. And Zela wasn't exactly wanted there, but she sure would come in handy if a bench-clearing brawl erupted at home plate.

The opponent was another start-up company: Hempdaddy.com. Their business model was simple: Venice Beach meets E-commerce. They peddled hemp-based products to anywhere in the world, and often only insisted on good karma as payment. Only four weeks in business, they were the Wal-Mart of their contemporaries. An aging hippie couple operating a hemp web site out of Fiji was considered the most serious competition because they had a 30-year head start of compiling loyal customers marketing a cookbook of hemp and crustacean recipes.

Hempdaddy.com was chock full of fresh faced, longhaired boys and girls nary a day over nineteen. They had 24 players ready to go in matching sweatshirts spun from hemp. Kippy and his troops pooh-poohed their opposition based upon their whole "Sammy Hagar Roadies for Jesus" appearance. Hempdaddy.com quickly dropped fifteen runs on USSBS.com in the first inning. Babs' five fielding errors and Biz Dev Grifting Machine's Brad fracturing his index finger in eight places highlighted the first stanza.

Kippy cursed and screamed, which only caused his players to drink more beer. Riding the bench, Stosh and Jay were enjoying the spectacle through the first four innings. When they were finally rotated into the line-up by Kippy, they were legally intoxicated like the rest of the squad but not as loose because of sitting around. Stosh fell down four times on one play attempting to field a ground ball hit to him in right field. Jay covered second base from a kneeling position with a genuflecting flair.

The final score was Hempdaddy.com 28, USSBS.com 3 (thanks to three solo home runs by Kippy who hot-dogged his way around the bases on each one). The teams shook hands, and Hempdaddy.com disappeared into the bushes to have a celebratory smoke. Kippy ended the game by giving his team a 650 word tongue lashing of expletives and physical insults then strut off with his "bitch" in the direction of the lake.

"I'm freezing. Let's go drink inside somewhere. Remember, it's all on Swifty." Ollie said.

The team tied one on at a vapid sorority girl hangout near Wrigley Field for a few hours. No one bothered to touch on the subjects of softball or Kippy's outburst. But the Campaign Coddlers, alike in their inability to handle alcohol well, did sink a few ships with loose lips about work-related matters. Since they have their own meetings, conference calls, and internal memos, the goings-on in the campaign coddling world are often kept from the sales managers and teams until well after the fact.

A few interesting things were gleaned from slurred ramblings of the sufficiently lit girls. Ollie was sure to keep the beers coming with each new tidbit. With Josh accompanying Brad to the hospital for hand x-Jays, Ollie, Rennie, Stosh, and Jay, were the first benefactors outside of Campaign Coddling to learn the juicy details. Elfie was on "triple-secret probation;" there were reports from headquarters about technical problems with the Ad-Ball; and all of the girls in the department wanted to get into the Chairman's pants.

The Campaign Coddlers were pathetic drunks, but they weren't liars. They wouldn't make up any such things just to stir up trouble. Elfie's napping and constant verbal assaults had worn out their welcome with the staff. Her subordinates held an after-hours, hush-hush conference call with Tessie about their level of disgust. It's not like Elfie would have been affected had she been invited to the gripe session as she'd more than likely been in a coma, but she wasn't told about it just the same. The Campaign Coddlers said they'd go over Tessie's head to Jimmy Jim and might even consider legal action—no doubt at Gabby's urging. Tessie assured them that if she received one more disturbing report about Elfie, she'd be fairy dust.

The bombshell about the Ad-Ball having some technical issues was definitely unexpected. No one had heard anything but positive spin about the beast since its origins amidst sticky hands at *Denny's*. In all of the haste to tweak the Ad-Ball for the Premium Tentacle release, software shortcuts were taken at any convenient turn. The Ad-Ball was doing peculiar things on different operating systems for the members. And it was becoming impossible to track on the server side. It was nothing that couldn't be fixed, but it would take a few weeks to get it done properly. Even though the IPO had been postponed until early Summer, bad reports about an Ad-Ball run amok wouldn't help seal the deal. A couple of clients, usually the high-maintenance sons of bitches, were complaining about the numbers being reported on their campaigns. Things weren't meshing with some independent tracking numbers they'd received. Campaign Coddling would pacify them by giving them several thousand additional free impressions on the Ad-Ball but knew that such a quick fix couldn't go on long term.

And finally, about getting in the Chairman's pants, they all wanted to in Campaign Coddling—maybe not Big G. Since the beginning of the coed workplace, soon after the earth cooled, men and women have gotten in their respective sexual groups to orate their "Who I'd Like To Boink In The Office—And In This Order" lists. Not ALL do it, of course, just the ones with a pulse and healthy attitude. It's a simple game to pass the time while drinking or listening to a boring team building exercise lecture. One simply states, in ascending order, who he or she would like to get naked with in the office. The game most often works better in offices containing three or more employees and provides for a wealth of shocked looks, guttural retorts, thought provoking dialogue, etc.

The Campaign Coddlers exchanged their dream lists over cocktails in the Loser Bar, a dark and smelly hooch pit in the bowels of the office building shared with USSBS.com, and the Chairman was the consensus choice hands down. He was everything a woman wanted: wealthy, wealthy, and wealthy. The Chairman was also dashingly handsome, articulate, strong, and wise; but those factors were just considered added features that no other man at USSBS.com possessed. There was something good about everyone, arguably. But nobody put it all together like the Chairman.

To be fair, the USSBS.com men played the Naked Game, too. To no surprise, Yummy was a runaway pick for first, and everyone else tied for third—except Hot Pot who was relegated to the cellar only because the men knew it would drive her insane when she found out. Given a man's preferences, Hot Pot could easily come in second place to Yummy with her nice feminine features and commiserating qualities.

An hour from closing time, everyone broke off into smaller groups and went in different directions. The Campaign Coddlers went home, except for Juleen who was arm wrestling boys for cigarettes. Rennie and Ollie dashed off to " . . . urinate on Wrigley Field, then have a night cap somewhere." Stosh carried Jay by the armpits into a taxi. Jay snapped back from the other dimension during the ride and demanded that he and Stosh have one more drink at a place called Big Red Shoe that had a 4:00 AM liquor license.

In no condition to argue, Stosh agreed.

No second hand superlatives did Heck justice. One definitely had to have an audience with the man to experience the full brunt of his elitist sales wrath. He'd bite the entrails off of a live alligator to make a sale and expected all of his troops would do the same for him. The day of the long postponed trip to meet with the Chicago team had arrived. Though the odds were still good it only being mid-Spring and all, there wasn't a blizzard in sight to save them this time.

All spent the better part of the morning tidying up the office. Zela spiffed up all of the machinery and countertops by licking a sponge and working it around with a little elbow grease, and tucked her half-empty bottle of Jack Daniels out of sight in a drawer. She even threw on a conservative, shapeless garb worthy of a spinster's coffin and put her hair up in a tasteful beehive. It was a true anal makeover for the girl that had really been letting it all hang out in recent weeks.

One telling Tuesday, she let it all hang out all the way down to the tattoo of a white-knuckled Beethoven peering upward from her "bikini zone" showcased during a bare-midriff and low-cut pair of lycra slacks combination. It was also on that day she teased any erect male who would listen that she had " . . . six things pierced on her body," leaving imaginations to figure out where.

Kippy reluctantly took down his "Great Beaver Hunt, 2000" calendar, but vowed to put it back up the second Heck stepped outside of the office. It was the same calendar that the generally biologically ignorant chaps used to venture guesses as to where Zela might have her other piercings tucked away. And since nobody guessed exactly correct yet, allegedly, most were eager for it to be re-displayed as well.

Swifty gave two of the Campaign Coddlers each a sawbuck to dust his office and make it look "President Reagan-esque."

Stosh popped in to trade barbs with Jay and Rennie figuring the best place to be was out of sight when Heck arrived.

"So, why do you think he's here? We're still holding our own, right?" Stosh asked.

"Totally. Don't sweat it. I didn't tell the Chairman or Swifty," Jay dropped his voice to a whisper, "but I'm on the New York office's e-mail list! I thought we all were, but I guess it's just me. I get to see a lot of the internal memos between Jimmy Jim and New York and everything. Heck has been ripping New York a new one for weeks! They're the biggest office in the company, and we're outselling them two-to-one!"

"That is good. New York is worse. Heck will not rip us a new one." Rennie's logic was airtight.

Ever the flirt and colossal corporate butt kisser, Hot Pot was quick to drop to her knees when Heck entered with Ollie and the Chairman. He stepped right over her and was whisked into the back conference room like Elvis into an awaiting Cadillac limo in the back alley. The Chairman stormed into Rennie and Jay's office.

"Heck want to talk to everyone. NOW."

The urgency in the Chairman's voice was nothing new. And with the knowledge of the New York office gasping for breath tucked safely away, Jay, Stosh, and Rennie took a few moments primping and composing themselves before following the Chairman into Heck's makeshift slaughterhouse. They certainly didn't want to be the FIRST to report and have to make small talk with the man. When they finally squeezed into the room, Heck was already two minutes into addressing everybody else. The Chairman seethed from the nostrils.

"Oh, thank you for joining us, gentlemen!" Heck condescended. "I'm not going to repeat what I've told everybody else so far just for your benefit. So, to continue, what in the hell is going on in Chicago? We've given you a great product! We're paying you the top wages in the industry. The market is still hot, despite a couple of minor bumps in April. And we're still $75 million under plan! I told each and every one of you in New York, granted a the majority of you have been hired since then, that I had a price tag of $1 million on each sales head in the country! So why do I have to go to each office and kick some ass? Do you think this is fun for me?"

Yes, Jag-wad, was the predominant collective thought shared in the room.

"I hope to hell you have some killer calls set up for me the next two days. Because I am going to go in and personally close all of the clients you haven't been able to close. And you'll see how they're falling over one another to give us their money! This is the Internet! This is all that anybody is, or ever will be. Your kids, your grandkids, their kids . . . they'll be BORN on the Internet. They're going to suckle from the motherboard, and have a mouse at the other end of the umbilical cord. We've got the greatest product for reaching people, and we're just not selling it! Do you know that we haven't had a single order for one of the Gold, Silver, or Bronze packages on the new Premium Tentacle Ad-Ball out of this office? This is easy, easy money. Bungleman went balls to the wall in designing this whole product for us. Why aren't we taking it to the street? I mean, what do I have to do to convince everyone about the validity of our niche in the marketplace?"

They thinks he doth protest too much.

"I want a commitment from you right here, right now that you will live, breath, and crap Ad-Ball until we're a billion-dollar market cap company. Do I have your commitment to this effect?"

If shrugging shoulders and barely audible "mmm-hmmm's" were donuts, the window-enclosed conference room would've burst with fried dough onto helpless pedestrians below.

"Goddammit!"

"Yes! We all share your passion and mission, Heck. No question about it." Swifty hoisted his arms and smiled to take the bullet.

"I see fear, nothing but fear. And fear is what makes you clench up your balls on approach, jam your toe on the springboard, and then bust your chops open on the pommel horse! I've been there, and it ain't an experience I care to revisit. Your people have got to WANT it. Otherwise, what the hell am I doing here? What are you doing here? What are we all doing here? Why don't we just pack it in and suck our crybaby thumbs rolled up in the fetal position on the balance beam of life?"

Heck took off his jacket revealing sweat stains the size of car batteries under each arm. He was losing them with all of the gymnastics references. Sensing this, he let the Good Cop take control over his bi-polar beat for a while. He spun a folding chair around to face him and straddled it like a weeping babysitter. Leaning forward, he smiled and winked at Hot Pot.

"You were in New York, right?" he asked her.

"Yes. I'm very happy here. It's all-good. Big things, I tell you. Big things are happening. I'm talking to Techstein College about a deal for fifty cracks! Much smack was swapped from the get-go, but I'm closing in on the cracks."

Heck, unfamiliar with Hot Pot's lunar truck stop waitress vernacular, just offered an unsure " . . . great," in response.

Swifty had lowered the thermostat in the overcrowded conference room to 55. A bra-less Gabby's nipples were bursting through her tight peach colored shirt like escaping convicts and immediately captured Heck's attention.

"And you, I don't believe we met in New York. You can call me Heck," he said to her never gazing upward from her sternum.

"We didn't. I'm Gabby, and I work in Campaign Coddling. And I just want to say a thing or two about the sordid—"

A disembodied snort followed by an unholy gasp for oxygen interrupted the exchange. Surely it would be the final nail in the coffin Elfie's subordinates were looking for as she drifted off next to Ollie. Ollie gave Elfie a lethal elbow to the ribcage jolting her awake. Heck didn't want to acknowledge the physical exchange while he was in Good Cop mode, and turned his focus on Jay, Rennie, and Stosh crammed together in the doorway.

"You guys have some calls lined up for me, right?"

Jay stepped forward, latent Captain Morgan's Rum still shellacked on his tonsils, and offered his hand to Heck.

"Hi, Heck. I'm Jay. I didn't get a chance to meet you in New York. This is a great opportunity. And I just want to say, thanks." Jay stepped back in formation.

Heck cocked his left brow while glaring a hole through Jay's right auricle and simply froze until Jay trembled ever so slightly.

"So you're the guy who didn't make it there on time, huh? Well, just as long as you're here now and pounding the streets. I hear good things about you. Just shine on like the crazy selling diamond I know you can be for the rest of the year, and the rewards will come." Heck turned away and looked across the room. "And I mean that to all of the sales people here. But you non-sales people are important, too; just not in the life sustaining way that the sales people are."

"Hi Heck. I signed the big car deal. I'm—"

"Rennie!" Heck leaped up and slapped a whopper of approval on Rennie's back. "I remember you from New York, of course. Plus, I see your name every week on the reports with some big dollar signs next to it. I'm definitely going to watch you in action today and tomorrow. I hope you've got some great calls lined up."

"Yeah," Rennie said with all the verve of a noose hung corpse.

Heck stared at Rennie for an uncomfortably lengthy time with what could be best described as "goo-goo eyes."

"You remind me of me when I first chalked up for the big meet against Fenger High. You've got the volcano within, and you're going spew in all directions and take no prisoners. You set a fine example for everybody here, a fine example for mankind." Heck took Rennie's right hand into his two massive, dry, cracked, cupped hands and shook it slow and deliberately as an example to all of the Shiftless Wonders in the room. "You are what it's all about, my friend."

"Okay!" Heck yelled, snapping out of his Rennie fixation. "We're going to dinner tonight—EVERYone! It's on me. We'll pound the street until six or seven tonight, then refresh for an hour, and rendezvous at some fine steakhouse at eight. Understood?"

"No thanks. I've got bongo lessons." Gabby brazenly offered up.

"Well, then I guess they're—I mean, you're—excused then." Heck replied. Deep down inside, he was tallywacker slapping the mouthy beast unmercifully, and everyone with an iota of business savvy in the room knew it. One doesn't refuse a dinner invitation from such a high authority figure, regardless of when the invitation is issued. Bad career move; only the most addlebrained reject would self-sabotage a career by saying no to the boss in a public forum with such a pithy excuse.

"I can't go either. I'm sealing grout." Elfie said groggily.

"You really screwed up this time, Jay! Of all your goddamn screw-ups, this one is the belle of the ball!" the Chairman berated a confused Jay on a mandatory invite jaunt for java.

"What?" Jay truly had no clue what upset the Chairman to such an extent. Was his handshake gesture to Heck really out of line, he wondered?

"You saw Heck storm in from the airport after me and Ollie picked him up, didn't you?"

"No, I think I was talking with—"

"Yeah, jacking around with Stosh and Rennie again! Goddammit!"

"That's what this is about?"

"Tell me what happened last night."

"We got the piss beat out of us by a Grateful Dead cover band in softball, I think. That's all I really remember until Heck greeted us with the morning reaming session."

"That doesn't surprise me. I can still smell it on your breath. You don't remember calling Jeeves last night and trying to set him up with a whore?"

Their dialogue continued at normal volume while standing in line for coffee, providing ample entertainment during the lengthy, single-file trudge of the midday walking dead.

"I can honestly say I do not recall such an incident." Jay wasn't kidding, but he was well past the point of recall by the time he and Stosh landed at Big Red Shoe the previous evening. And things only became foggier from there.

"Let me tell it to you, then, how Jeeves told HECK on the way in from the airport via cell phone!"

"Huh?"

"What you all be wanting?" asked Clitoria, the java mama.

"Two phat regulars, Lisa Bonet." Jay said. That, of course, was hip-hop lingo for "two large regular coffees, cream and sugar."

"Foe-fiddy," Clitoria said, extending her multi-color rainbow painted, three-inch fingernail claw of a hand.

"I got it," the Chairman was quicker on the draw for his folding money.

"Good, I'm broke."

The Chairman shook his head and they were prodded into the java holding pen opposite the cash register with the rest of the caffeine craving slop hogs.

"Let me tell you how it was told to Heck, and later, screamed to the rest of us on the car ride in from the airport, then. About 4:10 AM, you phoned a vice-president of this company."

"What vice-president?"

"Jeeves!"

"Jeeves? I thought he was just, like, a top office guy, not a V-P. Besides, you guys can't stand him."

"That's not the point. You called him at 4:10 AM while sitting in some bar with Stosh and a woman you guys called 'Snakepants.' You told Jeeves that she was a whore and if he could front the cash, you and Stosh would bring her up to his place!"

"Snakepants! Yeah, I think I remember this blonde, forty-ish woman—great body, but you can tell her face has been up against the car hood a few too many times—and she was in these real tight pants made from snake skin."

"So you're admitting to all this?"

"I guess so. But it was only Jeeves. He's a total horn dog. You know that. He takes out, like, four different women from dating services a week."

"That's got nothing to do with anything. You told a company vice president that he could have sex with a whore if he fronted you the money. And the vice president told Swifty's boss, and it makes Swifty and me look like crap. Get it? Jeeves hasn't spoken to Heck in eight months because he's afraid Heck will fire him for doing nothing. And now, Jeeves picks up the phone and calls Heck for the first time this year to tell him about the deplorable behavior of the people that Swifty has indirectly put in place! It really made Heck mad—really mad. He chewed out Swifty but good. Swifty reamed me. And now I'm giving it to you. You don't DO that? How stupid could you be?"

"So, is Swifty mad at me too?"

"He was mad enough to take Starpimp away from you and give it to Rennie."

"But Starpimp was my biggest agency! They were about to close a big deal with City Electric that we were going to be in on."

"That's too bad. Swifty doesn't think he can let you deal with the big agencies until you sober up and fly right. I mean, what the hell. All Swifty knows is that one week you're sexually harassing women in the office, and the next week, scoring whores for the executives in the dead of night! What would you do if you were Swifty?"

"I'd probably fire my ass."

"BINGO! But Swifty is too cool for that. Believe me, he GETS it. Nobody likes to party more than Swifty. But he knows you don't bring it into the workplace and definitely not at an executive level."

The Chairman paused for a moment to reflect upon an incident involving Swifty and himself at a previous company. He remembered how Swifty promised to, and succeeded in, maintaining a blood alcohol level of .20 for seven consecutive business days winning $500 from the Chairman in the process.

"That being said, it might be hypocritical for Swifty to pull the same type of behavior. But he IS the boss. That's reality. All corporate hierarchies increase in hypocritical behavior as they ascend. That's just the way things are."

"A'ight. Two phat regulars, Lisa Bonet!" Clitoria shrieked.

The boys grabbed their cups and headed back up to the office.

"So are we clear?" the Chairman asked Jay. "No more screwing up. Just make sales, and keep Swifty and Heck happy. And don't think this isn't serious because the IPO is in a holding pattern. There's a lot at stake here. You're almost halfway to vesting 25 percent of your options! Keep focused on the STOCK OPTIONS!"

Never one to be about money, Jay nodded obediently without saying anything. How could Jeeves turn him in? How could Stosh let him make such a call? How could he track down Snakepants again for his own Internet Executive air mattress romp?

Jay's silence was contagious enough to make the Chairman fall silent for the remainder of the plant-leg limp back to the office. The Chairman's patented silent treatment wasn't getting a peep out of Jay. They parted at the office entrance. The Chairman updated Swifty about Jay's pledge to atone. Jay interrupted Stosh, who was tutoring Yummy on the dual uses for business ends of a pencil, with all the dry heave fury he could muster.

"Thanks a lot. Jeeves told Heck about last night, and the Chairman just rode me to the prison shower and back for trying to set him up with Snakepants!"

"What is the snake pant?" Yummy asked.

"Hey, I kind of remember a woman in Snakepants last night. Remember we went into Big Red Shoe and you asked the bartender if you were looking for 'a date' if she could help you out? Then the bartender disappeared into the back. And five minutes later, this 70-year-old woman in snakeskin pants was all over you. She took her teeth out and put her head in your lap. I don't remember too much after that. In fact, I think I went bowling and left you guys there to pursue something more concrete."

"She wasn't 70!"

"She looked a lot like a survivor from the Titanic. If she wasn't 70, she was a real hard, real long, real abused 55!"

"Yeah, well, whatever. Apparently she was a whore, and I called Jeeves at four in the morning to set up a tryst. Between you and me, you know Jeeves would've been all over it in any other setting. But he decided to use it as political leverage to embarrass Swifty and the Chairman in front of Heck."

"Whoops."

Yummy giggled.

"Nothing I can do about it now, I guess. But they took Starpimp away from me. Say goodbye to about $400 in monthly commission!"

"Ouch." Stosh stood and offered a consolatory hand to Jay's shoulder. "Well, there IS good news. Heck is out of the office with Rennie and Ollie until dinner tonight. We can spend the whole day setting up some big appointments for tomorrow without him on our backs! If you take Heck on a good call, that would please Swifty and the Chairman."

"Yeah, I'm really looking forward to a night on the town with Heck. A drunken sunovabitch giving me what-for about everything on heaven and earth peppered with anecdotes about parallel bar parables over choice chops and expensive cabernet; it'll be a dream come true."

Bored with all of the business talk, especially in ENGLISH, Yummy took the pencil out of Stosh's hand and dropped it down her blouse.

"Anybody for want to play the hide and go seek?"

VIII – SURFING GOOD TIMES

"I'm gonna cut that bastards nuts off and fry 'em up for my cat!" Zela announced while storming out of the Chairman's office. She stopped at her desk to put her pepper spray and brass knuckles in her purse and quick-stepped out the front door.

As time wore on, she became a little too comfortable with the management team in the office, often smarting off at Swifty, the Chairman, and Ollie, or tap dancing on the thin line between "having a bad day" and "insubordination."

This was just another of what was becoming an all too regular weekly outburst. Zela didn't quit; she'd be a fool to since she was making more now annually than she did in the previous 23 years combined. She was going downstairs and outside for a temper tantrum smoke break to bad mouth the managers. Babs, feeling more and more the sales team outsider without having closed a solitary deal in five months, became Zela's workplace confidant. They'd smoke together, piddle together, lunch together, and get wasted together after work. Babs scampered out behind Zela.

Zela may have set a corporate America record for falling so far, so fast. Initially, she was the darling of the office taking on as many tasks as possible with a perky grin and a chipper "Can do!" Fast forward twelve weeks: she made Courtney Love look like Grace Kelly. She foolishly challenged requests from the Powers-That-Be to follow simple little tasks—like answering the phone 'hello' as opposed to 'yeah'—and stared the managers down ala an NBA/ playground bully if asked to put in a little extra effort or overtime. Zela was a bubbling cauldron of pierced private parts, Jack Daniels, and contempt for authority.

"My mama says they ain't paying me for no overtime, and I'd better not be working any overtime." Zela became fond of repeating in a loud, taunting tone daily at 4:45 PM. "She's waiting for me downstairs. And if I ain't down there at five sharp, she's coming up! And those boys don't want that, I tell you for sure."

This was the posture of the woman hired to keep the office running like a well-lubricated love doll. By the end of May, she was adversarial, indifferent, and getting too big for her britches—a extreme version of Rosie O'Donnell.

Her family life may have played a role in her opinion of the outside world. Zela's dad was a reformed Opium addict who lost the use of his tongue in a massage parlor raid back in the 1970's. Zela never got the full story, but the tongue was somehow squeezed to the point of rupture and left dormant ever since. Dad's choice means of communication with the family was made now through crude gestures and broken beer bottles.

Zela's mother was the Accounts Receivable Clerk breadwinner, but in an amazing coincidence, told her boss to "cram it up your stinkbone" if she was ever approached to work overtime. "Maw," as Zela usually addressed her, also carried a gun in her purse and had a tattoo on her abdomen of the word "Vittles" with an arrow below it pointing downward.

The soul sibling to share Zela's genes, a sister nicknamed Fugly, worked at a punk bar in River North which catered to all of the parent-hating, toothless, fake I-D carrying 19 year-olds from the suburbs. Fugly did double duty as a waitress/bouncer, and made sure Zela and all of her friends got blitzed at fifty percent off whenever they came in.

Zela slept on a cigarette hole burned sofa, so she at least bested Jay and Stosh in regard to slumber apparatus. She kept another fifth of Jack Daniels under the sofa cushion. She wasn't hiding it from the rest of the family out of SHAME. Zela just didn't want them to bogart the hooch while she was out of the apartment 18 hours a day. She really needed her wake-up shot to take the edge off in the morning.

So the Chairman finally chewed Zela out for the decline in her professionalism. Ollie stood stoically by the Chairman's side offering timely " . . . he's right, you know's . . . " to punctuate the Chairman's scolding. Zela sat there and took it, but in her mind thought they were hypocritical lunatics. It was a very informal, Internet start-up company, after all. Why was she expected to be the only who didn't joke around and have a good time with it all? Furthermore, taking orders from MEN was so 1962!

The Chairman also had it in for Zela ever since getting wind of her Central Brain Room orgy with two maintenance men. She never copped to it in a public forum, which was a surprise given her habit of clearing the air when drinking with the gang at the Loser Bar. Two independent sources, one of them being Babs, did confirm the incident, however.

As the story went, there was a problem with the air conditioning unit to the USSBS.com office. The air conditioner was located in what the technologically ignorant called the "Central Brain Room." To computer skilled users worldwide, it would be known as the "Server Room;" that term never caught on with most of the USSBS.com salespeople. Go figure. So the air conditioner in the Central Brain Room was on the fritz. Zela had to report at 6:00 AM on a Wednesday to let the maintenance crew in to fix things. One thing led to another, and by 6:08 AM when Zela asked one of them to " . . . see the problem unit," clothes were being ripped off like smokes and scratch-off lottery tickets from an inner city liquor store.

Zela's tube top was ripped to shreds. Instead of wasting another bus token on a trip home to retrieve another top, she fashioned pasties for herself out of masking tape and swatches from a pair of chocolate nylons. Luckily for Zela's sake, Babs showed up before anyone else that day and convinced her to put on something a little more substantial. Zela sat on the crapper and smoked until Babs returned from a nearby drug store with $3.99 T-shirt stylishly decorated with the *Skoal* logo across the front and back.

When the Chairman heard this tale, he was upset for two reasons. First, carnal pleasures exchanged on company property were frowned upon—especially if they didn't involve management and the tail of their choosing. Secondly, any "foreign substances" purposely or accidentally directed at, or absorbed into, the Central Brain could have caused irreparable damage. Any way they spun it, it wouldn't look good on an I/T work order form.

Despite Zela's subdued mood and tarnished view of the USSBS.com office politics, May, June, and July were still pleasant months overall in the grand scheme of things. The IPO was still on hold, but Jimmy Jim sounded more confident of things happening with each weekly conference call. The new accounts were still piling up, though not as aggressively as before. And Heck left town on a high note, which had everyone thinking that would at least keep him out of Chicago for another couple of months.

Ever the confident huckster, Jimmy Jim downplayed the stall in the high-tech IPO market. Often he would allude to his flock that it was "all part of his master plan." Instead of getting bogged down with questions that required specific answers about the state of the company from employees during the regular conference calls, Jimmy Jim let "guest speakers" take over the calls while he allegedly dashed off to important banker meetings.

The guest speakers ran the gamut from Jimmy Jim's second-in-command and Chief Warrant Being down to the curious, androgynous-sounding youngster in charge of keeping up the corporate Intranet site.

The Chief Warrant Being, a non-practicing attorney named Henry Thaddeus Steeplechase III, lulled everyone into a deep brain freeze reading legal briefs verbatim for hours at a time regarding Internet privacy. Brie, the transvestite responsible for maintaining the USSBS.com Intranet home page, lived next door to Jimmy Jim and needed a gig after dropping out of high school. He was likeable enough when just a voice on the telephone. But his preference for micro mini-skirt outfits in the workplace made everyone around HQ a little nervous, despite the predictability of it all given the office proximity to San Francisco.

Also on Jimmy Jim's Stand-in Hit Parade were a couple of the co-founders who repeated the tale of the genesis of the company for the ten thousandth time. Yes, the sticky sausage and pancakes at *DENNY'S* tale—everyone was familiar with it now. It was time to get to the next level in shameless self-promotion. The *DENNY'S* Ad-Ball origin story was quaint initially, but they should take something more substantial to the street now. Internet buyers had heard every version of the hokey " . . . we started this company sitting on adjacent stalls in a warming shelter john . . . " story by now from various entities. It was time to grow up and market the company like a traditional organization. But that was just 740 out of 750 USSBS.com employees' opinion.

Tessie, Heck, Kweeg, Jimmy Jim's college roommate, and a representative from the largest ad agency on the West Coast throwing a lot of business onto the Ad-Ball (who sounded under extreme duress) also got a shot at speaking to everyone on the weekly spin session. Smoke screens, one and all, but employees lapped it up as long as there were no negative words uttered about the STOCK OPTIONS going south.

All across the land, USSBS.com employees were padding the expense accounts with dinners, cab fares, and airline tickets that were only legitimately for business about half of the time. Headquarters reimbursed one and all without question. Not a single one of Swifty's receipts to the Chicken Ranch in Nevada even stood out as a red flag.

The company still had money to burn, and demonstrated so by sending an arguably terminally confused blonde girl named Amanda to every satellite office around the world—first class, no less—in order to "pick everyone's brain." Amanda truly had no purpose for any of the jaunts. Once she arrived in a new city, she would contact the local office heads, set up meetings, and then sit across from them at a five-star restaurant without making a comment beyond·" . . . so, what's on your mind?" Amanda was being compensated very handsomely for her trouble anyway, but she took full advantage of the company reimbursement expense program also.

To say there were a lot of Internet start-up companies with eclectic business models would be a grand understatement indeed. In Chicago, where Rennie had gobbled up more of the traditional and brick n' mortar companies, everyone else had a client list as diverse as a roll call of Star Trek villains.

On another night at Big Red Shoe, Jay was drinking by himself having an argument with a green olive about the worthiness of Internet companies in general. What possessed Jay to take the proside of the debate, the world will never know. But Jay's argument was so convincing, that an inebriated gent flanking Jay on the next barstool was won over by Jay's passion. He wanted Jay to sign up his Internet dating site, Skinboattotunatown.com, for an immediate test campaign on the Ad-Ball.

Jay also had clients that sold nothing but husky sized lingerie; ran three-legged pet adoptions; and several online pawnshops. Jay liked his clients, and they liked him. The Internet was bringing people together from all walks of life for the sake of e-commerce. It was becoming one big freaking cyber *KUM BA YAH* jam.

Stosh's bread was being predominantly buttered by Korndog King, Guessyourweight.com, and Vivalajew.com, a site run by a stunning 29-year-old business whiz named Torie Beanburg that catered exclusively to those of the Jewish faith. Though not Jewish, Stosh often boasted that Beanburg's site made him want to become a Jew since it was so well done. It was very informative, humorous, relevant, and they even sold Yarmulkes with next day shipment!

If all sites were as ambitious as Vivalajew.com, they might not go under so quickly, Stosh thought. He could count on two hands the clients who started campaigns with USSBS.com, only to go under a few days into the run. Some of the less fortunate included Bathtubmustard.com and Appendectomy.com. The former was a one-man operation who thought he'd get rich stomping out exotic mustards with his bare feet in his home bath tub and shipping them all over the world; and the latter was a site that dispensed do-it-yourself, back alley medical advice via video at $19.95 a pop.

Though new companies kept popping up every day, the competition for uncovering new accounts inside the Chicago office was fierce. The reps had very loosely assigned territories based on company names tied to the alphabet or proximity to home, but the unwritten rule was that whoever molested the fresh meat first got to keep it.

The daily newspapers and local TV stations provided some leads. But the best leads were provided from online sources such as Cyberskuttlebutt, a daily direct email industry newsletter, and from Big Rob.

Big Rob made a name for himself by being a fly on the wall at industry parties, than disseminating whatever gossip he heard via his web site and e-mail newsletter. If a face had a name and any kind of sordid juicy morsel to go along with it, it ended up in electronic print the next day. Big Rob's column was built on pillars of second-hand musings, scurrilous accusations, and occasional cheap shots reinforced atop a foundation of 'No Blood, No Foul' ethics and conveniently wrapped in the American Flag. Industry insiders loathed and loved him, which was the intended recipe for success in such a medium.

Big Rob was very big in physical stature also. His 6-foot, 5-inch frame supported over 400 pounds of free industry function buffets and power midnight snacks. The excess weight would sometimes cause Big Rob health problems, and he'd miss a few days of writing columns. He did write a column once from a hospital bed under the influence of Prozac and Morphine. The result was a 750-word essay of garbled names, non-sequiturs, and the meaning of life from the perspective of a bedpan. More than one reader thought Big Rob's assistant had mistakenly printed the lyrics to a recent Bob Dylan song.

More often than not, though, Big Rob came through with the scoop on the fresh meat. Stosh was fortunate in that his usual early arrival gave him first crack at the leads in Big Rob's newsletter when he signed on in the morning.

In a perfect world, the sales reps were to enter all of their contacts and account information into an easily accessible database so the other reps could see if a mark had been claimed already before going after it. Anyone who has been in a sales position knows that the REAL reason the company makes such upkeep on a database mandatory is so when they can the salesperson's arse, they can easily divvy up her accounts amongst all of the other reps. It was no fuss, no muss. And it was mandatory at USSBS.com. The Chairman made it his pet project to check the database thrice per day to ensure his team members were adding new accounts and updating info.

The common skirmishes would occur between the sales reps when a red-hot tomato was called upon by more than one person because somebody forgot to enter the account into the database. No one was ever brought to tears over losing a free spending interactive marketing sucker. But the Chairman would often make a judgment call and award an account to an undeserving rep, just to prove a point about being proactive in entering account information into the database. It was such a decision that took the lofty Dogpooptoyourdoor.com account away from Stosh and bestowed it to Kippy.

Josh and Brad had the Biz Dev Grifting Machine set on automatic pilot. They'd each make one or two in-the-flesh appearances in the office per week to check the mailbox or Yummy's thong line and were seemingly on the road the rest of the time spreading the gospel about the Ad-Ball to the world's biggest budgeted marketing companies. In truth, nobody had a clue as to what the hell they were doing. They didn't have a quota to fill like the regular sales reps did. And their leader, Kweeg, was never in Chicago. They only had to check in with him bi-weekly and convincingly deliver " . . . things are happening. It's real intense, dude . . . " via speakerphone to keep Kweeg happy.

Heck despised Kweeg and the whole 150 person Biz Dev Grifting Machine army he had in place on six continents. They sucked from the USSBS.com budget with absolutely no accountability. Apparently, the only reason USSBS.com even HAD a Business Development department was because every other Internet start-up had one. They didn't want to be the only one at the Internet Frosh Mixer without a Business Development wing to tout and/or gripe about. Heck's troops were the only ones generating income for USSBS.com, and he reminded Jimmy Jim of that fact during every top-level director's meeting. Jimmy Jim acknowledged that fact. But in his heart of hearts, Jimmy Jim just loved the thrill of the hunt involving everything that had to do with grifting, scamming, fleecing, or bamboozling. The Biz Dev Grifting Machine would remain, and in good standing.

The Chicago team had by this time fallen into a daily routine of reporting for work, disseminating the illusion of work related activities for 90 minutes, popping out to lunch from 10:30 AM to 1:30 PM, returning messages until 3:30 PM, then retiring to the Loser Bar until closing time at 8:00 PM. Since business or Yummy's adorable antics were discussed during lunch and at the Loser Bar, it all qualified as official work time to the managers.

Yes, technically, all were putting in a minimum 12-hour workday. Swifty, Ollie, and the Chairman wanted to take it easy, too. And when Heck wasn't breathing down their jockstraps, they weren't breathing down the napes of the sales reps. Deals were still being closed, so Heck was not heard from.

While commiserating, all would avoid discussing the IPO and STOCK OPTIONS citing a potential jinx. USSBS.com was officially over 1 year-old, making it an ancient Internet dynasty by relative standards. Taking the company public was out of the hands of the employees and taken for granted that it would just happen soon. Gus, the Loser Bar proprietor, was only charging the problem regulars .75 cents per bottle of beer, and Abba was in power rotation on the jukebox, so all was groovy in the world.

Things on the softball diamond continued to plod clumsily along for the USSBS.com squadron. The same nine or ten people would not show up from week to week, so there was no consistency to the line-up. Only Kippy and Ollie made every game. Others would drop in and out like resurrected bit players on a prime time dramedy. Despite it all, the drinks kept flowing on Swifty's dime before, during, and after each contest. There's the team consistency.

Deep down inside, most liked to watch Kippy get frazzled and eventually explode at the end of the game. There were, in fact, two consistencies to the weekly games outside of the shared alcoholism: Kippy's eventual meltdown, and the fact that somebody would break a finger, pop a hamstring, or fracture a nut.

The one time Zela signed on for a game in the middle of the season, she was a one woman wrecking crew to herself and a few others. She agreed to play out of Kippy's desperation to fill the fifth female spot. Plus, Babs would be there for moral and nicotine support. It was also only a couple of weeks after the Chairman gave Zela the royal chewing out, so she figured this might garner her a few good behavior gold stars.

Zela's uniform of choice was a transparent halter-top and pair of Daisy Duke cut-off jean shorts. She stood in the batter's box with a cigarette in her mouth, ran to first base with the cigarette in her mouth, and eventually burned the hand of the opposing first baseman that tagged her out during a head-first slide with the cigarette in her mouth. In the field, she skinned knees and shins on both legs down to the bone trying to field a fly ball and not spill her beer in short center field. And she left the game in the third inning after jamming a wrist on Jay's pancreas during a gutsy double-steal that was illegal and never called for by Kippy. The opposing team decided USSBS.com didn't have to forfeit because of the mandatory Five Chicks per Roster rule since they were already losing by 11 runs. They played it out to the cursed end.

Zela quietly fumed from the sidelines vigorously smoking and getting crocked on tepid beer to ease the pain of her wounds while her teammates battled. After the game, she and Babs tore it up on Rush Street into the wee hours until Babs called it quits on her fourteenth tequila shot and went home. She could listen to Zela rag about her hatred of the Ollie, Swifty, and the Chairman, the company, and organized sports all day, every day, since she shared the same disgruntled passion but didn't possess a like ability to articulate it so eloquently like Zela could.

"They suck. This sucks. Everything sucks." Zela repeated over and over again during the night.

But what Babs couldn't do was keep up with Zela's hard liquor consumption, even though she was approximately 80-100 pounds heavier than Zela. So when Babs began regurgitating in small amounts into her Chanel bag, it was time to shove off. Into Zela's dirty, abrasion scarred hand, Babs tucked a C-note, which Daddy had given her just that morning as weekly allowance, and wobbled off.

"She you in shix hours." Babs said.

"Yeah."

Zela hadn't burned off all of her pent up steam yet, and she sure as hell wasn't ready to call it a night. She noticed a couple of unshaven, clearly criminally minded boys on the other side of the beer garden looking for a Last Call Romance. One of the lads was clad head-to-toe in dirty ripped denim and adjusted his crotch via violent swats. His cohort was a dead ringer for Tupac Shakur though two-feet shorter with four times as many bullet scars on his bare upper torso. Zela decided to draw their attention by taking off her top, shaking out the fried mushroom crumbs, and putting it back on. It worked. They were on her like ants on spilt clam juice.

Since she couldn't take the blokes back to her place for fear of having to share them with Fugly and Maw, the trio opted to consummate their relationship in Zela's passion pit away from home: the Central Brain room. Getting the boys past building security at that hour was no big deal. Zela vouched for them as "visiting Internet executives" from the home office that needed to do an emergency sales proposal for a 6 AM presentation. This fiendish skin plot was no doubt Zela's way of snubbing her nose at the office authorities. She'll show them but good, this time.

Four hours and nine positions later, she sent the boys packing with commemorative USSBS.com edible jock straps, baseball caps, and emery boards. From the Central Brain room, Zela sauntered innocently directly past a SUN-TIMES engrossed Stosh and eased into her NASCAR paraphernalia draped work station.

"Good morning!" Zela chirped, hoping Stosh wouldn't notice she was still in her tattered, slinky softball uniform from the night before.

Stosh was a man, so of course he didn't notice.

"Bright and early today, huh?" he asked.

"Yep." Zela smiled and flipped the bird in the direction of Ollie and the Chairman's empty office as Stosh lost himself in a LOVE IS... cartoon.

IX – GIMME SHEVEN

If the planets are aligned properly, and God is feeling merciful, summer in Chicago normally lasts a good three weeks or so. People are free to walk about without mittens and scarves, and in extreme cases, even be scantily clad. But in this "Summer at Internet Speed," it came and went in what seemed like four days. Stosh and Jay had been toiling away at this Once in a Lifetime Gig well into July when one glaring truth dropped on them like a ton of Mothra dung: they weren't REALLY making any money.

Over some home made margaritas while seated poolside on the eighth floor cabana deck at Jay's place, they lamented their current existence.

"I'm making a higher salary than I ever have," Jay began, "but I'm sleeping on an air mattress, I can't pay my phone bill, and I haven't had a live woman in my apartment since my sister came to visit Memorial Day weekend. This is what it means to be an Internet Executive?"

"You're preaching to the choir, hombre."

"This is ridiculous! I lost five clients in the past two weeks because of poor campaign performance on the Ad-Ball. They still haven't taken the company public yet. The Chairman is asking me 'what's up' every day when he knows nothing is up. And my air mattress has a hole in it somewhere; by the time I wake up, I'm flat on the floor every goddamn morning."

"I've lost a couple of clients, too. I thought they fixed all those tentacle problems. Goddamn Bungleman!"

"Can you believe we were trying to talk people into buying those Tentacle packages for a million dollars a month ago, and now we'll throw them on a tentacle for free if they promise to do $20,000 in business with us?" Jay took a healthy gulp from his margarita and pointed over Stosh's shoulder. "Look, but don't look!"

"Is that our new slogan to promote the Ad-Ball."

"No, behind you. Next to the pool—there's a chick with no top on, and she just turned over on her back."

"And you don't want me to look!?"

"Okay, but be cool."

His heart already pounding at the mere thought of a topless female in the same city, Stosh spun around fast enough to cause his neck, spine, and pelvis to crack loudly. The sound of bone scraping together resonated over to the topless female who picked her head up and grimaced in Stosh and Jay's direction then covered her upper torso with a Scott Baio beach towel.

"Typical. Even in terrycloth form, he gets all the action." Jay opined.

The show was over, and they were about to retire upstairs to Jay's balcony when two shirtless, brawny men approached them. Stosh was internally activating his defense mechanisms when Jay leaped out of his chair and gave them his patented friendly greeting.

"Dudes! What's up? Hey, this is my buddy and coworker, Stosh. Stosh, this is Rip and Danger."

"My pleasure," Stosh said.

"What's happening?" said Danger, a 23-year-old version of Mel Gibson's butt taking on the form of a 6-foot tall surfer boy.

"Did I hear right? Is your name Danger?"

"Something like that. It's really Dan Gere, but I just kind of put it all together and dropped one of the E's. Chicks like it when they're dealing with Danger!"

"Funny, huh?" Jay laughed. "Where you guys headed all half-naked and stuff."

"We just got back from the Cubs game," Rip said. "Now we're going to a barbecue at some girl's house near Boy's Town. You guys want in?"

Having nothing pressing on their respective social calendars, they agreed to partake of the frivolity. Rip and Danger were already blasted, and Jay desperately wanted to catch up to their nirvana. Stosh went along because it was better than gorging himself on a jumbo bag of cheese popcorn while watching UHF television programs in his stagnant apartment all alone—seemingly.

Rip was legally intoxicated, but he had a chauffeur's license. Jay convinced Stosh that the two factors cancelled each other out, so it was safe to let Rip motor the posse to the barbecue in his late model Lincoln stretch limo. For the record, it wasn't an actual "posse" until they picked up two other aimlessly wandering men from the building: Nguyen and Francois.

All of them, save for Stosh, had apartments on Jay's penthouse floor. The initial deductive reasoning for moving into the most expensive apartments the building had to offer was shared by each: penthouse apartment + new smell = Parade of Poontang. But to date, not a single one had brought a non-relative female up to his apartment going back six months to when Nguyen was the first occupant on the floor. Through many shared elevator ride discussions, all decided it was going to be a case of WHEN, not IF, regarding the Parade of Poontang.

The party was about eight miles up Lake Shore Drive and over to the left. It took Rip 70 minutes to navigate the location. The gathering was indeed a casual affair with shorts and bikini tops the most popular outerwear. The hostesses were four healthy girls that together could overturn a Boeing 737 if they wanted to. The apartment was brazenly decorated with Playgirl centerfolds. And about a dozen plastic sex toys were "accidentally" left lying around on coffee tables, lawn chairs, in the refrigerator, etc.

Not comfortable with the whole scene, Francois darted off after five minutes and hailed a cab back downtown. The other members of the Aimlessly Wandering Posse stayed close by the keg all night for lack of anything better to do. It wasn't a great scene as far as parties go, but the beer was free. Eventually, five hours of slurping the suds and watching obese girls bop with one another on the hardwood floor to the latest mindless urban trash beats was enough. The boys hopped into the Rip's limo and headed back home.

"Lesh keep going! Take us out to the riverboashts in Joliet!" Jay screamed.

"No can do," Rip said. "I've got to pick up some connected guys in Melrose Park in a couple of hours and take them up to Milwaukee. I just needed to kill a few hours at that party."

Rip kicked everyone out of the car in front of Celibacy Towers, their anointed building, and tore off to Melrose Park. Danger suddenly remembered he was going to sit for the bar exam in the morning and had better get a few hours of sleep. Stosh, Jay, and Nguyen felt awkward just standing in the middle of the street looking like abandoned Pug pups in search of mammy's teat. So they ducked into a crowded watering hole down the street. Any of the three could have qualified for hardship enrollment into the Betty Ford Clinic by this point.

The only opened seats were at a very cozy table with three very out-of-place octogenarian ladies that were an odd sight in such a joint at such an hour. They were as loaded as Stosh, Jay, and Nguyen, and they were definitely hard up for some lousy, miserable, drunken conversation. The boys obliged, and everything seemed playfully harmless until one of the women began to get very touchy-feelie with Jay. She looked the same age as Jay but in truth had been on the earth about 41 years longer.

"I know you," she said barely able to keep her teeth in her head.

Not one to be discourteous to his elders, Jay smiled and said, "Oh really? From where?"

"You that white boy in the cross-dresser's revue on Clark Street! I'd never forget that face! We just saw the show last night. You were incredible, and so beautiful all done up in your makeup and gown!"

Stosh and Jay chuckled. Nguyen didn't know Jay or Stosh too well, so any allegations levied their way could be true.

"That's right!" Jay said for whatever reason. "I can't believe you'd remember!"

Alcohol must've been doing the talking, Stosh thought. For Jay to admit to being a cross dressing performer, there would need to be a big payoff. And there was nothing to gain here.

Jay then jumped up, began preening and gyrating around the table, and blowing kisses around the room.

"It's him! It's really him!" The gaggle of saggy skinned women laughed hysterically. It only motivated Jay to continue prancing and wiggling more erotically. He was definitely garnering additional onlookers around the bar when pitching woo to, and dry humping, a four-foot tall plastic palm tree.

"I'm out of here," is all Nguyen said while racing out of the building.

Next, Jay was bent forward rubbing his rear end up against the octogenarians' backs. He was really getting into it. Stosh sensed there was something wrong deep inside. He had seen Jay over lubricated on thousands upon millions of occasions, and this Peter Pan on Crack deal was definitely not his M.O. It's a good thing the Chairman wasn't around to see it all, or the barkeep would be scraping Jay-sidue off the walls for months.

In the coming weeks, the Cyberskuttlebutt and Big Rob both were quick to report the negative wave of news hitting the Internet industry in general. Cyberskuttlebutt covered the national scene, and Big Rob muckraked about all of the local goings-on.

While many, including the Chairman, Jimmy Jim, and Heck, had anticipated a summer lull in Internet business everywhere, the shared consensus was that the industry would bounce back in the Fall. And by Winter, all agreed, e-commerce companies would be ripping the world by the short hairs during the holidays turning traditional marketing plans inside out and getting whatever price they wanted to for their cyber advertising services.

The Cyberskuttlebutt repeatedly speculated that the summer blahs would continue. And such an extended downturn would prove fatal for most Internet concerns.

Big Rob seemed to revel in listing the names of the local Internet companies and executives on the bubble every morning. He'd get the ball rolling just speculating about the health of an Internet company whether he had inside knowledge or not. Things would snowball from there into name calling exchanges and re-printed "I Told You So" letters from vendors who had been screwed by an Internet company on its way to the top.

In short, there was a lot of hate to go around.

The traditional business community, that had built solid franchises the old fashioned way by screwing and manipulating its employees and the buying public, was just now beginning to get even. Since the mid-90's, everything was "Internet company this, e-commerce that." That attitude was biting into the anticipated revenues of companies that had easily controlled all that is commerce from generation to generation. And finally, the tide seemed to be turning against the 20-something brats and the handful of lucky "Gray Hairs" who started or got involved with Internet businesses on the ground floor level and become overnight paper billionaires.

Disgruntled brick n' mortar CEO's, vengeful presidents, you name it—they would take five minutes out at the 19th hole to dash off a smug note to Big Rob on their handheld PDA on whatever rumor they heard or fabricated on the golf course about " . . . problems at such-and-such dotcom." The underground anti-Internet coalition was gaining strength via the age-old adage of "the pen being mightier than the sword . . . " (even though the "pen" used nowadays was an electric handheld device or laptop computer and the message was sent via Internet e-mail).

Big Rob absolved himself from any wrongdoing each and every time he re-printed an anonymous posting stating boldly and proudly that "the public deserves to know what might or might not be happening in the world of Internet . . . maybe."

Internally at USSBS.com, there were no rumors, only sad facts. While the membership had grown to 25,000,000 (larger than the populations of 48 states!), the Ad-Ball wasn't properly fixed yet. In fact, it was freaking out. And Heck was roaring louder than ever.

The USSBS.com business model was to pay its members to download and use the Ad-Ball, which was clear. What wasn't clear was HOW they were going to be able to do that now with a membership community of 25 million members that was growing exponentially each month. In all the haste to retool the Tentacle version of the Ad-Ball and shove it down the world's esophagus, nobody seriously sat down to do the math.

USSBS.com was paying people, every month, in several dozen different types of currency. It was bleeding to the tune of $18 million per month in membership payback alone. All of the leased offices around the world still had to be staffed, most with lights and/or electricity, which required a few shekels. The third party entity in charge of serving and tracking Ad-Ball ads and generating reports expected its bi-weekly check, as USSBS.com did more business through the company than all of its other customers combined. And those edible USSBS.com jockstraps didn't grow on trees.

Suddenly, and without notice, USSBS.com changed its compensation policy to the members. In short, they were requiring members to use the Ad-Ball five times as much, for one-quarter of the money they were previously paid to do so. Some countries were cut out of the payment loop altogether, as it was cost prohibitive to pay someone in a Third World country for something he should be gladly doing for free anyway, the bastard. About seven days after the actual change in policy was implemented, Jimmy Jim sent a spineless letter of drivel, dripping with legalese, to all members explaining the sudden shift in payment methods. The final paragraph was pure Jimmy Jim:

"Remember, y'all. We wouldn't be here today without y'all. After the summer doldrums, we'll likely re-evaluate the original payment policy. Hell, maybe even do more than that! Y'all be cool now."

Jimmy Jim got out on an optimistic note and legally committed to nothing in cyber ink. He stopped short of blaming the "coke snorting A-holes on Wall Street" for the entire mess in the high tech market, but only because Henry Thaddeus Steeplechase III edited Jimmy Jim's final draft before it went out.

A few members took the opportunity to call Jimmy Jim a crook in different chat rooms and spam e-mails predicting the demise of USSBS.com by "month's end." But the majority of the members were still just glad to be sitting around getting paid to look at Monkey Chow ads.

Even with the new payment policy in place, USSBS.com was burning through more cash than it could handle. With only $16 million left in the bank, Jimmy Jim had to go back to the Japanese drunken sailors and tap dance for more good faith money. Quicker than someone could say "three card Monte," Jimmy Jim was flying home from Tokyo with another check for $40 million in his breast pocket. This would easily carry USSBS.com through the end of the year. And it would no doubt be a publicly traded company before then, leaving Jimmy Jim to go hog nuts with the extra cash.

Now, regarding the Premium Tentacle version of the Ad-Ball, nobody could say for certain WHY it was doing what it was doing. And 65 illegal Eastern European and Pakistani immigrants locked in a room at USSBS.com headquarters for days on end were at each other's throats trying to come up with a fix-all. True, the majority of USSBS.com users didn't bail out after the change in payment policy. The experiences with the constantly self-morphing, uncontrollable Ad-Ball, however, left thousands numb.

To begin with, the advertising community never embraced the Premium Tentacle idea. It didn't help that the salespeople didn't know enough about the technology to fully explain it to everyone, either. Simple questions from clients such as, " . . . how does the tentacle know when to extrude itself?" and " . . . why are you naming this new version of the Ad-Ball after male reproductive parts?" stymied salespeople in the middle of pitching the product. A typical response to any such question would simply be a cheesy, suspicious, unconfident, " . . . don't worry; trust us."

Since the USSBS.com sales troops couldn't explain how the Premium Tentacle Ad-Ball worked in a perfect world, they sure as hell couldn't explain the different anomalies experienced in the product. Advertisers would observe the Ad-Ball for hours waiting for their specialized tentacle message to appear when it was supposed to generate every 45 seconds all day long. Tentacles would extend from the Ad-Ball body carrying no advertising messages at all, play a lightning speed round of Solitaire, and then crash a user's system for no apparent reason. In other instances, the tentacles would present only "house ads" featuring a picture of an uncomfortable looking Henry Thaddeus Steeplechase III atop a slogan reading:

"Your anonymity matters. We'll protect
you. No, really."

And as soon as Steeplechase's picture dissolved, all twelve tentacles shot out from the Ad-Ball, entwined themselves, and automatically re-booted a user's computer commencing with a full screen ad for "USSBS.com Merchandise: Order Now!"

Problems with the Ad-Ball couldn't have come at a worse time. Again, the bad elements to the software were fixable, but the high tech industry was already on the ropes defending itself to the rest of the world. A shoddy product could not be tolerated at this point in time. Three-and-a-half years from now, no problem; everyone would be cashed out and gone. But not now.

While USSBS.com was dealing with its own catastrophes, the rest of the industry was on the defensive against computer hackers hell bent on proving what flimsy, simpleton security measures all Internet websites had in place. The hackers didn't care who they took down; the bigger and more respected the site they penetrated the better. No website was safe. The hackers defaced e-commerce pages, stifled informational sites, and embarrassed government run web operations.

With chaos reigning, it was a grand time for the lowest of the low, sniveling software hacker dweebs to make the scene: virus creators. They bombarded Internet users with computer viruses designed to destroy hard drives, showcase pornography, and scare the living daylights out of Joe and Betty Sixpack—who were just considering buying their first family desktop computer. Corporation e-mail systems were crippled. Murmurs of Internet industry collapse had begun. There were too many loopholes, too much at risk, for citizens and corporations to invest so much time, money, faith, and security in anything to do with the Internet.

The Internet was at DEFCON III.

USSBS.com disappeared for a week. From the outsider's perspective, it just ceased to exist. The Ad-Ball was gone. The company web site had disappeared. Nobody was answering the phones at headquarters. Even in the current climate, it seemed quite sudden. The Chicago rank and file looked to the Chairman, Swifty, and Ollie for answers. They usually had them. But not this time.

Finally, word came from Heck that everything was okay. Headquarters was scrubbing the software, web site, and workplace, because they wanted to be ready for the September 1 launch of the Revitalized Tentacle Ad-Ball. Things were more than all right, Heck insisted, so much so that he wanted Swifty and the Chairman to inquire about leasing additional office space in Chicago to accommodate the 35 new employees the board had approved for expansion upon Heck's urging.

"Expansion?!" Swifty laughed to the Chairman. "Can you believe they want us to hire 35 more people here while companies all around us are crumbling into ashes?"

"Heck's the man. He's got a better feel for the pulse of this baby than anyone has. He knows the competition is disappearing.

That's why he wants us to become the 800-pound gorilla. They must be poised to launch the IPO!" the Chairman said.

Within hours of Heck's order, Swifty and the Chairman were in preliminary negotiations to take over 14,000 SF of space on the second level of the same building vacated days before by the bankrupt and defunct Internet solutions company Wethinkwecanwethinkwecan.com. The whole USSBS.com office would move downstairs to the enormous space that was complete with a built-in Foosball table and Lazy Susan under-desk mounted urinals—for the less-than-active inside salesperson. The office of the building was going to give them a great deal if they signed the new lease by week's end.

The next day, Heck rescinded his order. USSBS.com would be staying put in its present Chicago digs. Furthermore, there was a hiring freeze on. Oh, and by the way, could Swifty, Ollie, and the Chairman come up with a short list of names of people they think USSBS.com would be able to live without?

"Layoffs?" Swifty asked Heck.

"No, no. We're just trying to get our best team in place, you know. We want to get rid of the dead weight so we can appear lean and mean to the bankers when we're ready to pull the trigger on the IPO." Heck replied.

Rumors swirled internally about all of the sudden doublespeak from headquarters. One minute, they're told to increase in staff size by 100% and rent a larger fleecing outpost. The next minute, they're trimming fat and staying put. In hindsight, it also appeared that the company wasn't being on the level with anyone about its weeklong disappearing act.

As he was wont to do, Stosh was surfing around on the computer at 7:15 AM one morning when he decided to visit the USSBS.com Intranet site. On the front page of the site was printed a letter from the El Grande Technical Guy at headquarters, Gupta Hammerschulz. The letter apologized for a "massive shutdown" in the USSBS.com infrastructure brought about by software glitches, an imported e-mail virus, and a "Denial of Service" attack on the company launched by hackers. Hammerschulz went on to say that for security concerns, the employees and media were being kept in the dark about the matter, and that the company was working closely with the FBI to get to the bottom of it.

Alone in the office, Stosh had no one to run and gossip about this bombshell with. He attempted to print the page for later viewing out of the office, but the printer was jammed thanks to a beating it suffered from Zela the evening prior. Stosh fixed the printer, but by the time he returned to his desk, the Intranet page was gone. The entire Intranet site was inaccessible. When it did become available again hours later, the letter from Hammerschulz was omitted. Without any proof, Stosh had a hard time convincing everyone but Jay of the traumatic episode.

From that day forward, no one heard from Hammerschulz again. His name continued to appear on the company phone list, but nobody saw him or ever heard his voice around USSBS.com headquarters again. It was very unnerving to Stosh in that he knew he was the only one in Chicago to SEE Hammershulz's letter. And with all of the internal computing tracking measures in place, he knew that headquarters knew that he knew. He convinced himself he would never live long enough now to sip celebratory IPO champagne from Yummy's navel.

Later in the day, after complaining of severe chest pains, Zela finally broke down sobbing before the Chairman. She couldn't explain the pains other than that they were sharp and incapacitated her a few times every week.

Stosh happened to be in the Chairman's office trying to recant the whole Hammerschulz mysterious erasing memo bit when Zela burst in clutching her chest crying. The Chairman blew off whatever Stosh was saying dismissing it as the misunderstood hobgoblins of an ignorant high tech brain. The Chairman didn't accuse Stosh of outright lying, but thought because of his limited knowledge of technical things, he probably thought he read such a letter on the company Intranet website while he mistakenly was logged in to a different URL address.

"Take Zela to the hospital. You can expense the cab fare," the Chairman ordered Stosh. He wasn't all that concerned for Zela's health, but there could be a liability issue if he just ignored her.

"But isn't Heck barking about us hitting our nut for the quarter? Wouldn't you rather I try and sell something?"

"Don't worry about it. Just go."

Stosh helped Zela downstairs and into a cab. Never before had this ruthless ogre of a woman appeared so fragile. The tears kept flowing all the way to the Northwestern Hospital emergency room. Stosh tried to be as comforting and consoling as possible, but couldn't get past thinking how close he might be to seeing Zela naked if the doctors have to zap her bare chest with a defibrillator or for x-Jays or whatever. He was one of the few men in Chicago that hadn't seen the full sea urchin tattoo. Today could be the day!

During the obligatory five-hour wait amongst whimpering stabbing victims and wheezing TB patients to see an actual health care professional, Zela's crying stopped. She opened up to Stosh and told him all of the horrendous details of her sketchy past that included extensive drug abuse, petty larceny, and a dishonorable discharge from the Army for alleged prostitution on government soil. She complained about the Chairman, and the Internet, and the continual pain in her chest. Tired of waiting and out of telling asides, Zela demanded the attending desk clerk have a doctor look at her right away.

"It'll be just ten minutes," the clerk told her.

"Fine. Come get me. I'll be right outside having a cigarette."

"It's bad, Jojo. I'm freaking miserable." Jay sighed into the telephone.

"That's nuts. You're making great money. And you got all of them whatchacallum options."

"Stock options. Not yet, I don't. And it looks bleaker every day. Nobody is buying into this scam anymore. Plus, I'm broke. I told Stosh I couldn't hit the bars this week because I was taking medication. I've put on 40 pounds, all in the gut. And the sun has only been out four days here since last December. What I wouldn't give to be at the Chocha Cantina with you guys right now sucking back some fatty margaritas!"

"I'm headed down there right now with Jena, Tawny, Rachel, and Melanie. It's going to be an awesome sunset tonight. We're going to pound the cocktails for a few hours, then Tawny wants to get her navel and nipples pierced on Venice Beach. She wants us to go along for support and stuff. So I gotta run. I'll call you from the boat tomorrow. D-bone is bringing some strippers for a photo shoot, and he needs my vessel. I'm trolling everyone out to Catalina. Too bad you're not here; I could use the extra seaman! Keep warm. Later!"

Jojo hung up, and Jay curled up on his air mattress gazing at the torrential downpour that had a stranglehold on downtown Chicago for a third consecutive day. A Canadian cold front had the temperature hovering in the upper 30's, and it wasn't going to budge until the last Chicago knuckle was blue.

Jesus, Jay thought. It's not even Labor Day yet.

Chronic depression and a gentle hissing sound lulled him to sleep. When he woke up on the hard floor some hours later, it was just after midnight. His deflated air mattress was flattened, cold, and damp with spilt Cabernet. The rain was coming down so heavily he couldn't see any other buildings from his balcony.

Jay needed some company and reserves, and he dashed out to pick up a few bottles of Captain Morgan at a convenience store on State Street. He returned home, filled a giant tumbler with a 6-to-1 mixture of Captain Morgan to orange juice, and surfed the few surviving job seekers websites in his sopping wet clothes. A knock on the door pulled him away before he could make any serious headway.

Standing in the hallway with their shirts off, crimson eyes fluttering, toting two cases of beer were Rip and Danger.

"Dude! You want to party at Rip's?"

"It's kind of late, no? Don't you guys have to work in the morning?"

"Thursday is my day off, man." Rip said.

"I've got nothing happening." Danger added.

Not one to turn down an opportunity to socialize or drink free beer, Jay nodded.

"Just let me get some dry pants on."

"What for?" Danger asked him.

"Good point. Let's go get hammered." Jay locked his apartment door, and then they skipped and hollered their way down to Rip's pad.

"Hey," Jay turned to Danger. "How'd you do on that bar exam. Are you a lawyer now or what?"

"I just took it for fun. I'm thinking about going back to school and get my Psychology degree or something. No rush, though. I might do Europe this Fall and do the school stuff in the Winter. Right now, I'm just drinking."

"I hear you."

"Dude, so Nguyen says you're one of those transvestite dancer dudes on Clark Street. For real?" Rip asked.

Jay yanked a beer out of the case under Danger's arm.

"No, but it seems like an attractive career move right now."

Rumors were flying, so Heck decided it was time for another cross-country tour of the sales offices. This time his objective would be to disseminate positive spin and damage control. He landed in Chicago about 6:00 PM, and instead of going to the USSBS.com office told everyone to meet him at his favorite five star steakhouse along the Chicago River. This time, no slovenly grunts were invited. Translated, that meant Heck wanted revenue producing personnel and managers only—no Campaign Coddlers or Biz Dev Grifting freeloaders.

Heck must've taken serious advantage of the free flowing booze in first class, because he was slouched in his chair with hair mussed and necktie loosened when everyone arrived at the steakhouse. He was already halfway into a $90 bottle of Shiraz and starting his third basket of warm bread.

"What took you guys so long? Didn't I say six!?" Heck barked.

"I'm pretty sure you said you were landing at six, and that we should be here at eight," Swifty countered.

Heck stood up slowly, never breaking eye contact with Swifty. He made a fist in his right hand, pulled his arm back, and looked as if he was poised to clean Swifty's clock.

"Oh, is that what I said?"

This impending physical violence thing made for an uncomfortable greeting for all. Heck's forte was definitely the verbal assault, not the public pummeling.

Heck laughed and threw his hand forward stopping just short of Swifty's gut. The sudden offensive caused Swifty to flinch and step backward on Hot Pot's bare toed hoof. Heck was simply a little buzzed and contrived this episodic dinner theater scene as a humorous and creative way to greet his people.

"Goddammit!" Hot Pot cried as she plopped into a chair and grabber her toes.

Heck shook Swifty's hand.

"Relax, gang. I just got here a little early, that's all. You're perfectly on time. That's my team. I couldn't be any prouder. You guys are what it's all about." Heck sat back down and gestured for all to gather round the cozy, 25 seat banquet table.

Heck was definitely acting weird, alcohol or no. The managers were still working on a short list of names for Heck to hack. All of this "team" and "being proud" talk was simply poppycock. Each time Heck made some kind of similar reference, the managers sensed a wink-wink, nudge-nudge twinkle in his eye. As close as the managers were to their respective team members, they never let the cat out of the bag that cuts would be coming.

The initial exchanges between Heck and the rest of the staff were simple, short blurbs about what each rep had "cooking," and Heck's personal assessment of such. Swifty thought he'd loosen everyone up by ordering a round of Zombies with Harvey Wallbanger chasers. Swifty liked to kick it old school in business-social settings. In addition to Swifty's order, each pair of reps was free to select and share a bottle of wine of their choosing.

Jay ordered a nice little $84 Russian River valley Cabernet to split with Stosh. The whole scene was reminiscent of the duo's Living-Higher-on-the-Hog days earlier in the year. The steak joint was the type of eatery Jay and Stosh were frequenting every night when the visions of STOCK OPTIONS were still dancing in their heads. They'd since pulled back the reigns eating mostly street vendor gyros and guzzling generic beer. This was definitely a premium venue for sumptuous cow—a taste for sore tongues.

"There have been a lot of rumors going around, dammit, and I'm going to each office to set the record straight." Heck threw back a belt of Drambuie and lost himself in the moment. He crammed a Chihuahua size wedge of bread into his mouth and washed it down with eight ounces of Shiraz.

"Heck, are you going to talk about the stock options?" Swifty was attempting to get him back on track. "I think everyone is distracted by that whole NASDAQ freak-out thing."

"We're not here for the stock options!" Heck yelled. A hush fell across the restaurant. Heck lowered his voice, but not a great deal. "If any of you, and I mean ANY of you, took this job just because of the stock options, then you're . . . I don't know what. This is the best trained, highest paid sales force of any Internet company. I know this, because I know things. We're here to do a job, and that job is to sell our products. Stock options are just a part of the eventual reward package you get for doing your sales job well. I want you to get stock options out of your mind. When you show up for work tomorrow, tell yourself there are no stock options. Do you understand? There ARE NO STOCK OPTIONS."

Since they weren't feeling any pain, the world's biggest group cry didn't take hold. All continued to nonchalantly slurp up their Zombies and nosh the petite fillets.

"That being said," Heck continued. "Everything is fine with the stock options. Like we told you back in April, the company and the bankers wanted to ride out the summer and let things cool down. Things seem to be cooling down. Now don't quote me on this, but they're looking at an October 1 launch date for the IPO."

Just as it is preached in physics and drivers education classes everywhere, the formula of time plus excess quantities of alcohol doesn't end in a pretty picture. Over the course of the evening, the USSBS.com party consumed 44 bottles of wine, 25 Zombies, 25 Harvey Wallbangers, four Drambuie's, and 25 Kahlua coffees.

At 3:00 AM, no one had left, but many had checked out. Jay and Stosh were too petrified to even blink in Heck's presence when sober. They sure as hell weren't going to put their heads down for nappy time on the crème brulee bowls while Heck was taking his infamous mental notes. Their bodies and immune systems were approaching self-imposed shut down, but they just had to hang on. They were still the Chairman's handpicked boys; any sign of weakness would reflect poorly upon the boss.

Heck had killed off eight bottles of Shiraz by himself. Stosh deduced Heck was thinking "Bart Conners, eat your heart out . . . " by the way he polished off each bottle and playfully set it on the table with a double twisting, double back, double tuck dismount.

It had been a 17-hour day for most at the table already. Each time Heck opened a new bottle of Shiraz on the hour, he told the same three identical stories about the history of advertising, the need to succeed, and the time in New York when he had the fancy cab horse in a headlock. The man was a soused broken record and nobody in the audience wanted to be the first to walk out on his performance. So it continued, and repeated, until Heck broke the cycle himself.

"You two!" Heck shouted and pointed at Stosh and Jay. "You two how come you no want to gimme sheven?"

It was the most direct, forceful, and imposing question Heck had asked anyone all night. And nobody knew what the hell he just said.

Stosh froze and smiled the same smile a fetus smiles when it passes gas for the first time. Jay simply hoisted his glass and barked right back.

"Damn straight we are!"

About 90 minutes later, the crew disbanded and wobbled off into the wee morning hours. Swifty, the Chairman, Jay, and Stosh were the last ones standing, and it took all four of them to lift Heck up the stairs and into a cab. He had his suitcase with him at his feet the whole time and never checked into a hotel. Heck was scheduled on a flight out of Midway bound for the Atlanta sales office in two hours.

Swifty handed the cabbie a C-note. "Take him to Midway, get him some coffee, and make sure he gets to the Southwest ticket counter."

The cab sped south down Dearborn Street. The sun would be up soon. That was Swifty's cue to call for a mandatory nightcap at the Cotton Club.

"We'll do this last round at the Cotton Club, and I won't expect to see any of you guys in the office until noon."

The Chairman was holding a now limp Jay up by the scruff of the neck.

"I think Jay's out. Stosh, make sure he gets home."

The Chairman handed Jay's corpse to Stosh. He and Swifty jumped into the next southbound cab for the Cotton Club.

Several minutes passed without another cab going by when Stosh said the hell with it and began dragging Jay home backward by his armpits.

"Gimme sheven," Jay mumbled. "Gimme sheven."

X – THE FIRST WHACK

On a casual Saturday afternoon, 18 games of bowling and 22 OLD STYLES behind them, the Chairman ordered an immediate post-competition whistle wetting in the Merryman Bowl lounge. It was also necessary so he, Jay, and Stosh could rest their weary, throbbing plant legs. Six games apiece is a lot of stress for the plant leg, especially on middle aged frames in the beginning stages of portliness.

Merryman Bowl was a great joint just northeast of Chicago's Boys Town neighborhood. Boys Town wasn't good or bad; it's just a part of town where the non-trendy, pedestrian heterosexual types should be careful bending over to pick up a nickel on the sidewalk. Built in the late 1950's, Merryman Bowl utilized the good, old fashioned, manual scoring tables. Jeb and Jocko, two 60-something cousins, owned and operated the bowling alley supply shop within the bowling alley. They'd been leasing the space since 1958, and had seen/heard it all when it came to plant legs, bloody thumbs, and freaky balls (the freaky ball stories were on the increase ever since the women-folk were chased from the neighborhood for good during the Carter administration).

Jay and Stosh had an uncomfortable episode at Merryman Bowl a few months earlier. On Wednesdays from 9:00 PM to midnight, all games bowled cost $.75 cents. Seeking to take advantage of the great rate at the respected local rollers' venue, they went in with their guard down. They knew the current reputation of the neighborhood around the bowling alley. But never in a thousand moons did Jay and Stosh think that as hard drinking heterosexuals they'd be in the minority in a bowling alley anywhere east of Denver!

The sight of two lithe, cropped mesh shirt wearing fellows making out on the ball waxing machine greeted them near the entrance. From there all the way to the counter at the center of the alley, Jay counted five male-male couples kissing, hugging, or engaging in heaving petting. Not that there's anything wrong with it, as the spineless-yet-popular Unwritten Rule of Tolerance goes. It just wasn't Stosh and Jay's "thing."

As the night wore on, Jay and Stosh bowled absolutely atrociously. There were just too many distractions. Plus, their nerves were on end. They could just FEEL all eyes mercilessly ogling their buttocks and/or orifices on each roll. A gaggle of no less than eleven transvestites, in full Shock-the-Breeders wardrobe, bellied up next to Jay and Stosh on the adjacent lane. They didn't do anything too over the top, other than simulate copulation with different thumb holes on various Black Beauty house bowling balls every other frame—much to the howling delight of their peers. How witty it was indeed.

Physically, Stosh and Jay left the lanes that night unscathed. But they were uncomfortable about ending up in a few of the transvestite crowd shot photos being taken at will by numerous digital camera abusing she-males. They had no recourse as to where those photos might turn up in print or on the Internet! It was not a comfortable position for Internet Executives with STOCK OPTIONS at stake to be in, in their minds, anyway.

The Chairman popped for the post-competitive round of *OLD STYLES*. All sipped silently and unconsciously nurtured their throbbing plant legs by holding the frosty cold bottle to their inner left thigh.

"I want you guys to keep this to yourselves," the Chairman said, "but there are going to be some layoffs." He immediately fell silent and tried to read Jay and Stosh.

Stosh only shrugged, as he was more concerned with draining the lizard at that point. Fatigued, he opted to stay put, rest his leg, and pour more *OLD STYLE* into his bursting bladder. Fine logic.

"Just give it to us straight, Chairman. We figured something was up. You, Ollie, and Swifty have been having a lot of closed door meetings lately—and without Yummy." Jay said.

"We were shouting it out until four o'clock this morning in Swifty's basement!"

"Jesus."

"Believe me, I was worried. We had Heck on the speakerphone. Ollie just kept going on about what valuable, young gamers Kippy and Hot Pot were. I was talking up you guys and the rest of the team. And Swifty was chewing Heck out, playing his steel guitar and drums, and blasting *Ishtar* away on the big screen TV. It was chaos."

The Chairman paused again. He had the complete attention of both. This was it, Stosh thought. This is why the Chairman invited them bowling—to soften the blow. Personally Stosh could take or leave the job, but he was still counting on the STOCK OPTIONS to erase the insurmountable credit card debts he'd racked up in such a short time. And he actually could tolerate this Internet stuff, as crazy as it all was. With his cronies in charge or on board, it was the best all around work environment Stosh had ever experienced.

Jay just wanted out. He wanted to leave but wanted to be laid off instead of quitting on the Chairman. If he let the Chairman or market conditions rub him out, Jay will have fulfilled his commitment to the Chairman to the best of his ability. But now he could be back in California just after Labor Day. There'd still be plenty of warm sunsets to be enjoyed with Jojo and the gang at the Chocha Cantina.

As far was Jay concerned, if the STOCK OPTIONS did happen in the next couple of months, so what? His debts were triple that of Stosh's by now, but his focus was still on drinking and seeking out poontang under the California sun. He still resisted convincing himself that the STOCK OPTIONS could one day be worth more than sun tanned, margarita fueled, writhing SNATCH.

Jay shut his eyes, crossed his fingers, and said a prayer to himself that the Chairman was about to break the bad news.

"I fought for both of you guys . . . and saved you both. And I'm not saying that because I'm looking for any big thanks or whatever. It was just the right thing to do. You guys have been working hard. And even if the numbers aren't there from week to week, you make up for it in other ways. Swifty and Heck eventually agreed."

"Who's going?!" Jay demanded answers.

"The short list is Babs, Elfie, Noah, Gerard, Josh, and Brad. Biz Dev is pulling out of everywhere but California and New York; they'll run things from there. And Swifty just told Heck the names of other people who weren't pulling their weight in Chicago whether they were in sales or not. Jimmy Jim and the board just told Heck to chop people at all levels. And you shouldn't freak out about the health of the company about this, either. Worldwide we trimmed about ten percent of the force, but it was ALL trim-able! We kept the doers, period. You guys have come this far. And even though they're eliminating all bonuses, we've still got the STOCK OPTIONS. So just keep your noses clean and work hard, and I'll continue to be able to go to bat for you."

"Thanks, Chairman. I've got to drain the lizard." Stosh said limping off towards the men's toilet.

Jay sat numbly atop his barstool mentally scheming as to how he'll pay his phone bill next month.

"I like the lemon vodka drop shot!" Yummy said throwing back her sixth.

Jay, Stosh, Kippy, and Hot Pot decided to blow off a little steam at the Loser Bar after the layoffs came earlier in the day. They invited Yummy and Zela along as the unexpected layoffs left both a little shook up. Both were drinking the other four under the table.

During the heated debate over the list of short names to give to Heck for axing, Zela's name was mentioned a couple of times. The Chairman, who had even a little tolerance for most people he found unappetizing, still held a great disdain for Zela. Ollie and Swifty weren't happy with her mood swings and lack of respect for their authority.

Zela ultimately survived the cut for two reasons. All things considered, she was getting better at the job. All of the menial tasks assigned to her were being completed 60 percent on time and 45 percent within expectation of the goal from the managers. That was pure gold in terms of Internet proficiency.

Secondly, Zela was third on Swifty's Office Top Ten List for Boink-able Chicks. Zela's animal magnetism, or the image of such created from all of the physical self-abuse through pierced body parts and tattoos, was enough of a turn on to keep Swifty's interest piqued. A piece of tail in the Nail-able Top Three had enough cachet to create some semblance of job security in Swifty's opinion.

Yummy's name never came up once during the whack list debates.

"It's a good thing, actually. We're trimming fat. We're just trying to position ourselves for the IPO!" Stosh related the Chairman's thoughts to the nervous wrecks before him.

"Hell, if they tried to layoff my ass, I'd come back here with Maw's gun and give them what-for like nothing their pasty white asses ever seen coming before." Zela said, lighting up a Newport menthol. "I work my ass off for this place."

Everyone agreed with her in that "If I Don't Nod My Head And Smile She'll Shoot Me In The Throat with Maw's Gun" kind of way.

"I no understand. We going out of business?" Yummy asked.

"No, Kiddoe. The fact that we're still all sitting here yacking shop about it is a good thing. Elfie, Babs, and the others are at home probably crying right now." Hot Pot said. "Okay, in Elfie's case, sleeping on the toilet."

"This bites dog balls, man. I'm going to start looking around. I've been busting balls since Day One. If they want to throw my freaking balls on the street, screw 'em." Kippy said, obviously wanting the word "balls" on the record.

"Stosh and I have been through this before," Jay said. "And like the Chairman told us, everything is cool. The company is going strong. They've made adjustments in all of the right places to prolong the company's life. Since none of us were whacked, it was a vote of confidence. Now let's change the subject so we can drink and cheer up."

"Anybody sell anything this week?" Stosh asked.

"I almost got a meeting with the big shooter guy at Totally Tulips. His secretary told me he was thinking about doing his first Internet campaign, and she was going to tell him everything I told her about the Ad-Ball. She sounded a little confused about the Tentacle idea, but I think she'll explain it to him okay. If he likes it, I might get a meeting by next Tuesday. But nothing besides that, really." Hot Pot said.

"My main man, Rennie, has been busting balls all week. He signed four deals, all for about $75K each." Kippy said then leaned to his left to punctuate the remark with a burst of flatulence. "Oh yeah, I'm in good voice tonight!"

No one else had anything positive to interject. Gus bought the table a round of drinks and asked about the longer than usual faces.

"Oh, our dotcom company just had to layoff a few people today. None of us here, but it just kind of makes us a little worried, you know?" Jay said.

"Dotcom, eh?" Gus chortled in his jovial Greek accent. "Yes, I put a few other dotcom peoples to work in the kitchen last week when their company went in crapper, too. Don't any of you worry about job if you get rubbed out, also. Gus take care of you!"

He slapped Jay on the back and disappeared behind the bar.

"Oh great," Hot Pot lamented. "At least I'll be able to throw Grease Trap Matron on the old resume."

"I'm out of here. I've got to get me some tonight. It's been three days!" Zela stood up and tucked her cigarette lighter in her Playtex holster. "You want any money for the drinks?"

Jay waved Zela off. "Don't worry, we got it."

"I'm out of here too, Jags. I'm going to throw one into my bitch and go on a pub crawl with my homeys." Kippy slung his backpack over his shoulder and departed; he didn't offer to contribute to the tab.

Jay, Stosh, Hot Pot, and Yummy held forth for another few rounds until Gus kicked everybody out. Since Happy Hour accounted for the bulk of his revenue, it had been cost prohibitive for Gus to operate late into the night for the previous 15 years. Little did he know that the USSBS.com crew would've quintupled his daily take if he could only extend things until midnight.

When they finally left the building, Yummy was the most coherent warrior. She hailed herself a cab and was gone before Jay and Stosh could composes themselves and go in for a cheap feel goodbye hug. They tried to hug her, but ended up wantonly flailing their arms in a cloud of cab exhaust.

"She's gone, Pervo's." Hot Pot said. "Who's going to walk me home?"

Unable to reply intelligibly, Jay and Stosh wandered off in different directions without saying so much as "good night." Hot Pot found a cab and told the driver to haul her to Division Street. Once there, Hot Pot let conventioneers buy her drinks until the early morning. She entertained all with stories about the top-secret inner workings of an Internet start-up company on the ropes and her loose, welcoming body posture.

She woke up at 11:00 AM next to Big Rob. His bed and apartment stank to hog heaven of B.O. and liverwurst. Lying next to her with his shirt off, Big Rob looked like an ivory, olive stained, king sized bed sheet wrapped around 400 pounds of cream cheese dipped in a barbershop dust pan.

He had approached Hot Pot at some point during her bender and decided to seize more than just the insider information for his newsletter from her.

Hot Pot groaned and slapped her forehead. It's not like she hadn't been down this road before, but she was certainly hoping to wake up next to something more befitting an up and coming female Internet sales executive who still had a job.

Big Rob scratched himself, long and hard. Hot Pot noticed the time on his clock radio and stated aloud for her own benefit how late for work she was.

As she dressed, she noticed a third-filled pitcher of Navy Grog on the nightstand. She took few chugs, threw on the last of her garb, and headed straight to the office.

In the weeks that followed, there was no major ripple affect from the initial layoffs. It didn't even merit a blurb in the industry publications that had been out for Internet company blood on any level since April. Jeeves, who had been scarce most of the summer travelling in the Caribbean hoping to avoid Heck at all costs, decided to put in a little more face time at the office. With one quarter of several hundred thousand STOCK OPTIONS already technically vested through seniority, and an incremental few thousand more vesting every month, Jeeves figured his name might be bandied about if another round of layoffs were to ever transpire.

Not yet desperate, but seriously wanting to sustain life, the USSBS.com brain trust came up with a few new wrinkles in the business model. For the members, the compensation policy was being altered for the second time in a matter of weeks. Members would now be paid a plug NICKEL for each hour they looked at the Ad-Ball and a PENNY for each time they clicked on an incentive tentacle. They would no longer be rewarded for coercing friends and relatives to join the USSBS.com family, either. Every member was on her own. This was implemented to help stop the excessive bleeding that continued into late September.

Jimmy Jim and his backers got their wish: USSBS.com membership dropped 50 percent in the click of a mouse. That saved umpteen millions in revenue going out the door right off the bat every month. Again, it caused USSBS.com and Jimmy Jim to be crucified in spam campaigns and on electronic billboards all over the ultra-reactive, anonymity protected, cyber universe. Lose sleep they did not.

USSBS.com then struck up partnerships with a few smaller Ad-Ball competitors that had ripped off the idea and gave it a new twist to avoid patent infringement. The companies' basic business models were all the same—endlessly bludgeon Internet surfers with advertisements while offering them some pithy incentive to do so.

Some of the craftier Ad-Ball software cousins included the "Adverwave," the "Cyberrhombus," and the "Floating Cyber Gonad." But USSBS.com gobbled them all up along with their respective memberships. This accomplished two things: it eliminated the competition, and added members. The addition of millions of more users would offset the losses in membership being suffered by USSBS.com for its chameleon incentive compensation policy. The new merger-incorporated members wouldn't stomp and huff about the latest incarnation of the USSBS.com compensation policy, because they would know of no other than the current model in place. And keeping the membership levels inflated were crucial if the sales reps were going to continue asking advertisers to pay higher rates than anywhere else in the industry.

USSBS.com also tapped Bungleman to spearhead an emergency revenue generation project to come up with new and exciting ways to defraud new and existing advertisers for the fall. In patented Bungleman fashion, instead of coming up with something unique, he simply borrowed concepts that were already being implemented at other Internet companies with regard to interactive marketing products and gave them goofy, Ad-Ball related names.

"Ad-Ballgrams" were Bungleman's term for direct e-mails launched at USSBS.com members on any topic ranging from Asphyxiation to Zorba the Greek chock full of paid for text advertisements. The members received the Ad-Ballgrams willy-nilly, whether they requested them or not. And they were about as relevant to the reader as a banana would be to a man in a knife fight. A creative subject line was supposed to entice a member into opening the Ad-Ballgram to see the message inside. Admittedly, nondescript, computer-generated mail spam that says something like "Ad-Ballgram's 101 Facts about Fun!" on the subject line seems enticing enough to want to learn more to the average web surfer. But when opened, the 101 Facts about Fun were interspersed with 101 freaking text advertisements, causing a wealth of deeper contempt for this tried and true, high tech, slimeball interactive marketing tactic.

Next, USSBS.com needed a means to generate revenue without actually having to provide anything new or additional in exchange for it. This would be a tricky one, but if anyone could do it, Bungleman could. It only took a couple hours of listening to Top 40 radio while surfing porn sites for him to come up with Ad-Ball Two-fers. Translated into Advertiser-friendly lingo, Ad-Ball Two-fers would run an Advertiser's message on two Ad-Ball Tentacles at the SAME TIME (thereby doubling the impact, arguably). By doing so, in reality, all it did was grind through an advertiser's allotment of purchased Ad-Ball inventory twice as fast so they'd have to renew their campaigns sooner and with greater magnitude for the next time.

Bungleman just needed the boys in software design to tweak the tentacles a bit for the whole thing to materialize. They tweaked for 58 hours without sleep. The result was another untested and sloppy software metamorphosis that led to latest Ad-Ball Freak-Out plague knotting up computer intestines of the USSBS.com members who were yearning for just one more reason to chuck the whole Ad-Ball concept for good.

The Ad-Ball Two-fer's were short lived and went back to the software boys for re-tooling. When a handful of stressed out software engineers decided to commit Hari Kiri with the gas pipe from the oven in the kitchenette at headquarters, the Ad-Ball Two-fer's were ordered shelved until after the New Year. In a solemn ceremony backstage at a Phish concert, Jimmy Jim said a few complimentary words about the engineers before sprinkling their ashes over the communal deli platter.

Another Bungleman beauty, the "Advertoberfest," wasn't so much a new interactive marketing product as it was a convoluted way of saying, "We're Really Out of Interactive Marketing Ideas, So Hear Us Out."

The Advertoberfest concept sent the USSBS.com sales force into the streets every day in September wearing lederhosen to promote the latest innovation in kissing advertising community tush: free beer. In essence, each regional sales office would invite the ten largest spending clients during the month to a free beer bash in October that culminated in the opportunity to win a Grand Prize of six days and five nights in Dusseldorf, Germany, with Jimmy Jim.

Advertoberfest was a gargantuan bust, and not in the good Yummy kind of way. Advertisers were already leery of Internet campaigns after months of declining results and clear desperate attempts from Internet companies to try and prove they were more than just the Fleecing Fad of the Moment. Nobody bought into this latest half-baked attempt to be juiced. And the prospect of being patted down for folding money by Jimmy Jim abroad didn't make it any the more attractive.

"Where's Jay, dammit!?" the Chairman asked Stosh prior to the beginning of the "All Hands On Deck" conference call.

It was approaching 11:30 AM. Jay always answered the bell for work after a late night of wine and carpet tasting, but he never reported in so tardy before.

Stosh shrugged at the Chairman. "A sales call, maybe?"

Chairman sensed Stosh was covering for Jay, which he wasn't. But the Chairman didn't push the issue.

"Well, this is unacceptable! He knew Heck was going to speak to us today about important things. Unacceptable."

Stosh shrugged again. He figured Jay just retired to his air mattress with his bedside box o' wine after Stosh dragged him home from their new favorite after-hours hangout, a down and dirty joint called the Bust Bar, only seven hours earlier.

The Bust Bar existed in the same dilapidated structure on Clark Street since the late 1940's taking on one failed theme after another. In it's present day form, though, the Bust Bar struck gold since instituting it's theme of "Less is More" in 1993. Not a penny was spent on rehabbing, redecorating, or fumigating the joint. Posters of once storied Chicago Bear squadrons and incarcerated aldermen hung crookedly on the wall unsuccessfully fighting off the ravages of mildew and second hand carbon monoxide. Toilets could only be flushed by forcefully thrusting one's fist into the bowl from a running start; hence, they never were flushed. Most patrons either held it in or ran into the alley.

The establishment was owned and operated by a diminutive Hungarian named Hussar. He paid his street taxes, and everyone left him alone to run his business in whatever manner he deemed suitable.

Hussar's business model for the Bust Bar was simple. He put very attractive girls, up to three at a time, in the middle of a 30-foot long rectangular bar. The girls were shapely, sassy, playful, provocatively dressed, and instructed to flirt first, sell booze second. The crowd seated around the bar watching the tight denim adorned vixens was overwhelmingly male, and they sucked up the flirting like the love starved sponge saps they were. The heavy doses of flirting and T & A kept everyone in the bar spending money, and Hussar never put a dime of it back into décor or structural improvements.

The girls tending the bar were prime sirloins surrounded by drooling, impotent ground chuck lads with money to burn. Subordinates would bring bosses to the Bust Bar after a day of screwing up and getting chewed out to wipe the slate clean. Fathers walked arm-in-arm with sons as they indoctrinated them into this true buxom Utopia. Bachelorette parties wandered in regularly to perpetrate their ribald "penis pranks" because they knew the Bust Bar is where the men would be.

There was rarely any nudity, and a brass pole would serve as too great an expenditure for Hussar. The girls behind the bar playfully entertained by groping one another, pouring cold water on the front of each other's blouse, or knocking Hussar to the dirty, sticky floor and simulating an orgasm while kneeling atop his concave chest. This was the mystique of the Bust Bar—the illusion that patrons were paying for more than they could see on cable television. It was raw and unrehearsed. It nicely filled in the gaps of escapism wherever the booze couldn't.

The girls always paid a lot of attention to Jay, as they knew every night would close with an additional 60-85% tip for them on his American Express card. Jay drank more beer, absorbed more vodka gimlets, and snorted more Bombay gin & Tabasco shots at the Bust Bar in eight weeks than he did in six years at Southern Illinois University. Stosh enjoyed the Bust Bar because the OLD STYLE was always colder there for some reason. And the eye candy certainly wasn't hard to slurp up with the peepers after a long day of sensory deadening labor in the shaft mines of Internet skullduggery.

Jay and Stosh tied it on at the Bust Bar until early that morning. After Jay signed his $220, plus tip, Amex slip with a limp wrist scribble, Stosh dragged him home by the armpits and dropped him atop his deflated air mattress. All Jay requested before Stosh slipped out was a box of Merlot he had chilling in the crisper inside the refrigerator. Stosh obliged, not wanting to dampen the good buzz Jay had going.

"Gimme sheven . . . " Jay cackled and slobbered as he crawled into the bathroom while Stosh slipped out the front door.

It being an "All Hands on Deck" conference call, a surprisingly good two-thirds turnout in the Chicago office was better than the managers anticipated under the declining morale circumstances.

Zela dialed in on the conference room speakerphone, and all listened intently to Heck's chipper tone with cynical ears.

"Alright, everybody. I'm glad you could make it. As you know, I've recently been on a whirlwind tour of all outer offices to explain the recent mini-reorganization mandated by Jimmy Jim and the

Board," Heck said. "We were fat. And the days of fatter is better are over. Now we want to be lean and attractive so the bankers are more comfortable about taking us public—now don't quote me—but they're thinking three weeks from today."

Jay's klutzy arrival distracted everyone momentarily with its sounds of feet banging into furniture and accompanying imbedded stench of box wine. Jay sidled up in the doorjamb and flashed the Chairman a crap eating grin.

"Bungleman has come up with many new ways for us to approach our clients. I know we've stepped on a few toes in the market already. We're going to go back to each and every advertiser, apologize for the past, and talk about the exciting things we've got coming out now and in the future. We are righting the ship. If you're hearing my voice, then you know that you are the best of the best, because your managers and I decided that you are the people we want around for the resurgence of USSBS.com and the Ad-Ball. We're still the biggest in our arena, and we've got some wonderful partnerships with other strategic companies. There is no telling where the Ad-Ball will be a year from now. Jimmy Jim even has a small group of software engineers under a veil a secrecy coming up with ways to incorporate the Ad-Ball into home appliances, automobiles, and certain prosthetics."

Since the respective offices all muted the conference call from their end, Heck couldn't hear all of the laughing on his end. But he wasn't kidding.

"And enough with the rumors," Heck raised his voice. "The health of this company is better than very good. Let's not forget we're just over a year old. There are going to be growing pains. There are going to be bumps in the road. There are going to be problems. This is true for any technology company. But rest assured, I want everybody who is hearing me right now to still be on board a year from now, two years from now, ten years from now. I know everyone is getting calls from headhunters with tempting offers—hell, I'll admit that I am. But take a deep breath, and look at the big picture. We've got money in the bank and a solid product to offer. Rededicate yourself to this company, yourself, and me. You're going to like the results."

"Time for him to wrap it up, huh? This is getting to sound a lot like a Donny Osmond infomercial for teeth whitening!" Swifty opined.

"The rocky times are behind us. There is nothing but good times ahead. And I'll tell you something else for free; there will be no more layoffs at this company. There will be no more layoffs at this company."

One last time for effect, Heck repeated the phase again slowly articulating and punctuating each word with staccato flair.

"There ... will ... be ... no ... more ... layoffs ... at ... this ... company."

XI – AXE TWO

Forty-eight hours after Heck's pep talk, Stosh was on holiday with his wife on Wake Island celebrating their seventh year of occasional bliss together when Jay rang through on Stosh's cell phone. Oversexed and bloated with shellfish, Stosh was too immobile to do anything else but answer the phone.

"What's up, my good man?" Stosh asked.

"It's not good."

"What, did the Ad-Ball reach out and choke someone this time?"

"Layoffs, man, and big time."

"No, really. Do you need me to wire you bail money or something?"

"I'm not kidding. Jeeves? Gone. Kippy? Gone. Zela? Gone. And you're not going to enjoy this next part . . . Yummy? Gone!"

The shellfish in Stosh's gut churned with the fury of a thousand lactose intolerant men.

"What the hell!?" Stosh said. "Didn't Heck say everything was cool? What the hell!"

"I know. We were all taken off guard, so it was pretty much by design. I talked to the Chairman. He said the order came through late yesterday afternoon, and he, Swifty, and Ollie were slugging it out until all hours of the night again. And now the great part: he went to bat for us again, and we're still here. Can you believe that? Together I think we've closed three deals in 12 weeks. And everybody who just got whacked gets 8 weeks of severance pay. I begged him to include me on the whack list, and he drove me around in his rocket car for an hour so he could give me the silent treatment at 110 miles per hour. By the end of the ride, he had scared the hell out of me and I retracted my offer."

"Yummy! How? Why?"

Jay sighed. "They just couldn't think of a way to justify her salary to Heck. He said all non-essentials were to go; that's why Zela got it, too. Oh, and there's only three people left in Campaign Coddling."

"Jesus."

"Let's see, what else can I tell you at $18.95 per billable long distance cellular minute? Oh yeah, they're asking Jimmy Jim to step down so they can bring in some South African guy named Pierre to revamp the company. We're immediately to cease and desist on selling any new products except for basic Ad-Ball packages until after the pow-wow in San Francisco."

"What pow-wow in San Francisco?"

"About an hour after you get back from the Tropics, they're flying all remaining USSBS.com employees to San Francisco to meet this Pierre guy and give us the straight dope on where the company is heading. No need to worry about our brethren in Europe, Asia, and other foreign lands, though, as all of those offices have been shuttered. USSBS.com is now 86 total employees in the continental U.S., and we're two of the lucky ones." Jay chuckled.

"Jesus."

On opposite sides of the world, Jay and Stosh headed straight for a drink upon ending their call. Jay grabbed a weeping, blabbering Hot Pot and headed down to the Loser Bar. Stosh stood in the ocean slurping a Scorpion out of a coconut shell.

Amidst the chaos in the office, Rennie closed his office door and calmly continued to cold call clients and ask them to sweeten their Ad-Ball action for Q4.

The managers retreated up to Swifty's country club on the north shore to discuss what the next step would be. First, they had to re-assign accounts, Campaign Coddling duties, and office manager duties to the remaining employees and submit the post-apocalyptic office plan to Heck for approval. Next, they had to get at least nine holes in before the sun went down. Finally, they had to start toying with the notion of life after USSBS.com if Pierre couldn't salvage the company from destruction by the end of the year.

The $15,000 Stosh had racked up in credit card debt since coming to Chicago was looking a bit more ominous now that the company's future—mostly the STOCK OPTIONS—were seeming like less of a reality. Like the rest of his life, Stosh had nothing to show for the $15,000 debt; it all went towards foolish pleasures such as food, booze, more food, and cash advances to pay his rent when he was running a little short. To date, there was nothing tangible gained outside of the 35 extra pounds of flab on his already endomorphic frame.

Stosh was counting on his first year's vesting to erase his debts and then some—so was everyone at USSBS.com. The high tech market was still in the dumps. In ten months, Stosh went from throwing out his chest and proudly announcing to one and all that he was " . . . an account executive for a start-up Internet company!" to denying he was even working at all. It was less embarrassing to be regarded as unemployed than aligned with an Internet company. The rest of the world reinforced his opinion. Each new day brought headlines about the shuttering of Internet companies and public opinion polls deeming the Internet " . . . a more objectionable concept than sleeping with Hitler's brain."

Hot Pot still had a job, but she was completely shaken by the second round of layoffs. Good jobs were few and far between in her life. If she were to lose this cushy gig, she might have to go back to slinging truck stop pancakes. She didn't mind being passed truck to truck during her break on the old job so much, but the tips just couldn't equal her salary as an Internet account executive.

"Why? Why? Why?" Hot Pot asked Jay before tossing back a tumbler of Rotgut.

"It blows, that's for sure."

"Are you looking for another job?"

"On the record, no. But I'm not liking this anymore. I want to get back to California as soon as possible."

"You'd bail on the stock options?"

Jay laughed. Rennie came down to join them.

"Hell, yes. It's not worth three more months of misery to me. Nobody is buying a goddamn thing. The company doesn't have a focus or a stable product. I, in good conscience, just can't approach clients and ask them to give me money for this crap. I just can't. It's goddamned pathetic if Heck thinks we're going to go out and hit our nut. I don't know about you, but I'm $650,000 under goal for the year with 3 months to go. And if you're only staying around for the stock options, you'd better reevaluate things; there's no way in hell this company is going to be around on January 1, let alone go public." Jay took a deep breath and then muttered. "Goddammit. God freaking dammit."

"Do you know something? Did the Chairman tell you something? Do you know something?" Hot Pot cried.

"No. It just comes with my sober instinct. I can sense when things are going belly up."

Rennie ordered another round of drinks for the table.

"Alright, Rennie!" Jay slapped him on the arm. "What's the occasion?"

"Oh, I just closed two deals. Not big deals, just 5-K each." Rennie said without an ounce of braggadocio in his voice. Since he was the only one still successfully shilling the Ad-Ball, he was fully entitled to brag. It just wasn't his style—there'd be too many big words involved in tooting his own horn.

"Great. Now Ollie is going to wonder why you closed two deals while I was out drinking. I'm freaking out." Hot Pot grabbed her handbag and ran into the crapper.

"Don't worry about her, man." Jay said.

"Why would I?"

"You may very well have kept the Chicago office open another week or two by closing those deals. If nothing else, they should pay for the plane tickets to fly us all out to San Francisco to kiss this Pierre guy's ring."

"I hope this is a good thing." Rennie sighed. "Times were good last year, but not now. Bad times are not good."

Jay nodded. They pensively sipped their beers and waited for Hot Pot to return. She never did. Instead, she slipped out of the Loser Bar powder room, returned to her work hovel, and tried to make something out of nothing for the 40 minutes that remained of the business day.

Hot Pot stood up and looked around the spooky, lifeless office. She was alone. There would be no more gaseous emissions from Kippy to engulf her. The catcalls from all corners of the room towards Yummy were no more. Swifty's DVD player was left behind in haste spinning another round of *Ishtar*, but it was muted. All of the constants that Hot Pot counted on as the stabilizing factors in her tumultuous life were gone or fading away.

Jay could be right about the future of the company, she thought. But Hot Pot was going to do her damnedest to stave off the occupational Grim Reaper. She rolled up her sleeves, cleaned the screen on her HP craptop with a tear drenched tissue, and dialed for more dollars. Unfortunately, the phones were down. And the fat pipe connection to the office was on the blink denying any access to the Internet.

Hot Pot was already headed in no particular direction, and now she had no means to get there.

The 11:00 AM flight out of Midway Airport on Aeroflot West would put the Chicago staff in San Francisco around 9:00 PM after stops in Des Moines, Denver, Reno, Seattle, and Phoenix. Having been thrust into the roll of Office Manager with Zela's departure and Stosh out of town, Hot Pot was in charge of booking the tickets for everyone at as low a cost as possible. Aeroflot West was under Chapter 11 at the time, but they offered the best round trip price on such late notice at $499 per head. So Hot Pot quickly pulled the trigger.

"Looks like I'm going to have to bite the bullet on the $499 per head; ring it up sister!" Hot Pot instructed an Aeroflot West customer service representative less than a week before they were to depart.

Hot Pot was also the first to show up at the airport that Sunday at 8:30 AM. The airport bar was open, and she instructed the barkeep to make the Bloody Mary's flow her way until ten minutes after take-off.

Stosh arrived next and joined Hot Pot in the bar. Neither was looking forward to the trip as the downward spiral gripping the company might rub off take hold of their Aeroflot West DC-8 over some worm infested Nebraska cornfield.

"So, what do you think?" Stosh asked her.

"I think this minimum wage Jag is giving us all tomato juice and no vodka!"

"I mean about the whole Pierre and company restructuring thing."

"Bungleman called me. He's worried. He says we don't have any aces left up our skirt." Hot Pot said dejectedly while tonguing an olive.

"Do you think they'd fly everybody out there to hear what this guy had to say if it was entirely hopeless?"

"This company? Yes."

All of the Chicago office employees materialized over the next 90 minutes save for Jay. No one actually anticipated him being overly prompt, so a collective sense of worry hadn't spread.

Swifty, Ollie, and the Chairman said good morning to the troops, but then huddled off in a corner of the bar having what appeared to be a very hush-hush discussion. Every now and then the Chairman would glance over towards Stosh with the "Where's Jay, dammit!?" expression on his face.

Stosh was too concerned about getting his own compass and internal body clocks adjusted to worry about Jay. He landed at O'Hare Airport that same morning, caught a cab to the south side to catch this flight out of Midway, and was still gassy and bloated from living the leisure life on Wake Island for so many days.

About four seconds before the flight attendant pulled the door to the aging, rickety jetliner shut with an extra long "plumber's helper," Jay hurled himself from the boarding ramp into the plane. It was clear he had spent the last several hours throwing up and sleeping on some kind of concrete surface judging by the residue and imprints on his face. He was clutching two plastic grocery bags. One of the bags contained his toiletries and a change of clothes. The other was filled with high fat, salty, breaded or pork snacks and a couple of *Leg Stew* magazines.

He eased himself into the aisle seat next to Stosh and across from the Chairman.

"Hey dudes! I didn't think I was going to make it!" Jay chirped.

The Chairman grunted. "Yeah. That would have been a riot, huh?" After going to bat twice for Jay to save his job, such a stunt would not have been warmly received by the Chairman. And it was reflected in his tone.

"Pork jerky?" Jay held up his snack bag and offered it to the Chairman.

The Chairman turned away and buried his face in *TakeNoPrisonersDammit*, the Internet industry's monthly trade Bible.

"Pork jerky?" Jay said turning to Stosh.

"No thanks." Stosh lowered to a whisper. "Where the hell have you been?"

"Hey, remember way back when I first moved into the new apartment and you suggested some night I should have a slumber party out on my balcony if weather ever permitted? Well, last night weather permitted. So I did. I grabbed a box of white zin, a blanket, and slept like a caveman under the starry skies. Oh, but I must've gotten up around midnight or something. I apparently got hungry and called that All Night Pizza Parlor on Chicago Avenue then went back to the balcony and passed out. This morning, there were six angry messages from the pizza delivery guy on my answering machine cussing at me from the lobby desk phone. I could hear Rufus the security guy laughing his rump off. But enough about me, how was your trip?"

"Not bad. It's weird coming back with so many people gone. I only counted, like, ten of us on the plane . . . including the Campaign Coddlers."

"That's about right."

Jay crammed his two overstuffed, plastic pieces of luggage under the seat in front of him per the flight attendant's directive. The brow over her one good eye was arched and angry.

As the plane limped away from the gate, the engines thunderously backfired causing the aircraft to helplessly lurch, shudder, and vibrate for several seconds. It unnerved the passengers, but the flight crew passed it off as "business as usual." Stosh noticed that many pieces inside the aircraft were fastened together with masking tape or knotted pipe cleaners. He had engineered more airworthy Soapbox Derby racers in his younger days.

Pierre obviously had the company on a strict budget from Day One of his tenure. All USSBS.com employees that had been flown in for the big restructuring meeting were put up in fleabag youth hostels near the airport in San Francisco and transported via overcrowded mini-van to the Four Seasons hotel where the meetings were to take place. Pierre was also conveniently staying at the Four Seasons, as the 15-minute drive from his home would save on mileage reimbursement costs.

More than one person was overheard commenting about the funny tasting cheese on the convention room appetizer table at the Four Seasons. Little did anyone know that in a cost saving move, Jimmy Jim provided all of the food and beverage for the event which he had procured backstage at the Phish concert so many weeks before after it had gone untouched.

Jimmy Jim, making his first public appearance in over a month, appeared gaunt, listless, and depleted of spirit. The I'm-Going-To-Take-Your-Money-And-You-Can't-Stop-Me sparkle in his eye that Jimmy Jim possessed since the cradle just wasn't twinkling. He offered little glint as to what the future might hold for USSBS.com and took no questions from his bewildered throng of employees. After a pointless seven-minute introduction that sucked the life out of every trembling soul in the room, Jimmy Jim brought Pierre up to the front podium.

"Here now," Jimmy Jim yawned, "... is the man who is going to keep us on a path to profitability and IPO, Pierre."

A smattering of applause greeted Pierre. Jimmy Jim was whisked out of the room by two bodyguards and lifted into an awaiting conversion van. Jimmy Jim was off to lay low for awhile at his country estate in Abilene, Texas. It was on the insistence of Pierre that Jimmy Jim must fully remove himself from the day-to-day operations at USSBS.com if Pierre were taking on such a huge professional risk to make the glorified tent show a solvent business.

Pierre left a very nice, cushy position as CEO at a profitable computer hardware manufacturing company to take on this role at the request of his old friend Jimmy Jim. Though born in South Africa, and a product of fourth generation American parents, Pierre insisted upon speaking with a heavy, and oftentimes indistinguishable, French accent. He fancied himself as smarter, thinner, and more successful than most American pigs. By taking on a French accent, it was the best way to remind everyone of that fact.

Pierre was tall, lithe, and at 57 years of age, a dead ringer for a clean shaven Sigmund Freud. He didn't mince words, and could care less if he was liked by anyone. He was here to get USSBS.com healthy in the manner he best saw fit, and whoever didn't agree with him was free to catch the next dog meat airline out of town.

Stosh was only able to translate what Pierre was saying by closing his eyes and picturing Inspector Clouseau mouthing the words. It worked with 70 percent effectiveness. Stosh blamed himself for not having one more Harvey Wallbanger from Swifty's Thermos on the ride over; that surely would've increased his Pierre translation understanding ratio another few percentage points.

"I am not going to lie to you," Pierre snapped, "I am not here to be your friend. I am here to be zee one to make zee company profitable. To begin, we are not taking ziss company IPO. Zat is a joke."

Jay had to restrain himself with all his might from standing up, calling Pierre an A-hole, and sprinting to the airport. In his peripheral view, Stosh could see Jay fidgeting like an inmate getting juiced in the electric chair.

Stosh and Hot Pot were also fighting back the tears as their best hope to achieve "living comfortably" status was all but quashed by Pierre's opening remarks.

"Yes, I want to make ziss a public company, too. But we are not there yet. Maybe early next year we will be ready, according to my timetable." Pierre paused to take a drink of water and smirk behind the glass at the terrified looks on the downtrodden faces before him.

"I cannot believe you have been selling ziss product for over a year. I applaud your sales ability, but zat is all. From a software perspective, ziss thing is crap. If it were up to me, we would shut zee Ad-Ball down for six months time and get it correct. But it is too late for zat. We have obligations to meet, and we will meet them. Or we will die together."

Noticeably absent from the proceedings was Heck. For such an important day in the company's history, surely Heck would be there to put in his two cents. Stosh opened his eyes for a moment to scribble a note on the back of his hand for the Chairman that read "Where's Heck?"

The Chairman whispered, "He's in the hospital having a procedure. He'll be out of action for a few weeks. Swifty just told me at the airport yesterday. Keep it to yourself. Now quiet!"

For the next day and a half, Pierre, Tessie, Bungleman, and an army of superiority complex laden engineers stood up describing their vision as to how USSBS.com was going to get back on track. None of it seemed to jibe with the original business model or the selling strategy Heck was brought in to create, nurture, and execute . . . with an emphasis on execute. All speakers seemed to be taking pleasure of Heck's absence and consequent inability to defend himself by firing cheap shots at the "old school policies" and "ineffective strategies during our formative months."

Product-wise, the Ad-Ball had already regressed to its fetal stages. Gone were the tentacles, horoscopes, and skins of deceased ex-presidents. The Ad-Ball was again just a black blob with rudimentary search engine capabilities and advertisement delivery functions. The only other product the sales staff was to take to the street was the Ad-Ballgram. These, too, would be stripped down to a single category called "Stuff" as it was too labor intensive to create Ad-Ballgrams that were categorically diverse.

And that was it for the products. Pierre instructed everyone to " . . . sell zee snot out of them" before even thinking about going to the next level. The advertising community would no doubt be enthralled with these featureless pretenders.

Rennie was relieved that all of the difficult to understand complexities were being cleansed from the products; now his face-to-face client pitches wouldn't have to be so elaborate.

The biggest overhaul was again to the business model itself. Members would no longer be paid ANYTHING for using the Ad-Ball. Pierre said this was necessary to get monthly costs fixed; under all previous versions of the payment plan, there were too many unmanageable outlays. Even if USSBS.com lowered the amount it paid out every hour, it still couldn't control how many members were using the Ad-Ball for X number of hours, X number of days per month.

So instead of such a pie in the sky, behavior modification and reward system, Pierre was immediately turning USSBS.com into a Cyber-raffle company. Instead of being paid directly to use and view the Ad-Ball, members could earn a cyber-raffle ticket for a chance at a $150,000 daily prize. If no one won the daily prize, it would roll into the following day's jackpot for up to seven days. If a jackpot went unclaimed on the eighth day, USSBS.com would keep the money and start all over at $150,000.

The raffle "entry" was simply a number chosen by the MEMBER. Each day, the USSBS.com Central Brain would randomly generate a number from 1 to 1,000,000,000,000 at headquarters. If any member matched the number generated by the Central Brain with her guess, she'd win the daily jackpot.

"Isn't that, like, a one in a TRILLION chance?" the Chairman scoffed. Ever the company man, to see the Chairman publicly take a superior to task was an uncommon sight. But even the Chairman was having trouble digesting this tripe.

"No, zince technically zay can enter zee contest up to four times per day. Everyone has four opportunities to win zee jackpot. Isn't zat great? It 'tis zee American dream, no—winning zee huge money jackpot?" Pierre countered.

All member bank accounts were immediately frozen. Any bank account carrying a balance of under $1,000 was to revert back into the USSBS.com coffers. It was unethical, but not illegal according to the member agreement each user had to acquiesce to upon joining into membership with USSBS.com. So outside of a handful of USSBS.com bank accounts in the four-figure territory, a couple million dollars was reverted back to the company that would be used for operating capital.

"And let me assure you, we have made all of zee necessary corrections in regard to zee size of zee staff . . . at least as of ziss date. If I have to make anymore layoffs, I will. I don't really care. But for right now, today, we are a company that is zee right size with zee new policy in place to be profitable. It is zee profitable Internet companies zat Wall Street will take IPO, and zat we will be next year by my calculations."

Satisfied with himself, Pierre lit up a Virginia Slim and took a self congratulatory bow. Few in the room applauded.

"Now, go out and drink like zee reckless American pigs zat you are. And when you go in to work tomorrow, report with freshened breath and renewed vigor. I'M not going to make ziss company great, YOU are! It's about time you start realizing that. We have provided for you what you now need to make it so. Make it so!"

"It was a heart attack, initially," the Chairman said. "Heck was having chest pains on his way through Dallas, collapsed, and they found a blockage. When he went down, he also dislocated his shoulder, tore his right hamstring, and caused a hernia. A doctor said out of instinct, Heck attempted to do some kind of fancy dismount as he was going down—with horrible results. He's undergoing angioplasty right now. And he'll be out of action for a few weeks. 'Nuff said."

All remaining USSBS.com employees gathered at a festive beer hall just outside of San Francisco to recap the recent events and get tanked. Respective office personnel would be flying out on the Red Eye or early the next morning to their regional home offices.

The Chairman spilled the beans about Heck to everyone, because he knew it would leak out sooner or later. Plus, he was buzzed. While all were stunned at the news, they were also secretly relieved that Heck wouldn't be making the weekly tailbone kicking rounds from office to office for awhile. Nobody wished Heck ill health, but catastrophic bodily failure was the only thing capable of cooling his jets. Heck was a man who finished an entire state quarterfinal high school gymnastics meet with deep spine contusions and a grade three concussion in his athletic prime; all were certain he'd bounce back from this.

Swifty and Curtis, the Regional VP from the Atlanta office, threw down their credit cards so the food and drink would be taken care of for all 78 minions in attendance.

After what they'd just been through, most knew the prospects for prosperity at USSBS.com were grim. But being salespeople for the most part, their innate sense of denial and uncontrollable need to disseminate false information had most vocalizing around the bar what a "positive experience the past two days had been," and "what a great guy Pierre is."

"If anyone is going to turn this eroding, stench of death train wreck around, it's Pierre!" Swifty loudly proclaimed. "Now who wants a Rob Roy?" Swifty made his stock, sweeping circular arm motion above his head and shouted over to the cocktail waitress. "Rob Roys for the room!"

Jay and Stosh stood in front of the big screen television munching on fried cheese curds and bleu cheese stuffed crab cakes hoping to avoid dealing with the reality of the patronizing situation all together. Endless Rob Roys or no, there was no reason for all of the fraudulent toothy smiles and exchanging of hollow predictions for good things to come in 2001. They would have none of it. For all they knew, the comp crab cakes would be the entire severance package coming their way in a few weeks. To expect anything more grandiose was rubbish.

"Don't say anything to the Chairman, but I've got three job offers on the table." Jay said.

"You're kidding! Where? With who? And most importantly, HOW?" Stosh's voice trailed off a bit. "And . . . why?"

"They're all in California, man. You know I want to get back there. After what we just heard from Frenchie the Clown, I taste Venice Beach more than ever. You know I haven't had a good night's sleep since, well, I moved back here. The past couple of weeks when I've been waking up in the dead of night, I've been plugging away on the computer looking for jobs, sending out resumes, whatever. I've had a bunch of phone interviews with all three. And get this, I've got to fly out to L.A. two days from now to see one outfit, and then again to another one next week for second interviews! I don't know how I'm going to pull it off with the Chairman . . . sick days, I guess. But I don't really care. The third place is ready to hire me right now just based on the good phone I gave them; but it's a pure Internet play selling advertising on an e-commerce site that only sells heavy stuff."

"What's 'heavy stuff'?"

"You know, it's like one of those shopping clubs, but on the Internet. They'll only sell stuff in bulk weights of one ton or greater.

But I've been asking myself, where is the average person going to keep a ton of dog food or diapers? I worry about the long term viability of it all."

"Where's the office?"

"I'd be working from my car with only my cell phone and a tow hitch trailer full of glossy peripheral materials. It'd be a rolling virtual office, of sorts. So it could be risky. But they're willing to match my current salary, can you believe that? The other two are with more traditional companies. One is junk mail; the other is a men's magazine . . . but not *Leg Stew*. I did send my resume to *Leg Stew*, but I think I blew it in the cover letter because I got on a diatribe on how they show too many feet in the pictorials. So that was probably a bad move. Bottom line is, I'm definitely going. It's just a question of how soon."

Stosh knew Jay had been miserable, so he didn't question his decision.

"Yeah, I'll be out of here, too. I just want to see what transpires over the next couple of months. If the stock options kick in January or February, I can vest my 25 percent, erase the debt I've amassed, and bolt."

"Well, I hope they do kick in. And since I'm leaving the company, I'm sure they WILL. But I don't care if I'm here to see it. I'm going back to paradise. Life's too short to take it in the tailpipe from Heck, the Chairman, and all of those idiot MTV suckled, 21-year-old media buyers twenty-four seven."

Twenty-four seven? It was rare for Jay to use a lame, hackneyed catchphrase like the uncreative masses usually did ad nauseam, thought Stosh. Jay *must* be bottoming out.

Bungleman, who was only assumed to be an untalented, fat, loud mouth drunk, decided to confirm that for everyone when he grabbed a microphone and tried to codify some jovial team unity through a one-man comedy routine. He began by positioning the microphone under his shirt and striking up an all armpit version of "Dueling Banjos." He followed it with a couple of homophobic slams at San Francisco, a one-verse crooning of his favorite fraternity drinking song, an impersonation of Heck having a coronary episode, and ended by insinuating how lame everyone in the room was for not laughing along. Unable to extract the desired response he was hoping for, Bungleman grabbed a bottle of Tequila off of the bar, stormed into the men's room, and gulped it down while masturbating in the stall nearest the door. It was Bungleman's finest hour.

The flight back to Chicago would never make it in during regular business hours. Swifty gave everyone the day off while an Aeroflot West maintenance crew struggled to douse flames from the front landing gear of the 35-year-old 727 on the tarmac in Newark—the third of five stops scheduled before the jet was slated to plummet down at Chicago's Midway.

Everyone from the office was emotionally exhausted after the flight. None was particularly fond of the daunting task ahead: convincing corporate America that USSBS.com was tan, rested, and ready to become the Internet's darling once again.

Jay appeared to be the only one looking forward to the future. He convinced Stosh a nightcap at the Bust Bar was in order. Jay wanted to pick Stosh's brain about his career conundrum for awhile while his own brain was submitting to the soothing calm of Blow Job shots shared with his favorite pair behind the bar—a blonde triple-D cup aptly nicknamed "Smother Theresa."

XII – THE FINAL AXE

The USSBS.com fleece force went back into the streets during October and November with the best of intentions. Too bad it was to interview for positions with other companies instead of rekindling the Ad-Ball romance with the advertising community.

Jay successfully hoodwinked the Chairman and others to fly out to California for his second interviews by feigning recurring bouts of malaria and Swimmer's Ear. Prior to the second round of interviews, while he was still in town, Jay would duck out of team meetings and Pierre-led conference calls to take calls on his cell phone from the prospective employers to finalize travel details, ask follow-up questions about company health, and the like.

Since he didn't want the cat out of the bag about leaving the company yet, Jay was too paranoid to take the calls between the USSBS.com office walls. Without explanation to the Chairman or anyone else, he would dash out of the office citing a "client emergency." He would then take his business down to Wacker Drive, pacing back and forth between traffic lights while dodging chain smokers and immigrant propelled baby buggies, and communicate with his future career suitors via mobile phone. The battery on Jay's cell phone was woefully weak, and he'd continually get disconnected after 12 minutes of consecutive use.

"Goddamit!" Jay screamed upon losing a call many afternoons at the corner of Wacker and Adams. If nothing else, his fiery rhetoric fooled tourists into thinking he was a colorful street preacher, and they'd drop a few coins at his feet out of respect for his performance or pity.

The managers bought the "client emergency" excuse time and time again, because client emergencies were the only types of incoming calls any of the reps were receiving anymore—even Rennie!

Talking purely in terms of numbers, which are all that matter in a Ponzi scheme fueled society, less than nine paying accounts remained through the Chicago office. Eight marks were still locked into long-term deals until year-end. The ninth account had a "trade out" deal that was negotiated by the long since departed Noah who swapped 30,000,000 Ad-Ball banner impressions to a ticket broker who managed to wrangle Noah four seventh row seats to a Streisand concert. That was the major reason Noah's name was added to the second round of heads to chop. Now, had he swapped out the inventory for Cheap Trick tickets, and invited Swifty and the Chairman to go along, he'd probably still have a job with USSBS.com.

In retrospect, it was fortuitous for his long-term mental health that he took the Streisand tickets.

Stosh was down to one client, the Korndog King. And he already confided to Stosh that as of Thanksgiving, he was taking down his own web site and ceasing all advertising for at least 12 months. His commitment to USSBS.com was more than Korndog King should have absorbed. On average, for each $10,000 he spent with USSBS.com, he gained 11 new customers.

All USSBS.com advertisers were realizing the same weak returns. They had been paying a king's ransom to gain a handful of new customers over the past 15 months. Most operations far exceeded their media budgets, because this Ad-Ball thing was supposed to be the hottest Internet commodity to come along since real time messaging capability. No company wanted to be the one to miss the boat and not have its impact felt on Jimmy Jim's cyberspawn.

The Ad-Ball isn't what clobbered the high tech market and buried so many Internet hopes and dreams over such brief a period of time—arguably. Perhaps anyone with enough resources and commitment could make a pretty good sounding case that it DID to any court in the land. But the worldwide consensus was to err on the side of caution and chill out on anything Internet related. There just were too many present day X-factors in the industry on a myriad of criteria to merit a significant investment of time, money, and human collateral.

Hot Pot was devoid of any clients, period, and had all but thrown in the towel showing up for work four days a week in XXL sweats with unwashed hair and Schnapps on her breath. She was definitely subconsciously preparing herself back into truck stop waitress mode. The daily chew-outs from disgruntled customers hit Hot Pot the hardest as she wasn't accustomed to being abused and discarded by people until after having spent the night together.

Rennie was losing all of his biggest players who cited the uncontestable, spineless excuse of "market conditions" as reason to cease business with USSBS.com. After being only one of four USSBS.com sales reps bestowed with the esteemed "$1,000,000 Fleece" award at the San Francisco meeting, Rennie lost a couple of clients each week. Each time he picked up the phone it cost him $100,000.

Now the phones were ringing off the hook but no one in Chicago wanted to answer. Everyone's voicemail box, from Swifty on down to the junior ranking Campaign Coddler, was jammed with angry, slandering, borderline criminal messages. But who could blame the marks for airing their grievances now?

Clients continued to receive invoices from the USSBS.com accounting department regardless of their campaign performance. Given that the overall membership was down in the 600,000 range while the Cyber-raffle concept sucked wind, campaign performance was destined to be miserable. The same 600,000 Suma Cum Laude candidates wooed in by the Cyber-raffle scheme were being pelted with fifteen unique Ad-Ball messages again and again all day long. That was it—fifteen different advertisers remained in North America.

As USSBS.com only promised to deliver X number of message exposures and not a rate of return, its conscience was in the clear. Them were the rules. If a campaign didn't go ape crap, too bad.

Here's the invoice. There will be a 10-day grace period before the USSBS.com collection department wolves begin scratching at the door.

Furthermore, campaigns were still being garbled and misdirected on the stripped down Ad-Ball, and companies obviously were fed up with being victimized and ignored. With Jimmy Jim in hiding, Pierre too removed from the common man to care, and the sales force ducking incoming calls, voicemail served as the fed-up customers' only recourse.

One of Jay's less happy clients, an underworld flesh broker masquerading as an Internet dating service, voiced his displeasure on Jay's voicemail box repeating the same 14 words, seven of them beyond vulgar, for three-and-a-half minutes. As a local client whose message was supposed to appear exclusively within Chicago zip codes, he was none too happy to learn after the fact that the $25,000 commitment he made to the Ad-Ball was generating his campaign throughout two Chicago zip codes, Colorado, Wyoming, and the Virgin Islands.

Luckily for Jay's corroded artery, a bleeding heart at USSBS.com headquarters named Graefen issued the client a full refund upon having the voicemail forwarded his way—especially after Jay filled Graefen in on who the client's business associates might be.

The number of unhappy and litigious advertisers simply had to be greater than the number of members using the Ad-Ball the sales reps concurred. On an especially harrowing day in late October a few of city based clients that had been taken in by USSBS.com formed a white collar lynch mob and showed up at the Chicago office demanding answers and refunds.

Luckily for the USSBS.com gang, Swifty thought it would boost office morale by ducking out en masse around 10:00 AM that day for an all day bowling party at Dearborn Street Lanes. Another bullet was successfully eluded.

The lynch mob left a note under the door which was seen only by Swifty who then forwarded it on to the company legal department via Fed Ex.

Swifty had grown tired of the long faces and whispers. But most of all, Swifty was tired of the fact that his office hadn't sold any new campaigns, and was losing the clients that it did have—and all due to circumstances beyond control of anyone under his wing. A long day of drinking and rolling the rock at Dearborn Street Lanes was the perfect antidote, Swifty thought.

Dearborn Street Lanes was hardly the venue of choice for hard core bowling aficionados with its electronic scoring machines and thumping hip-hop music. But it was within walking distance to the office, and after the fifteenth round of drinks, the inferior scoring robot and jungle drum noises wouldn't loom so large in the minds of the gang.

Heck had returned to work after 10 days on his back and was as rabid as ever—even more so to overcompensate for his sidetracking malaise. One by one, he attempted to call Swifty, Ollie, and the Chairman on their cell phones during the bowling soiree. None responded to his beckoning.

"It's Heck again," Swifty would say as the number was displayed in the small plastic window via his Caller ID feature. "Let him bark at THIS for a while!" Swifty crammed the phone down the front of his trousers, polished off a bottle of malt liquor, and took his turn on lane 47. The team ate it up.

Under normal circumstances, Swifty, the Chairman, nor Ollie would be disrespectful to Heck regardless of whether they were in the presence of the rank and file or not. But they had been the brunt of enough temper tantrums and threats in recent weeks. Whatever Heck had to say would be negative or could stand to wait until later.

Three rounds later, irritated—yet pleased—by the constant vibrating of the cell phone near his crotch, a very tipsy Swifty scribbled out a note on his PDA and e-mailed it to Heck:

"Silence; bowling bash in progress."

"It's done, man. I'm taking the junk mail gig. I might only stick it out for a few weeks, but at least it'll be a springboard back to Cali." Jay said.

"Well," Stosh grappled for poignant words "we gave it our damnedest."

"Yeah."

They sat on Jay's balcony on a frigid and foggy October night splashing Captain Morgan & Coke's against the back of their throats. In six months of living on the penthouse floor, Jay could only remember scoring a killer view of the city seven or eight nights in all. No woman, other than a blood relative, had set foot in his SNATCH Lair in that time either. He was at least $26,000 in debt at 24 percent compounded daily interest. He was psychologically spent from serving multiple Virtual Masters and sick of the cold, icy grip the Internet had around his air pipe for nearly a year. Jay was ready to go "home." Even though California had only been "home" to him for a scant few years, they were the best years he could recall.

"I'm giving the Chairman two weeks notice tomorrow. I figure my final paycheck, plus unused vacation pay, should give me close to ten grand to get back there and into a new apartment and everything." Jay was speaking with an optimistic lilt for the first time in a long time. "Of course, that's before taxes and my SNATCH stops in St. Louis and points unknown."

"You're not going through Amarillo again! Why not take the northern route?"

"No way. I talked to Goon and he said it's already snowing in Denver. It's not even November 1, yet! I-80 would be brutal. I'm safe on the southern route. I mean, what could happen? It's not like they're going to get snow in Texas in November! That ice patch last time was an anomaly . . . and that was in the dead of winter. Hell, I'm not even concerned about it anyway. I'm going to call Jojo right now and tell him to save me a seat at Chocha Cantina for three weeks from tomorrow!"

Jay went inside to drain the lizard and call Jojo.

Stosh shivered slightly as he sat, sipped, and wondered how he was going to make it until after the New Year without his partner in misery. With Jay out of the way, Stosh was sure to become the Chairman's new whipping boy, too. Jay's impending departure made the beginning of the end of this Internet folly a more palpable reality—and the reality was gruesome.

A distant gunshot broke Stosh's train of thought. He peered down in the direction where a gas station blanketed underneath the fog was.

"Zela must be picking up some smokes for the family again," he said to himself.

After 80 seconds of uncomfortable silence, the Chairman looked Jay dead in the eye across the conference room table and said, ". . . all things considered, I really think you should think things over. You've almost got a full year in. If this thing goes IPO, that'll still give you 25 percent of your options vested."

"I know that. And no offense to you or Swifty or anybody who is still here, but I just don't see it happening. If what's left of the company is putting all it's faith in Pierre, then—" Jay's voice trailed off and he shook his head.

"You're certain? You're absolutely certain?"

"I've already got half of my stuff packed. Okay, technically it was never unpacked in the first place. But in two weeks, I'm hitting the road."

"I'll break the news to Swifty."

The Chairman never raised his voice, scolded, or criticized Jay during the exchange. He was unhappy his long time friend was leaving him high and dry in the eyes of his superiors—or what was left of his superiors. And the Chairman could always count on Jay to be free if it was convenient to drink on the Chairman's schedule. Plus, Jay had single handedly been conquering Canada on behalf of USSBS.com the past couple of weeks.

While most of the world had soured on USSBS.com, the Ad-Ball, and the Cyberraffle concept, for whatever reason, the advertising community in Canada was eating it up. When the second wave of USSBS.com layoffs resulted in consolidation of sales territories, Canada somehow wound up in Jay's lap. He had been flying up to Toronto 3 days per week for a month, and he was taking no prisoners.

Though no clients purchased anything immediately, Jay had secured several commitments from Canadian companies that verbally agreed to doing Ad-Ball campaigns after the start of the New Year. All told, the commitments would bring in $225,000 for USSBS.com just in Q1 of 2000.

In theory, Jay was poised to have a great year at USSBS.com in 2001. That perplexed the Chairman and Swifty greatly.

"What?!" Swifty exclaimed upon receiving the news of Jay's departure from the Chairman. "Will he stay if we throw him another 5,000 STOCK OPTIONS?"

Swifty was serious.

"No. He's pretty set on going back to California."

Swifty's mind had drifted off. He was already thinking about landscaping plans for the backyard of his new North Shore mansion.

"Hey, wouldn't it be cool if I put in a bocce ball court and a concrete bunker like Hitler had? I could set up my drums in there and everything. Wouldn't that be cool?"

Before the Chairman could respond, Swifty had his contractor on the phone to make the necessary arrangements.

It was early November, and Wall Street continued to slap dotcom companies around like emaciated villains in a Jackie Chan film. In 2000, it was ALL supposed to happen on, by, or because of the Internet during the holidays. Retailers were supposed to set record sales on their websites. Children were to send and receive letters from the North Pole at the speed of DSL. Families in all hemispheres were to gather around the 17-inch monitor emitting the yellowish glow of the cyber-fire to sing Christmas carols.

Little, if any, of it came to pass. Most E-tailers and gimmicky Christmas websites were out of business by late Fall of 2000.

At the USSBS.com office in Chicago, the few remaining cogs of the once mighty Ad-Ball selling machine checked in for work every other day at best. Swifty, Ollie, The Chairman, Rennie, Hot Pot, and Stosh were passing the work day away at the Loser Bar or catching the train out to the nearby gambling boats. Each knew the end was drawing near, but no one came right out and said it. Strangely, Jay was diligently making preparations for a smooth transition of all his future Canadian clients to whomever the Chairman assigned as the benefactor and often was alone in the office in his final two weeks.

Jay's "good-bye" party amounted to little more than Jay, Stosh, the lead singer from the Outfellers, Jizzy, and Jay's old high school chum, Wiff, slouched over at the Bust Bar lamenting the state of the Internet, the economy, and conservative attire of Smother Teresa.

"It's so cold in here!" Smother Teresa giggled.

"We know. That's why we think you should be wearing just a T-shirt . . . damp, if possible." Jay deadpanned. "You know, I'm leaving town, going back to L-A. Yep, sunny L-A. And I know people who can make you famous."

Unimpressed with Jay's overture, Smother Teresa turned around to pull a credit card out of the cash register. She spoke with her back to Jay. "We still have your Amex card from last night. Should I just put everything on here again?"

"Yeah."

Smother Teresa wiggled off to grope one of her curvy coworkers at the other end of the bar for the benefit of a younger, more slovenly assortment of sausage casings from the Chicago Board of Trade. There was more to gain in wriggling for them than for Jay and his crew. Jay should never have divulged that he was leaving town so early in the evening. Now that the Bust Bar crew knew he wouldn't be coming in five nights a week, the incentive to treat Jay as anything but tourist trash was vaporized.

"I thought you said these girls were playful and hot and I'd be seeing nipples!" Jizzy said. It was Jizzy's virgin pour at the Bust Bar.

"I don't know what's up. Hell, who cares? The SNATCH is better where I'm going. Cheers!" Jay toasted Heineken bottles with all.

Wiff checked out after two rounds citing an early AM flight out of town for work the next day. Jay, Stosh, and Jizzy absorbed another seven Heinekens each, then sashayed a few blocks over to the All Night Pizza Parlor that Jay had infuriated with his delivery order and passing out antics so many times in recent weeks. An angrily scribbled sign hung near the phone behind the cash register that said:

"No deliver to – Mr. Jay, 1 W. Ontario,
55th Floor! Under NO CIRCUMSTANCES!
He is drunk, he is crook!"

Being upright and in the flesh, Jay was incognito to the good folks at the All Night Pizza Parlor. Otherwise, the trio might not have been seated.

Jizzy and Stosh recanted their favorite Jay stories from the past 10 months while gorging themselves on the best deep-dish pepperoni pie in the city. Jay soaked it all in with a beaming smile and glass of Jim Beam neat in each hand.

One common denominator to every story about Jay that they told was a drunken, sexless, unhappy ending. Most men would've succumbed to tears when the ugly reality of it all finally dawned. Jay smiled and laughed along. He knew he was changing his destiny for the better in the morning.

After they folded Jizzy into a taxi bound for Ukrainian Village, Stosh and Jay exchanged their final handshakes and manly hugs on Chicago soil.

"I couldn't have made it the past year without you," Stosh said.

"By my calculations, neither one of us MADE it. But I'm sure once I leave the city limits, the market will rebound, Pierre will be pronounced King, and you, Hot Pot, Rennie, Ollie, the Chairman, and Swifty will become overnight millionaires."

"I'm out of here January 1, I told you. If it doesn't happen by then, it won't happen for me either. But at least I'll be able to vest in 25 percent of ZERO!"

"Exactly."

Big Rob had been laid up in the hospital for weeks no doubt with some kind of symptoms brought about by Internet related stress. The Cyberskuttlebutt's daily dish was cut back from a full page of Internet movers and shakers to a few paragraphs about the latest daily additions to the dotcom graveyard three times per week. Every Internet entity was operating on a leaner, meaner path to profitability in hopes of being revived after the holidays.

Jay made it back to California successfully, but not without incident. As the gods would have it, Oklahoma, Texas, and New Mexico were hit with an "unseasonable blizzard" the moment Jay's Mustang roared out of Joplin, Missouri, and into Tulsa, Oklahoma. Mangled, twisted semi-trucks and frostbit livestock littered Interstate 40 for mile after mile. Jay was hell-bent on getting back to California and would not be deterred.

He drove for 26 hours straight at a top speed of 30 MPH before fishtailing into Amarillo for the second time in less than a year.

"Goddammit!" Jay screamed numerous times on Stosh's voicemail. His weak cell phone battery, combined with the inclement weather, left Jay with the ability to communicate in one-and-a-half second spurts. Rennie, eat your heart out, Stosh thought.

Though Jay made it through Amarillo this time without any sordid tales of lascivious truckers bearing down his backside, he did manage to leave town with a fresh tale to tell his grandchildren about. Not comfortable with just sleeping for a few hours in Amarillo, Jay wanted to go out on the town and partake of the local flavor of SNATCH and alcohol. In the phone book he located a few adult nightclubs. Three were within walking distance of his hotel room. One was not. But the one that was not, which was located 1.8 miles up the frontage road, was ALL nude and aptly named "Clammy's." The others were merely topless. And Jay didn't come that far to NOT enjoy SNATCH.

The roads were iced over and couldn't be safely navigated, even for such a short drive. So, Jay procured a six pack of Foster's

Lager from a liquor store across from the hotel, zipped up his windbreaker, and trudged the 1.8 miles across a thigh-deep, snow covered cornfield over to Clammy's. It would have brought a tear even to Norman Rockwell's eye.

The next day, on his way out of town, Jay pulled into a gas station and stocked up on salty pork snacks and gargantuan containers of diet soft drinks. He was 60 miles out of the gas station, on roads that were still pretty treacherous, when he suddenly remembered why he had pulled into the gas station in the first place: he was out of gas. Not knowing how far it would be until he got to the next gas station, he thought that it would be wiser if he turned back. And so he did.

Jay just couldn't seem to beat Amarillo. Some force in the universe just wanted him to stay put there. Since he was so close and it was still early in the day, Jay convinced himself to go back to Clammy's for the breakfast show.

The entire cycle repeated itself twice more before Jay was finally out of Amarillo 18 hours later. Experts will argue for years whether Jay was the Chicken to Amarillo's Egg or if it were the other way around. Either way, Jay had pressed enough flesh in Amarillo to toy with the notion of running for mayor one day.

The Chairman was the only one absent the day they finally pulled the plug on the Chicago office. He was off in Toronto following up on some of Jay's clients just before Thanksgiving to solidify commitments for dollars in 2001.

Swifty, Ollie, Rennie, Hot Pot, Stosh, and two of the Campaign Coddlers that still bothered to show up for work huddled around the conference room table passing a bottle of Chivas Regal listening to a very frail Heck drop the bomb.

Heck had suffered a second pulmonary setback a week prior but swore off any type of convalescence as USSBS.com was in such a critical state. Heck just wouldn't let the whole thing slip away without a fight. His voice was raspy and tired, like that of an aging

East German woman gymnast fighting off the ravages of 66 years of vodka mixed with steroid abuse.

"We never saw it coming, I tell you," Heck paused to hack up a quart of phlegm. "The investors decided that enough was enough. We're closing all of the offices, scrapping the Ad-Ball, and liquidating everything outside of California. Your managers have probably all given you the bad news by now."

Everyone in Chicago looked at Swifty who flashed an "aw, shucks," smile and shrugged.

"Bottom line: don't take this personally. The fact that the company is closing and everyone hearing my voice is going to be out of a job once this call ends is not something any single individual is to blame for. I'm out, too. A few people will be staying on at headquarters, mostly engineers, as Pierre's vision for the company is as a software solutions provider."

Cue guffaws echoing around the nation.

"So as of this point in time," Heck continued, "you're no longer under my wing. Your managers will go into detail regarding the severance package the company has put together for everyone. Hey, at least it's something. Most Internet shops have sent their people into the street without so much as a souvenir mouse pad. Jimmy Jim also relayed to his secretary who told Pierre how sorry he was that the whole thing didn't work out and how everyone should keep chins up, heads high for doing such a super duper job. He wanted to be on this call personally to relay the message, but he's in Japan with Pierre trying to sell the Japanese investors on the whole software solutions thing. Again, that won't involve any of us as they plan to assemble a very small sales force combined mostly of high school students who can work for much less and without any benefits. I hope someday our paths cross again before we get to that big State Quarterfinals Meet in the Sky. We should all stay in touch. Keep it real. I'm damn proud . . . damn proud."

Cue middle fingers extending in the direction of speakerphones around the nation.

"What a chump, I'm sorry." Swifty laughed. "Yeah, I got your severance package right here!" Swifty tugged on the crotch of his pants for good measure as his cell phone rang.

"Hello . . . oh, hey Heck. Yeah, that was great a great rap, given the circumstances . . . everybody here was very moved." Swifty listened to Heck talk for a minute, then disconnected the call.

"Well, me, Ollie, and everybody but the Chairman is gone, too! Heck is sending me a file about the so-called severance package I have to tell everyone about. A crack organization, right to the end, huh? Sit tight, everyone. I'll be back in a few with the juicy details. Start calling headhunters on the speakerphone and see if you can get us all signed somewhere as a package deal."

Swifty went off to wait for his file from Heck while the others sat silently stunned in the conference room. They all knew this day was coming, but they never were really prepared.

"This is not a good thing. But it is a good thing if you think it might be," Rennie said attempting to console his fallen brethren.

"Oh, yeah. This is exactly how we wanted things to end," Hot Pot said. "Didn't anybody think about fixing the friggin' Ad-Ball sooner? Why were we still going to the street with products that never did what they were supposed to do in the first place? And why is the Chairman still on board? Does Pierre have it in for him or something?"

Ollie burped a little Chivas and backed it up with a heavy sigh. "They probably want the Chairman to close up the office—you know, tear down the cubicles, send back all of the non-sampled edible jock straps and stuff, the poor bastard. You know what's strange? Each time there were about to be layoffs, we knew at least several hours or a day or two beforehand. This time, we didn't hear anything. Even Heck was in the dark. Software solutions meeting my ass—those Japanese investors are giving Pierre and Jimmy Jim the Ginsu High Colonic! This whole—"

Ollie's rant was interrupted by a call to his cell phone from the Chairman who had also dialed up in between meetings in Canada to hear Heck's farewell address. Heck confirmed for the

Chairman that, yes, USSBS.com would employ him for another ten days so that the Chairman could officially close up shop in Chicago. While Ollie took the call into Swifty's office, Hot Pot finished the last of the Chivas.

"We'd better go get reserves so we'll be able to stomach the severance package horse crap," Hot Pot said. "God I feel like a used, fat Polish whore."

"You know if Jay had only stayed a little while longer, he wouldn't have had to go through all that stress about interviewing, sneaking around behind the Chairman's back, and gotten a little severance money, too!" Stosh said.

"Nah, what he did was right. There is no more cash left." Rennie said. "We lost big time. He is free. He found a new job while he still had this job. That is how it should be done. We will be screwed, and we have no job. I want to drink more and punch things."

Many hours later, Swifty laid out the severance package particulars for everyone as they were laid out down at the Loser Bar. Each victim would be receiving a priority overnight package filled with slimeball legalese that, in effect, stated USSBS.com would be paying 7-weeks of severance pay in exchange for universal absolution waiving any liability against the company or its principles from all former employees for 99 years. In order to receive the pay, the victims had to sign and initial the three-page document in 16 different places and send it back to the company legal department within 48 hours. It was a no-fault corporate divorce at Internet speed. The victims were being given hush money for whatever reason. The reason might not emerge for years. But since the slithering cowardice that is the legal community was calling the shots, this was a lifetime waiver and protection throughout perpetuity from any type of grievance for USSBS.com. Jimmy Jim, the founders, the corporation, and anyone a heartbeat away from any knowledge in the unholy scheme would be taking most of the deep, dark secrets behind USSBS.com to the grave without fear of repercussion en route.

God bless corporate America.

As money was tight at holiday time and none had any significant job prospects, everyone took the package. It wasn't the plan, but the checks would be processed in several different increments until December 31, 2000. Rumor had it that since the ranks at headquarters were thin, Jimmy Jim's concubine and gardener were in charge of processing the final gasps of severance pay between their regular chores around Jimmy Jim's estate. English and math were both natural barriers for them, too, of course, and things went less than smoothly.

For Stosh, specifically, it was infuriating as he was maxed out on his credit cards, had zilch in the bank, and had to haul back out home to California to reconnect with his Old Lady. He was getting no answers from anyone at USSBS.com as to the whereabouts of five of his seven weeks of severance pay. Often Stosh found himself spouting off for no reason like a Tourette Syndrome patient into public phones or at families innocently enjoying the State Street Christmas decorations.

So THIS is why they made everyone sign the severance package waiver, Stosh deduced. The pain and suffering of his predicament was ravaging his gut and soul, and he legally waived any right to do anything about it. The bulk of the money promised to him, he'd likely never see.

Stosh motored out of town in his VW Bug with $120 in cash for gas, food, and lodging to get him the 2,100 miles back home in the final week of December. Here he was, a full grown adult with 20 years work experience under his belt and zilch of a nest egg or enviable material possession to show for it. He at least thought he'd be able to entice a bra-less hippie chick hitchhiker for company for the long ride since he was living the no frills, free spirit, grungy motorcar lifestyle anyway. Even the bra-less hippie chicks ducked out of sight at the interstate roadside rest stops after Stosh confessed to them he had been tainted by an Internet company the previous 11 months.

If the Internet had a spin-doctor, he'd never do lunch in America again. "The Internet" was the New Economy's dirtiest little phrase. Everyone by this time had been conditioned to shield their children's ears upon hearing the phrase broadcast on television or uttered in public. Most times, an oral bile secretion from a listener would greet one who still audibly used "the Internet" in casual conversation.

Enough was enough. If humankind was going to ascend to a brighter, more efficient level of species in the coming centuries, it would do so without "the Internet." This high tech gold rush left the masses chewing on cyber-pyrite.

Kissing one's sister was not so disagreeable by comparison anymore.

XIII – WHATEVER

If the Internet's intent at the end of the 20th Century was to break hearts, steal innocence, foster health problems and alcoholism, intellectually deflower the young and further embitter the old, make the crooked richer and the confused more befuddled, then the Internet did a damn good job. If the Internet's intent was anything else, it fell woefully short.

The official end of USSBS.com was so overlooked and unceremonious, Big Rob or the Cyberskuttlebutt never even reported it like they had done for so many other Internet stink bombs over time. The only mention of note was nine weeks after the fact when the *USA TODAY* ran an unusually lengthy, ten-paragraph manifesto about the 423 Internet companies that had crumbled in the past year. USSBS.com received an alphabetical listing in the accompanying color bar grid to the story.

As far as the ravaged souls at USSBS.com went, all landed on their feet in some humble fashion. Some would chalk the whole USSBS.com episode up to valuable work experience while others regarded it as a surrogate, abusive guardian in therapy sessions. Still, even after the admittedly unstable life experience at USSBS.com, many turned once again to the Internet for a livelihood.

After closing up shop in Chicago, the Chairman wasted no time in sifting through 21 different high paying, executive level offers to join other surviving Internet companies before deciding on the highest paying one. Luckily, the company was a subsidiary of a legitimate, 100-year-old brick and mortar concern, so there was at least SOME illusion of security.

The Chairman was out of work for a pithy 36 hours. He wisely used those final 10 days at USSBS.com to interview and call in old markers, etc. before deciding on just the right situation at that point in his evolution as a Commander in Chief.

Ollie, Rennie, and two of the former Campaign Coddlers hooked on with an Internet company that again dealt in hypothetical products, untraceable results, and high tech fables. It was nothing more than a stepping stone for any of them to the next corporate sham, but their new jobs paid well. And another healthy dose of severance pay would come in handy around Spring Break time at the Indiana State Dunes.

Stosh reluctantly took another sales job at a shameless joke of a barely legal Internet shop that had no official corporate address, URL, or business model. On the upside, they hired him after a five-minute phone interview, matched the salary he had been getting at USSBS.com, and told him he could work from home—if he secured an unlisted phone number. A more conservative chap might pause for reflection, but the debt-laden Stosh jumped on it without a second thought.

As much as Stosh wanted to get the Internet out of his life for good, the economic reality of the situation had him sign over the remaining remnants of his soul. He never fully understood what his job was in the six short weeks he was on the payroll for. He was supposed to convince offshore websites to send him checks for a minimum of $10,000 and that he would then send them more details once the check cleared. Stosh didn't even know what the "details" were, as they'd be sent out from his bosses' virtual office in Phoenix. The "boss" was a computer-synthesized voice, which didn't have the capacity to entertain verbal inquiries, and many of Stosh's questions went unanswered. The streetwise offshore business folks never fully bit. It was a tough sell, for sure.

Stosh got his paycheck on time every week for a month-and-a-half, but was dismissed from the company via e-mail chain letter generated from the computer in Phoenix.

Hot Pot did everything she could think of to avoid going back to the truck stop pancake house including a failed, four day enrollment at bartending school and an embarrassing erotic attempt to get on board at Big Rob's website. However, at the end of January, Hot Pot did end up back at the truck stop pancake house slinging runny eggs and getting felt up by truck drivers with last month's Blue Plate Bacon Sandwich Special still on their breath.

Swifty intentionally avoided the Internet altogether as he found the whole thing "didn't hold his attention." He simultaneously opened a north shore Dog Grooming business and an Import/Export Nut Shop.

Swifty didn't know a thing about dog grooming but figured he could make a go of it if he hired the right people. People in Swifty's neighborhood would pay top dollar to have their Bichon Frises primped and perfumed, and splashing a little Aqua Velva on a hound's underbelly from the confines of his backyard concrete bunker had very low overhead.

Most of Swifty's time was spent with the Import/Export Nut Shop. He "imported" mass quantities of name brand supermarket peanuts, cashews, what have you, repackaged them in a plastic bags with his face stenciled on it, and "exported" them to war torn parts of the world hard up for nutritional substance at a 5,000 percent mark-up.

"Nothing tastes better in your mouth than Swifty's Nuts!" was the slogan proudly stamped on each crate, box, and plastic bag.

Jeeves retired and relocated to Sydney, Australia. He only kept in touch with Hot Pot for awhile, and only because he was still hoping to seal the deal between her knees.

Kippy took the only job he could get—disc jockey at a transvestite titty bar.

Yummy all but disappeared from sight leading some to speculate that she never really existed at all—a curvaceous microcosm of USSBS.com she.

Bungleman was in counseling for months and never returned to the active workforce citing "recurring mental demons." It was to Internet employees what Delayed Shock Syndrome was to Viet Nam veterans. He gained 85 pounds, most of it alcohol, and wallowed the weeks away in the pungent squalor of his Manhattan efficiency studio.

On the advice of his doctors, Heck took it easy for a couple of weeks after the USSBS.com collapse. At one point, he interviewed for an opening at the same junk mail company where Jay was working—and he would have become Jay's immediate superior. But the gods interceded, and Heck talked his way into a high six-figure frozen foods selling position instead. He occasionally checked in with the Chairman and Swifty from time to time for career networking purposes only.

And Jay? Jay was finally home and happy. When Jojo found Jay's rigid, odiferous body in the street curb in front of the Chocha Cantina after an all night Groundhog's Day drinking party, he realized Jay was back for good.

Jojo propped Jay up on the back of his Harley hog and asked if Jay wanted to go home or out to get coffee.

"Gimme sheven . . . " Jay mumbled.

"You're not making sense. Maybe we should go get some margaritas instead."

His eyes clogged shut with asphalt and street grime, Jay drooled, smiled, and swirled his arm above his head the way Swifty used to do when it was time to buy the room a 'drink.

"Gimme sheven!"

Jojo, ripe with a three-day musk of B.O., throttled up the hog and they roared down the jogging path towards Venice Beach. The marine layer was burning away, and it was going to be a beautiful, sunny, southern California day. It was something so tangible and real . . . and so far from the Internet.

Printed in the United States
3231